WHERE THERE'S A WILL

LINDA COLES

BLUE BANANA

PROLOGUE

It had been rehearsed so many times, though only in their mind. Over recent weeks, they'd worked diligently to make the right acquaintances, usually over coffee, lending an ear and handing over loose change where they could, with one simple goal in mind.

Now it was time.

The car cruised along the quiet side street, the driver on the lookout for their mark. After a couple of nights observing the location and their routine, they knew just what to expect, where to find them. Even the homeless, without a calendar commitment between the lot of them, were creatures of habit – a blessing for things to run smoothly. Street lamps glowed amber, moisture dotted the windscreen, the town centre almost deserted.

Stomach butterflies, in full flight, tried their best to distract the driver, but the final endgame consumed their head, overpowering any urge to back out now. They had to press on, had to right the wrong. As adrenalin pumped through their veins, they knew it was time to act, there would never be a better time than right now.

The lad was a little way along, shoulders hunched forward in the wet. The driver pulled up beside him and wound the side window down. A parka hood covered his face, but they knew just who was sheltering under it.

"Hello again," the driver said brightly. The pedestrian stopped and, upon recognising the voice, broke into a smile. Bingo! It was working.

"Let me give you a lift out of the rain. Or better still, let me buy you a mug of hot tea, eh?" In the moment's hesitation that followed, the driver was almost able to read their mind: should they?

"Thanks, yeh, a cuppa sounds good, if you're sure?"

"Of course! I wouldn't offer otherwise." Another bright smile. "Come on, get in before you're soaked," they said, leaning across to open the passenger door. The lad climbed in, grateful, made himself comfortable. As the car pulled away, the driver asked, "Burger to go with that tea?"

"Oh, I wouldn't say no. Lovely, ta. Very kind of you." Big smile, stained teeth. So naive.

"I'm happy to help. In fact, actually you'd be doing me a favour." A smile returned, though with a very different meaning. If only the lad knew how.

The first part of the plan was in motion. It would now be down to someone else to decide the young man's fate.

ONE

Two days later

His breath trailed out in front of him, silvery grey like the exhaust fumes from the now idling engine of the small excavator. Satisfied enough soil had been removed from the grave, he turned it off, the digger's work done for the next hour or so. Will kept a respectful distance in the cemetery as others carried out their tasks, mobile floodlights enabling them to see in the small hours of the morning. From his elevated spot, he had a bird's-eye view of the proceedings about to take place, and he poured coffee from a flask then settled back to wait.

"Right. Let's take a look, shall we?" said a woman with almost denim-blue hair who appeared to be in charge. Will assumed she was with the police, a detective perhaps. A heavy-set man from the small gathering stepped forward and peered down into the hole she was standing next to. The undertaker. Will recognised him, had seen him hundreds of times at burials of people he'd never met before, not that he knew of anyway though in his other role, his day job, it was always a possibility. The undertaker turned to a colleague and beckoned the lad over. It was obvious from the way he walked that he was his junior – an apprentice maybe, someone who lacked the confidence of a seasoned pro. People said dealing with the dead wasn't for the fainthearted, though Will would argue it was quite the opposite. A short conversation ensued, and the young lad made his way down into the hole, squatting out of view from Will in the digger. A moment later, he popped back up wiping his gloved hands together, clods of damp dirt falling away.

"Well?" asked the woman with the blue hair. "Is the nameplate still intact?"

The lad shook his head 'no' and returned to his original spot in the gathering, beside a woman Will didn't recognise. She wore boots with a thick fabric cuff, like fancy wellies. Another from the undertakers', he assumed.

"Then we have no choice but to see if the grave has been tampered with."

Will could tell by her tone that she wasn't happy about what was to happen next, but when a nameplate from a coffin buried six months ago turns up above ground in the cemetery grass, relatives get concerned. He sipped his coffee while he watched the scene unfold. From experience, he knew someone was now going to have to open the coffin itself and check its contents for any signs of disturbance.

The woman stepped forward and prepared to slip down into the hole herself. Another figure moved forward out the group and handed her what looked like a gas mask from the Second World War. It was the coroner, the authority to watch over proceedings for the exhumation that was about to take place. One couldn't go around disturbing graves without the proper say-so, and so he'd been required to join them at the same unsociable hour, as opposed to being tucked up in the warmth of his bed where he belonged.

"I won't need that," she said tersely and tossed the mask back at him.

"I wouldn't be so sure, Detective Mason," he said.

Inspector. It's Detective Inspector."

He muttered an apology and returned the mask to the young apprentice before putting on his own. The group followed suit as DI Mason once again vanished from view for a moment before popping her head back up. Will could hear her every frustrated word.

"I can't get the damn catches undone."

It was the burly undertaker that stepped forward, holding his mask away from his face while he spoke. "I'll do it, the catches are meant to be tricky to open, for obvious reasons. There's a knack to them." Will smirked at the withering look the DI delivered in the false bright light, it was obvious she wasn't amused. Will sat a little further forward on his foam seat inside the digger's cab. Since there was no point in two people standing on a coffin lid they were about to remove, DI Mason climbed back out as the undertaker adjusted his mask to fit better and entered the small space himself. He wasn't going to take any chances with the odour about to fill the air. The coffin had been buried only six months, not six years.

Things were about to get interesting.

Everyone watched as he kneeled down on the lid to undo the clasps. Moments later, the lid suddenly flew up out of the hole, twirled like a baton, then landed on the pile of soil Will and his digger had just removed, closely followed at high speed by the undertaker himself. He landed with a thump.

As Will sat in shock, eyes wide open at what lay in front of him, a cloying putrid stench seeped out of the coffin and smothered the small congregation of various officials. Nearby, the blue-haired woman clamped her mouth tightly shut and headed towards the trees, searching for clearer air as she went. The coroner and vicar watched on in dismay as events unfolded in front of them, their noses safely enclosed by masks. Will held on to his recently consumed coffee and sat perfectly still, in awe and dismay at what had just unfolded. The undertaker finally staggered upright, mask dislodged in flight, and wiped his face with a handkerchief, mud covering the front of his once pristine black suit. Even in the bright portable lighting, the man looked like he'd heard a coffin bell tinkle. He nodded at Will. The man was always a professional, though a little embarrassed no doubt.

What the hell had just happened?

When the small group had finally collected themselves, order was returned to the proceedings. They still had to finish what they had come to do, and that was to look inside the coffin itself. With its lid lying unceremoniously on the pile of earth by Will, the pesky clasps were no longer a concern. Another individual, the local pathologist, stepped forward from the group with an air of confidence. It was his job to determine if the body had in fact been tampered with, and Will watched as the DI and the others stayed stock still where they were, grateful it wasn't down to them to do the actual deed. The pathologist carefully climbed down inside and balanced himself on the edges of the coffin to get a closer look. From his spot higher up in the small cab, Will prayed the man wouldn't slip and join the dead woman he was now precariously hovering over. There had been way too much excitement for one night already. A few moments later, and after a brief examination of the remains, the man shook his head to the gathered group then carefully, and thankfully successfully, climbed back out and approached the DI. It was easy enough to hear the pathologist's words, it seemed everyone stopped breathing while he delivered his verdict. Since the woman's remains were covered entirely by a fine cobweb coating of some sort of fungus, it was obvious she hadn't been disturbed and no harm had been done. The undertaker, though, might have thought differently.

Will remembered back to an old movie he'd seen many years

ago. A man travelling on a train had been questioned by the rail police about a murder in another carriage. Had he seen anything, murdered the woman himself perhaps? The man politely explained he'd done neither and pointed to his cigarette. There had been nearly two inches of ash holding on to the butt precariously, proving he hadn't moved a muscle in some time, else the ash would have fallen. It seemed the fungus covering the poor unfortunate woman in the now open coffin was telling a similar story.

The night would be one to remember. It didn't, however, solve the mystery of how the brass name plaque had found its way above the ground.

TWO

It was almost 5 am when a weary and somewhat shell-shocked Will Peters climbed in beside his wife for a few hours' sleep. It had been a memorable evening, no mistaking that, and one he was sure he'd laugh about in months and years to come, but right now he was still processing what had happened. Never before had he seen such mayhem in a cemetery and he wasn't sure he'd want to experience it again. When the undertaker had finally refitted the lid and closed the awkward clasps, Will, who had been waiting patiently in his digger, had been instructed to fill the hole in before the town awoke and saw what had been happening in their sacred spot. There was always one nosey early bird with plenty of questions, and so it didn't do to linger and give someone cause for gossip. He'd smoothed the area over again and had the digger out of the way before dawn and hoped no one would notice the disturbance. A wreath of fresh flowers had been laid on top as a mark of respect – it seemed the right thing to do.

Oh, but that the smell! A sickly sweet odour that had crept into his every pore. He'd showered, even pinched some of Louise's tangy shower gel to rid his nostrils of the stench, but still it lingered. He'd scrubbed and rescrubbed, but it wasn't leaving him anytime soon. He eventually slipped between the sheets carefully and lay gazing at the ceiling, his head still spinning. Louise turned at the slight disturbance and upon realising her husband was back, snuggled up to his side and rested her head on his shoulder.

"Sorry, I didn't mean to wake you," he said, stifling a yawn.

"Mm?" She was still sleepy. Then she said, "You smell like a girl, what did you shower with?" She gradually pushed herself up on to one elbow and sniffed Will like a dog. "If I'm not mistaken…" She left the thought lingering for Will to explain.

"I'll tell you later, but yes, it's your grapefruit body wash. I needed something stronger than normal, but right now I need to sleep. I've a pickup at eleven, so if you don't mind I'll fill you in on the gory details later."

"In that case, I'll leave sleeping beauty to rest," she said, tossing back the covers on her side. Long slender legs exited the bed first. He watched as she stood and wrapped her robe around herself, a foot chasing a slipper around the floor by her dressing table. A moment later, the door gently closed, she was on her way downstairs to make her first cup of tea of the day before their young family woke up. While Will would have liked to share a brew with her and tell her the whole fiasco, sleep was far more important right at that moment, and he slipped off almost immediately.

At 10 am, his phone alarm filled the bedroom and he reached across his bedside cabinet to find it and turn it off. He had regular customers to think about, people that counted on him to drive them to their appointments, or some other destination, and he couldn't risk being late. Being a part-time minicab driver fitted in well with his role as gravedigger. The hours worked with the rest of the family's commitments too, enabling Louise to carry on in her career as a senior nurse. Her shifts were rarely an issue, and since she was the main breadwinner, it made sense for Will to fill in the gaps. It was the perfect set-up for all concerned.

He headed to the bathroom, where last night's grapefruit gel grinned at him from the windowsill, and checked his nostrils with a deep sniff inward. It seemed all was clear. He moved the fancy container out of the way and checked himself in the bathroom mirror. Dark-rimmed eyes looked back at him and his stubble felt sharper than normal. Turning side to side, he checked his profile and grimaced at how dishevelled he appeared. His soft brown curls hung down the back of his neck, well over an imaginary collar. He needed a haircut. It would have to wait, but a shave he could deal with right now. Louise hated day-old stubble, and he wasn't fond of it himself, so he lathered his face and got to work. Once the prickles had been removed, he flicked the shower on and stepped under the warm jets, allowing the needles of water to massage his head and shoulders and wash the grime of deep sleep away. He'd had five hours, but that was barely over half the usual eight he liked to function on. How did other people manage on so little? He'd be in bed early tonight, that was for sure.

By 10.45 am, he was breakfasted and on his way to his first pickup of the morning, coffee riding up front in a tall travel mug, Peter Gabriel blasting out on 'Solsbury Hill'. The drive into town from his village was generally a pleasant enough one, whichever route he took. Barely fifteen minutes and he'd be in the centre, either picking up or delivering to the general hospital, university or shopping centre. It was all there, and it kept him busy.

He steered himself to Greenwood Road, a row of brick terraced houses that all looked like the next, with an Aldi supermarket car park for immediate scenery. He pulled up in front of a house he knew well, that of Sanjeev Kumar, and prepared to wait. While his actual pickup time was 11 am, Will knew there would be a delay. From the time the customer saw Will arrive, his own internal countdown would begin; a part of his torment would rev into gear and he'd eventually force himself out the door. But not until seven minutes had passed, and a whole lot of double-checking. While Will waited for his fare to appear, he hoped Sanjeev was having one of his better days.

THREE

Sanjeev finally stepped outside into the sunshine and Will observed as the young man checked then double-checked the door was locked, before unlocking it and repeating the exercise several more times. Will counted the number it took Sanjeev before he could move away from the door and towards his waiting lift. Twenty was today's magic number, and Will hoped it wouldn't take Sanjeev twenty goes at getting out of his vehicle once they reached their destination, but what could he do?

Sanjeev attended a weekly appointment to help manage his obsessive compulsive disorder. It was Will's task to deliver him to his therapy session, wait, and return him home. Sanjeev's father picked up the bill, including wait time, and generally made sure Will kept up the important task any way he could. He knew quite how difficult his son could be, particularly if something or someone upset him, and was grateful that Will cared enough to continue and had not fled off into the distance like many drivers before him.

Will turned his playlist off and prepared himself for another ritual. The dark-skinned man with black hair that gleamed from whatever Sanjeev did to it, opened the rear side door, brushed the leather seat three times with a cloth, and once satisfied, climbed in and sat down. Will watched as the cloth was folded neatly into quarters and placed carefully into the small sports bag he carried. Will often wondered what else he kept in there but had never asked. It was more the size of a manbag than a holdall.

"Morning, Sanjeev. Are you well?" Will smiled at his passenger who was now seated and studied him for a moment while he waited for a response that took a moment or two to arrive.

"Good. I am having a good day. Thank you." Each word was drawn out matter-of-factly and sounded a little mechanical, like a robot. His serious expression and tone said otherwise – he didn't look like he was having a particularly good day; he looked strained and agitated. Will started the engine and pulled away, destination the hospital campus. They hadn't moved more than ten metres when they came to a complete standstill. Another car was reversing into the road. Should he try and make conversation today or not? It was always worth a try.

"What do you have planned today, Sanjeev? After your appointment, I mean." Will waited patiently for the shopping-trolley-of-a-car in front of him to move off after the driver finally became aware of another road user close by. A pink head with dark plastic glasses and a moustache told him it was an elderly male at the wheel. He hoped the old boy's reflexes would cope in an emergency stop situation should one arise. He didn't fill Will with confidence. A horn blared behind him. Someone was getting impatient, but Will kept his cool and eventually the trio of vehicles moved forward. Slowly.

"Nothing planned."

It was the same answer every time, but Will tried to engage his passenger anyway. Conversation soon halted, however, with no sign of anything forthcoming from Sanjeev. Will eventually pulled up outside the therapy building and waited for him to go through his usual routine of closing the car door perfectly, several times, before finally being satisfied and heading inside.

Will found himself a parking space a little way over and made himself comfortable. Engine off, he relaxed back and sipped his coffee then let his thoughts drift to the previous night's shenanigans. He was surprised to find a smile creeping across his lips as he relived the vision of the undertaker flying through the air after the coffin lid had blown off. It really was comical, and if it hadn't been such a serious activity as an exhumation, he would have laughed out loud, he was sure of it. He wondered whether the undertaker had since recovered, emotionally and physically, and just how he was going to get the soil stains from his suit. Pity the dry-cleaner that found themselves with that particular bag of goodies this morning. He flicked his playlist on, more to keep himself awake and alert while he waited than anything else. It wouldn't do to drop off and leave Sanjeev stranded. Even if the car was only a hundred metres away, he'd never find it, and Will didn't want to think what would happen then. He checked the time on his phone; he had nearly fifty more minutes before Sanjeev returned. As another yawn, much stronger than the last one, escaped his mouth, he relented, set the alarm for 11.45 and pushed his seat right back for forty winks. He was asleep in an instant, the morning sun keeping him toasty warm as it bathed the car with its rays.

Will slept like a baby. For far too long.

FOUR

He awoke to his phone ringing and a hot car. As Will scrambled upright and tried to fathom what was going on, the caller rang off. He soon realised what had happened, and checking the alarm setting on his phone, groaned at his simple mistake. He'd set it for pm instead of am. At nearly 1 pm, he'd failed to pick Sanjeev up, and according to caller ID, his missed call was from Sanjeev's father. Will knew the surgeon hated being disturbed at work, understandably, and that Sanjeev had likely called him in distress.

"Shit." He pulled out from his parking space and headed for the front entrance, where he prayed Sanjeev would be waiting patiently, and was disappointed to find no one there. Where could he be? Should he call the father back? Maybe he knew where his son had gone? Or would that make matters worse? Worry filled his veins. He'd lost his charge, grown man or not. His eyes did a slow tour of the car park just in case he was out looking for Will's car. After two passes round with no sighting of Sanjeev, he had no choice but to call Dr Kumar back and hope he'd not returned to surgery. He pressed the last incoming call number and waited for the man's voice to boom out through the car's speakers. He answered immediately.

"Mr Peters, it's Dr Kumar here, Sanjeev's father." As if Will didn't know that already since he'd called him, but he allowed the man his greeting, such as it was. "I'll get straight to the point," he said, carrying on so Will couldn't get a word in of his own. "It seems Sanjeev is either confused or you failed to meet him after his session. Which is it?"

What could Will say? There was no point denying it, he had failed. And lost him.

"I'm afraid that it's the latter, Dr Kumar. A mix-up at my end that I apologise profusely for. I'm trying to locate Sanjeev as we speak." He cringed, hoping his words would be enough to pacify the man. The silence at the other end of the line concerned him and he refrained from filling it with his own explanatory waffle. He'd learned in the past that people like Dr Kumar appreciated only a few words in their communication but a *useful* set of words. Forget the superfluous ones, they didn't have time for them. Will found himself responding in the same way. Maybe it was a surgeon thing? *Scalpel. Clamp. Swab.* He wondered how the man's communication style affected his son, he couldn't see him being particularly patient with Sanjeev – was he part of the problem? Will pulled onto the main road in an attempt to retrace Sanjeev's steps if he'd headed home on foot. It would be quite a walk for him, and depending which way he'd turned from the hospital, he could be heading either north or south of the town centre. Will picked south and crossed his fingers while he drove. The surgeon finally asked, "Where are you now?"

"Retracing his steps in case he's headed towards home. I'm assuming he's been in contact with you. Did he say where he was going?"

"You are correct. He's set off walking and I can see he's on St

Giles Street. Please pick him up and return him home. I don't need any more calls today." Will wondered about how he knew where his son was precisely. There was only one way he could know – he tracked him with an app. Did Sanjeev know? Was it for his own protection or was it a breach of the adult's privacy?

"On my way there now, thank you. I'll take him straight home."

"Please do." The line went dead.

St Giles Street was one-way so Will zigzagged across town to start at the hospital end and work his way along. He hoped Sanjeev wasn't in the mood for shopping or eating, not until he'd located him at least. Turning onto Spencer Parade, Will slowed down to a crawl, searching as the road turned into St Giles. There was little time for a smile as he passed the funeral home, the very same undertakers that he'd had the strange pleasure of working with the night before, and he drove on slowly looking for the familiar dark shiny hair that belonged to Sanjeev. It was almost at the end of the street, by the gentleman outfitters, that he spotted him. It wasn't the best place to park, but he pulled the vehicle onto the pavement and flicked his hazard lights on, praying there were no traffic wardens about to pounce. The guildhall loomed over him. He shot out of his seat in a flash, leaving the door to slam shut on its own.

"Sanjeev!" he shouted. He caught up with him easily and waited for him to turn and recognise him; he knew he couldn't reach out – touching his arm, say, was a big no-no.

"Will. You weren't there." He sounded almost sad, worried.

"I know. My fault entirely, I'm sorry. It won't happen again, promise." Will waited to see what Sanjeev might do next and was relieved when he turned and started walking back in the direction of the car. He spotted a traffic warden making her way across to his vehicle and he called out to alert her of his return. She hadn't started on the ticket as yet. Deciding to stick with Sanjeev rather than sprint off to state his case and appeal for clemency, he could only hope she would be satisfied with his return then move on. The uniformed woman diverted and walked towards them, and Will could tell he was in for a lecture. He wasn't disappointed and he stuck it out while she did her worst. He deserved it all, apparently.

At least he had Sanjeev back with him.

FIVE

The day could only get better. With Sanjeev safely back home, Will dared to breathe a sigh of relief, though his stomach reminded him he hadn't eaten since breakfast. As if to make a point, it gurgled again.

"I hear you," he said as he headed up the A4500, destination Sainsbury's and another regular customer. While he was too early to pick her up, the café was a welcome fixture when he was driving the streets, and since the last twenty-four hours had been somewhat eventful, he felt he deserved a treat. With the added Sanjeev debacle, he yearned for something to counteract the adrenalin that had spiked and since evaporated. Now Will had a hunger as sharp as a tack. He pulled onto Gambrel Road and found a parking space not too far from the store itself. Usually, he parked away from the masses and walked the short distance that most people preferred not to bother with. His legs usually needed stretching but he didn't give them a second thought today, it was all about his stomach. Once inside, he followed the smell of hot food, ordered sausage and chips then grabbed last night's paper off a nearby table before settling down to eat.

Will never rushed his food, quite the opposite in fact. Having lived on so little a quantity as a child, he'd soon learned the value of it. At age thirteen he'd found himself as caregiver and had worked hard to keep himself and his other six siblings fed while their parents spent their wages in the pub. Between them, the children had 'stolen' money from wallet or purse while the adults slept booze-filled evenings off, and saved it to buy their own bread and jam, which they kept hidden in the old outhouse at the bottom of the garden. Without their own place to hide and consume food, who knows what would have happened to them all. At the ripe old age of fifteen, Billy, as he was then known, had had enough and had left home for something better, leaving Kirsty, the next eldest, to take over the role of provider. Living on the street and fending for himself couldn't have been any harder than what he'd been doing at home. And he doubted either of his parents had noticed him gone. He'd spent four years living on the streets before his luck turned, and during those years of self-sufficiency, he'd learned some valuable lessons.

He finished the last of his meal and then opened the paper in front of him while his pot of tea brewed stronger. It was the usual content: shoplifter caught on camera, the recent vandalism spike, but it was news on the upcoming mayoral election that dominated. None of it particularly interested him as he scanned the pages before flipping back through from the end. How he'd missed it the first time round he wasn't sure, but the headline grabbed him now. A body had been found in the country park at Hunsbury Hill. Will read the few short paragraphs that informed the reader the police were investigating and there wasn't much to report at this time. The elderly man that found the body had given a brief report to the paper insinuating that, by the way they were dressed, the person was perhaps homeless. Until a post-mortem had been carried out to determine the cause of death, the police would remain tight-lipped. He rested the paper down and poured a mug of dark tea while he thought about it. So, the man that had discovered the victim had simply made an assumption by the person's appearance? There were plenty of homeless people in the town, he knew that for sure since he volunteered one night per week at the local shelter. Then there were those that only occasionally had a roof over their heads, the so-called 'sofa-surfers', an estimated four hundred that stole nights on friends' sofas or slept in their car for shelter. They were marginally safer than those that slept on cardboard in doorways. The Refresh Centre served those that needed it most and it relied on volunteers like Will to function. He thought back to the garage he'd shared with a friend in Croydon some years ago. He'd only been a teenager back then, but the memories of living on the streets were as clear as if it were last week. That had been one cold winter. He'd been lucky to have had the protection of an empty building and a good mate to pass the time with. He wondered about her for a moment: they'd eventually gone their separate ways and, with no way of keeping in touch, he'd never seen her again.

He glanced at his phone for the time – he had ten more minutes until he needed to be out front for his next fare. He quickly re-read the short article again and made a mental note to try and find out who the homeless person was, if that's what they turned out to be. It would be a bit of a detour, but he'd drop by Refresh on his way home. Maybe they would have more to tell him? He refolded the paper and cleared his tray away before heading back to get the car.

As a part-time gravedigger, exposed to death far more than the average person, the news of a body found still unnerved him some-what. Was the lifestyle of a person the deciding factor in how much space would be given in the news should they be found dead? Dead sex workers were often headline news because their profession was scandalous, but a homeless person? Who cared? Had it been a more prominent member of society – the mayor himself, maybe – it'd be front page news, of that he was sure.

He pulled the car around to the main entrance and was right on time to see his next fare coming out of the store. She waved a wrinkled right hand, bright red lips smiling from ear to ear. Will couldn't help but grin back and pinged the boot, ready to load her shopping. Birdie Fox was a woman guaranteed to brighten anyone's day.

SIX

"Hello Birdie," Will said, and he leaned forward to plant a customary peck on the loose skin of her cheek. She smelled of lavender and made him wonder about the grandmother he'd never known but hoped he had somewhere in the world. He opened the rear door and waited while she shuffled herself across the seat. She preferred to ride in the back and often joked she was 'Miss Daisy', as in the movie, though that made him Morgan Freeman, and she was way off target with that one. Tall, slim and white, he was the polar opposite. Still, he enjoyed Birdie's company and pointed the car in the direction of her home on Timken Way North.

"You look a little tired, Will."

He smiled before debating whether to tell her the truth or not. He chose truth.

"I knew it!" she said, sitting forward in her seat so the seat belt strained a little. "Tell me more!"

"No, it was nothing like that, Birdie. Far from it actually. I spent the evening in a freezing cold graveyard, an exhumation. I wish I had been with Louise at home, let me tell you."

"Well, that's exciting too." Her eyes twinkled with mischief when he glanced in his mirror. "Why an exhumation? Somebody think a relative had been buried alive? Or perhaps a different body in the box? What?" She steadied herself by holding the rear of Will's seat like a child might. In her seventies, she wasn't as strong as she'd once been.

"I don't think I can tell you the details, not yet. But it was certainly eventful."

He proceeded to fill her in on the assumed gas build-up and the flying undertaker. Birdie held her side as if she had a stitch then dabbed each corner of her watering eyes with a tissue. "You've made my day, Will. Astounding. That beats anything I've heard this year, I think, even when old Mr Sims' leg fell off at the bowling club and three of us couldn't re-attach it."

The vision of three elderly people trying to put a human mannequin back together on the green was almost as funny as his own story and he laughed loudly. "What did you do with it, then?" enquired Will. "The leg, I mean?"

"Bob put it in the basket of old Sims' mobility scooter, and he drove off with it sticking out sideways, it wouldn't balance straight up." Birdie spluttered and burst into a full laugh as she described the whole unfortunate incident. "He needed a 'wide load' sticker on his bumper!" she said, trying to bring herself under control and failing miserably. She dabbed at her eyes again and eventually calmed down. "I guess he put it back himself, once he got home," she said by way of explanation. "There was no way any of us were going to take his trousers off to do the job."

"You didn't check in on him? Later, I mean."

"I don't know who would have been the most embarrassed, him or me, but no, I'm ashamed to say I didn't. I figured he managed every morning, he'd manage again."

"I bet that made for another interesting bowls meet?"

"I never saw the old boy again. Died of a heart attack the following week. Not related, I'm sure." Talk of the man's death sobered them both a little, but the frivolity had been fun while it lasted. It was always sad when a loved one passed and Will wondered about the exhumation again, and the brass nameplate found above ground, the reason they checked the coffin in the first place. It was puzzling, with no obvious answer.

The car pulled up outside Birdie's red brick house that was bigger than Will's own. Why she rattled around in there all by herself, he'd no idea, but since she'd only moved there a year ago, he assumed she must enjoy the space. He stepped out of the car and headed for the shopping bags in the boot. Birdie started for the front door and went inside, leaving it open for Will who eventually followed laden with all four bags together. He put them on the kitchen floor for her.

"Coffee? Or wine?"

Wine was definitely out. He checked his watch. "A quick coffee would be great, then I'll dash. I've a detour to the shelter on my way back, thanks."

Birdie flicked the switch on the kettle and started to put the groceries away. Stooping to reach the last in the bottom of one bag, she said, "I suppose that homeless person they found might be someone you know?" Their eyes met for a second. Birdie was no fool and had also seen the small piece in the paper.

"Maybe. I'm not sure. Details are few and far between at the moment. That's why I'm detouring to the Refresh Centre on my way back."

"Why do I detect you're going to snoop around a little, find out more?"

"Perhaps I will." The kettle boiled but neither of them poured the water. Birdie watched Will closely for a moment before adding, "Need some help? I did time for murder, remember; I know how a murderer's mind works."

SEVEN

Will knew some of Birdie's story, she'd casually dropped it into the conversation one morning while they'd been in the car, though Will being Will, he hadn't wanted to pry. That didn't mean he hadn't been curious for more, like why and how she'd come to murder someone, and just who that person had been. Her husband, he'd assumed, for no other reason than she now lived alone. It was a silly assumption, the man could easily have died just like old Mr Sims with his artificial leg, but since Birdie had casually thrown her criminal past back into the conversation, he couldn't resist asking this time. He cleared his throat as if he was about to make an important announcement.

"Did you conceal your victim's body somewhere perhaps?" It sounded far too casual for his own ears, but Birdie had been the same in her delivery, so he mirrored her tone. He sipped steaming hot coffee she'd eventually made.

"Good Lord, no. I left it, or should I say him, on the kitchen floor where he fell. Stabbed him in the chest and he bled to death in front of me. I must have hit just the right spot because it didn't take long. Made a hell of a mess though and I couldn't shift him. He was still slumped by the cooker when they came for him. There was no way I could roll him up in a conveniently sized rug and drag him to the boot of my car like they do in the movies. I'm not a weed when it comes to strength, but a dead weight is awfully hard to deal with. Not a prayer of moving him."

"So, what you're telling me is whoever dumped the person in the woods had to be physically much stronger than, say, you were back then, or possibly they had help?"

"Well, it depends on the size of the body for one. Do you know for sure it was an adult?"

Will thought about that. He'd made an assumption from the news piece that it had been an adult, but could it have been a youth, a teenager maybe? He hadn't checked online for any further information and he silently reprimanded himself for not doing so. He'd see Hazel soon, a cook at the Refresh Centre, maybe she was aware of more. If the body was that of a service user, she'd be the one to know. The streets might have eyes and ears but so does the cafeteria. "No, I don't know anything for sure, not yet."

"You'll find a way to confirm what the police have found, and on that note, do you know anyone in the police, have a contact?"

"Never needed one. Not sure I need one now."

"It won't hurt. Back in my day, you kept away from them. They were as corrupt as you like and giving a suspect a good slapping in the cells was an acceptable way of getting a confession. Thankfully they've cleaned their act up now." Birdie appeared to drift off the conversation for a moment and Will wondered where her head was. Is that what had happened to her, a beating? He decided to press on, curiosity getting the better of him, and asked, "When were you inside, Birdie? It sounds like it was a while ago."

"1985," she answered, clear and upbeat. "I went to Bronzefield then got moved to Holloway for a time. Rosemary West was there for a while, saw her a few times. As was Myra Hindley, though long before my arrival. I don't consider what I did anything in their league, not in the slightest, but a female killer is a female killer and nothing more. We were all lumped in together. Made a few friends actually," she said, smiling. "It wasn't all bad."

"Did you keep in touch with any of them, when you were released, or are they still inside?"

"Heavens, no! That was a time I wouldn't want to relive. It's much nicer on the outside than the in." She went back to her thoughts for a moment. "Though there was one woman," she said slowly. "We wrote to each other for a time. I wonder where she is now?"

It wasn't a question that needed an answer from Will and he let the conversation drift along, she seemed happy to talk.

"She killed her husband too, so I guess that's why we bonded, birds of a feather. Rat poison, not a nice ending for him, but he'd deserved every last gasp she'd said. I never asked but I suspect he'd been abusive, and she'd had enough. She was such a meek thing, though by the time I'd left she was as confident as the next woman. Prison could do that, plus it was a great training ground for learning other crimes." At that revelation, she fixed her eyes on Will's and let them dance. Birdie Fox had picked up a few extra tricks it seemed.

"Birdie, I do believe there's more to you than meets the eye. I'll bet you're a resourceful person to have around."

"You can count on that!" she said, moving to the sink and placing her coffee mug there. "I've not dredged all that up in some time, it's best left forgotten now. I've learned and moved on. Now, what's our plan?"

It looked like Birdie had invited herself along – but to what exactly? He'd only planned on making discreet enquiries at the shelter; it seemed she had other ideas. Will checked the oven clock. Time was marching on. If he was going to pop in on Hazel before heading home, he'd better get a move on.

"I'm not sure if we need a plan, Birdie, but I am going to call in at the shelter on my way back, see if they've heard anything. After that, I couldn't tell you, probably nothing."

"I've been your passenger long enough, Will Peters, to know that you're too kind-hearted to let anything happen to those you volunteer to help. If it turns out to be one of your 'flock', for want of a better word, you'll be all over it like a bee on a honeypot."

She had a point. As she reached up to give him a farewell peck on the cheek, she placed a wrinkled hand on his chest, its skin loose and baggy, deep blue veins protruding like inky rivers running inside her. It was then he noticed the scarring, her whole hand looked quite different to the other, and wondered what had happened. Birdie recognised the look on his face. "Scalded. On my second day inside," she answered without any emotion. She rubbed at her hand as if that would melt the scars away and led Will towards the front door. He took the hint; their time was up.

"Let me know how you get on."

EIGHT

Will's mind worked overtime as he drove from Birdie's towards the shelter. Ten minutes later, he pulled into a small car park that stood beside another modern red brick building. He made his way towards the rear service doors where he knew the kitchen team on the other side would be at full throttle. He ducked inside. No matter what time of day it was, there was either a meal on the go or one being cleared away. He could smell some sort of casserole, a popular staple on the menu, and potatoes, ready for the oven, were stacked nearby on a trolley that was as tall as Will himself. Busy hands worked pots and pans, and he thought perhaps he'd come at a bad time. The evening meal, he should have known better. A voice he recognised called his name and he struggled to find her short dark hair over the other volunteers. A hand waved in the air as if she could read his mind. "Over here, Will," she yelled. Something metal clattered to the floor followed by a curse in another language. He spotted her and made his way over, trying his best to keep out of everyone's way. Hazel's face was beet red from the heat and hard work, but she wore a smile as wide as Birdie's. Everyone liked

Hazel, she had time for whatever was needed to be done and she always did it with enthusiasm. He'd have liked a mum like Hazel.

"What brings you here at rush hour?" she enquired, wiping her hands on a tea towel – they were nearly as red as her face.

"Silly of me, I know. I didn't think, sorry."

"No problem, though I can read your face you've something on your mind."

He smiled the smile of someone being caught out. Not much slipped past Hazel, the very reason for his visit.

"Can you spare a moment to talk outside?"

She nodded then yelled across the kitchen to another volunteer. "Mick, can you take over here for a minute, please? I don't want it to stick to the bottom," she said, mimicking stirring the pot in front of her. It looked like the makings of a cheese sauce. When the pan was in safe hands, Hazel steered Will back to the rear door and they stepped outside. She pulled her cigarettes from a pocket and lit one. "Needed a quick ciggy anyway," she said.

Will began. "I wondered what the word was about the body they found at Hunsbury Hill. The report I saw suggested it was perhaps a homeless person. I wondered if it was maybe someone that frequented the shelter?" His blue eyes watched her deep brown ones, looking for answers, but he saw only concern.

"I did hear on the rumour mill they'd found someone there, but it really is too early to notice anyone missing. You know as well as I do, we don't see everyone daily and a transient community by its very nature shifts around."

Will nodded. It had been a long shot.

"What are you thinking, Will?" she asked, then sucked hard on the filter of her cigarette. She'd have to get back inside shortly, break over.

"If it was one of our community, I want to help, make sure someone is held accountable for their actions and that the police take this case just as seriously as any other. I don't want him or her to be considered unimportant just because of their circumstances. That they were living rough, if that's what it turns out to be, shouldn't influence anyone. A crime is a crime. They deserve a thorough investigation just as much as someone with a permanent roof over their head. I'm tired of people treating them as worthless!" The tirade came out in one long burst and she stared at him, staying silent for a beat before rubbing his arm in affection. It was clear from the strain on his face that Will was worked up about the possibility. She knew Will's story; she knew all the volunteers'.

"I hear you. Look, I've got to get back inside, Will, but if there's more mention of it on the grapevine, I'll let you know, okay?" Her own concerned eyes stared straight into his and had the desired effect. He relaxed his shoulders a little and took a cleansing deep breath. He nodded; he knew she could do no more.

"Sorry. It just gets to me, that's all."

"I know, it does me too, and if I hear anything, I'll be sure and let you know. Now off you go before I end up making another pan of sauce," she said warmly. "I'll see you tomorrow night anyway." She dropped a light peck on his cheek and headed back inside, leaving Will to make his way to his car. There was nothing else to be done. Was he getting all upset over nothing? Maybe the police would know more tomorrow, perhaps he could contact the woman DI with the blue hair from the exhumation. Surely, she'd have news, but would she share?

NINE

WILL ARRIVED HOME TO SEE LOUISE UNPACKING THE BOOT OF HER own car, Sainsbury's bags in both hands. Four small children danced about in the driveway as if it was the most exciting place to be in the world. He moved in for a kiss with his wife as his eldest, Poppy, pulled a face of disgust. At six, how could she even think affection between two adults was so yucky? When the triplets had come along and Poppy had been only fourteen months old, both Will and Louise had wondered quite how they'd cope, but somehow they'd managed. With Will's flexible shifts, excellent day care in the village and afterschool clubs for Poppy, they made it work. Will carried two more bags from the car and followed her inside to the kitchen. "I could have grabbed groceries, I've not long ago been in the shop myself, picking Birdie up." The room felt cool, the weak sun on the front of the house now. Louise turned the oven on. No doubt there would be something from one of the bags for dinner.

"And how is Birdie? Still her old self, I presume?" She unpacked one of the bags as she spoke, idle chit-chat and nothing more. It was part of her winding down process after a busy shift at the hospital.

"She is, yes. Though she did give me a bit of a surprise earlier about her past."

"Oh?"

Will checked over his shoulder to see if any small ears could overhear him before adding, "She murdered her husband some years back, did time, including a stint in Holloway. I always knew she'd killed, but I didn't know who. It was her husband apparently." Louise stopped what she was doing, a can of peas in her hand.

"Wow. Do you know how or why?"

"Stabbed him, though I don't know why, and I couldn't really ask. I tried googling it, but the crime was back in the 'eighties, so there really isn't much information about it."

"How did you get on to that?" Peas were added to the pantry and other tins followed.

"They've found a body in Hunsbury Hill Country Park and she was telling me about how hard it is to move a dead weight."

"I heard about that earlier myself." Packets followed the tins, and she closed the cupboard door, turning to Will. "I read somewhere that statistically, young men often kill themselves in woods, though it could turn out to be foul play. Or an accident, perhaps, though unlikely. There'll be an investigation opened, of course."

"Is the post-mortem being done in your hospital, do you know?" Will's brain raced ahead.

"I would expect so. Why are you so interested?" She set a family-sized lasagne on a baking tray and placed it in the oven. Garlic bread lay ready on the work surface and no doubt there'd be a salad to go along with it all.

"You'll think me daft, I know, but I just want to make sure, if I can, that if the rumour of the body being a homeless person is true, that someone looks out for them somehow." Louise moved closer to her husband and slipped her arms around his waist, pulling him in closer. She too was aware of his history living on the streets long before he met her.

"You're a compassionate individual, Will Peters, and it's one of the reasons I love you." She reached up for his lips and planted a quick kiss before asking, "Are we opening a bottle of wine tonight?" There was a chilled bottle in her hand, almost as if she was waiting for permission. Will knew he'd be having an early night anyway, with no plans to drive anywhere.

"Why not," he said then smiled. It had been an odd though enlightening day and a relaxing glass to soothe him sounded ideal, even though it was a 'school night'. Louise poured and handed him a glass, and Will took a larger mouthful than normal, letting the cool liquid massage his throat.

"That do the trick?" she asked, a grin on her lips. The pair sat down at the kitchen table with their drinks and Will filled her in on the rest of his day, 'losing' Sanjeev and the call from his father.

"God, I hope his dad wasn't in surgery when he called him."

"No idea, I can only hope not. I believe he's not the most charming of humans at the best of times."

"Definitely not. Superb surgeon, though. If I was being operated on, I'd want someone with his skills and wouldn't be too bothered about his bedside manner. But then I'm biased."

"He's safely home now, though, so no harm done. I just hope I don't lose the job. We'll see." Will's phone buzzed with an incoming text. It was Hazel.

I've some news. Call me after dinner service, 7 pm should work.

His face must have showed his concern at the content, as Louise said, "What is it, Will?"

He pushed his glass of wine across to her.

"You can finish mine. I may have to pop out later. To the centre."

"I thought you were on duty tomorrow night?"

"I am but Hazel has news on the body in the woods. I'll know more later, but from her message, I suspect I might be right about the victim being known to us."

TEN

Will took Hazel's hand that didn't hold a cigarette and held it for a moment. When he'd called her at 7 pm as instructed, she'd broken down in tears and he'd rushed over. Normally a woman that rarely showed her stress, the outburst said everything: Hazel was hurting inside.

"He often went off for a day or two at a time. They all do. I didn't think this instance was any different. Maybe I should have reported him missing."

"You said yourself earlier that many are transient. They are never missing really, just away. Plus, the police wouldn't do anything anyway, they haven't got the resources."

Hazel wiped her cheek with the back of her hand as tears fell in a steady stream.

"I'll grab you some tissue," he said, leaving the canteen for a moment, heading to the toilets. A moment later he was back with a wad of toilet roll rolled up. "Here."

She blew her nose loudly and wiped her eyes, the act of doing so making her look a little calmer.

"How do we know for sure that it's Clyde?" he asked. "Have the police formally identified him?"

Clyde Mollineau had been living on the streets since he was nearly seventeen, though if you counted the number of times he'd run away from foster care over the years, he was in his early teens when he first slept rough. Even at eighteen, the lad hadn't accumulated much to call his own in life. With little to no support at their various housing placements, youngsters like Clyde found it difficult to get even a part-time job, since a permanent address was invariably an issue. There was often little motivation to change their current situation and so they filled their days by loitering and begging. Clyde had learned to do the same. Somewhere along the line, he'd ended up dead.

"An officer called not long after you had left, asking questions. It was only when they mentioned what he'd been wearing, you know, that parka he always wore, the red and black one? He was found in that."

"But no formal ID, then?"

"No, not yet. If it is Clyde, there are no family members that I know of so I'm going to the mortuary tomorrow morning." She sniffed hard, then asked, "Do you think it could be someone else in his jacket? Perhaps he traded it for something?" There was a milligram of hope in her voice that pained Will in his heart. What were the chances? A homeless person rarely traded their clothes for anything, particularly not a jacket or coat.

"It's possible I suppose…"

"But not likely."

There was no need for confirmation. They both knew the score.

"What time are you going? Would you like me to come with you?"

Hazel didn't answer right away, and Will wondered if she'd heard him. He was about to ask again when she said, "Please, yes. I was going to go first thing, say around eight. I could go a bit later but…" Will did a quick recce in his head of his diary; he had some unscheduled time after the school run. "How about if I pick you up around nine and we go over together? I have the school run beforehand and I can't change that, Louise is working. Will that work for you and getting back here?"

"That's good of you, Will, yes. I'll let them know. Perhaps we can actually go in together, for support. In case it really is Clyde."

"Of course. Now, will you be okay tonight?"

"Yes, thanks. This place will keep my mind busy, though I don't suppose I'll sleep much."

Will thought back to events of the previous night, when he hadn't got much sleep either. He was paying for it now and stifled a yawn at her words. She caught him trying to hide it, it brought a smile to her pink blotchy face stained from crying.

"Looks like you need some sleep too," she said and rubbed his arm affectionately again. He gathered his keys off the table and bid her farewell. A couple of youths were hanging around near the door and they both nodded, aware Will was a volunteer at the shelter, a sort of 'thanks' as well as a greeting, a way of communicating their appreciation for all he and the team did. He carried on towards his parked car, thinking about Clyde and his demise. Based on the lad's distinctive jacket, the chances of it not being him tomorrow morning were slim to none, he knew that.

Birdie's comment about how hard it was to move a dead body on your own made Will wonder. Clyde had only been a slight lad, probably weighing not more than nine stone wet through. It was hardly the same as moving, say, Birdie's husband, a full-grown man. If that was the case, whoever disposed of Clyde's body at Hunsbury Hill could probably have done so without any help, though Will wasn't even sure if this was of any consequence. Perhaps Clyde had killed himself. Thoughtfully, Will slipped in behind the wheel and drove home.

Louise was still up and watching TV in the living room when he locked the front door behind him for the night. He filled her in on his conversation with Hazel and noted her face of concern when he mentioned identifying the lad's body the following morning.

"So, with that, I'm going to bed. It's been an eventful twenty-four hours and I have to say I'm knackered," he said, leaning in for a kiss.

"I'll come up too, then," she said, turning the TV off with the remote. "It's a shame I can't pop over to Path tomorrow to see you, though I doubt it would help you any."

"Nice thought all the same," he said, taking her hand and leading her towards the stairs. He could barely keep his eyes open and so he knew sleep wouldn't be an issue. Not tonight.

ELEVEN

Colin Hayhurst swirled whisky around almost-melted ice cubes, letting them chink against the sides of the tumbler while he contemplated the lad's death. They'd killed him, then. When the ransom note had reached his desk, he's brushed it off as nothing serious. Who kidnaps a homeless person and then demands money? He'd assumed it was a prank, someone that hadn't a clue how kidnappings and ransoms worked. It was almost laughable. Surely, they'd be better choosing a rich businessman's daughter over a street person. But it hadn't been a hoax after all. He detested the urine-soaked doorways he passed some mornings, and while it was a shame the kid been killed, it was one less to litter the streets. That was how he reconciled it with himself anyway. Perhaps he should have reported it to the police instead of ignoring it, though it was too late now. He tossed the remainder of the whisky to the back of his throat and picked up his briefcase. It had been a long day. Fancying something spicy for dinner, he decided to pick up a take-away curry on his way home. He very much doubted Babs had cooked.

TWELVE

He'd slept well, all things considered, and Will wondered how Hazel was feeling this morning. With Louise on an early shift, Poppy and the triplets fell into his charge, and he battled to get breakfast into three four-year-olds and persuade a six-year-old that she couldn't go to school dressed as a dinosaur. While he smiled inwardly at his headstrong young girl, his priority was getting everyone fed, appropriately dressed and out of the door before his own shift started. He needed to push them on.

"Let's get moving," he shouted over the morning din. "Ice cream after dinner if you can all make the car within the next ten minutes!" It was one way of persuading Poppy to lend a hand and remove her focus from what she was or wasn't wearing for the day.

It took precisely nine minutes to get everyone into the car and ready to go and Will clapped his hands together in triumph. When he had everyone strapped in, he set off first to the village day care and then on to Poppy's school. He pulled up outside and watched while his eldest made her way into the grounds and began to catch up with one of her friends who was waiting for her. She gave a backwards glance to her father and smiled just enough to say, 'see you later.' Satisfied, he headed back into town and the shelter. Hazel would be waiting, breakfast rush over with, likely a few stragglers making a mug of tea last as long as possible. At least it wasn't raining, the service users wouldn't need the indoor areas quite the same today. Will remembered the long, cold, wet days living on the streets; they could be bone-achingly tough. He pulled into the car park. Hazel must have been watching for his vehicle because she was standing by the passenger door before he'd taken his seat belt off. He was relieved to see she looked a good deal brighter than she had the previous night and was back to her strong self.

"Morning, Will," she said brightly. "All the girls at school okay?" She was making polite conversation, away from the task ahead.

"Fed, dressed and delivered. Poppy was adamant she was going as a dinosaur this morning, and I thought we might have a tantrum, but it was narrowly avoided," he said triumphantly as the car pulled away. It was only a short drive across town to the general hospital, and Hazel filled him in on the local gossip. It seemed the news of Clyde had spread among the other centre users and everyone feared the worst. From what Hazel had heard, the stories were getting more and more sinister, with theories ranging from abduction to overdose and everything in between. She'd been tempted to tell them all to shut up but had refrained. Until she knew anything certain, there was nothing to tell.

"Who are we meeting there, do you know?" he asked.

"A detective, DC Stephen Flint. He was the one that I met when he dropped in asking questions."

Will turned the car onto Billing Road before turning again. The trick now was to find a spot to park. As with most busy hospitals, it was a lottery, but he spotted a car slowly pulling out of a space up ahead and waited patiently for the elderly man to take his time. He looked about a hundred years old, small and frail and probably shouldn't still be driving at his age. Hazel and Will sat in silence as they watched the man struggle and eventually pull away clear. Will slipped effortlessly into the spot. He turned to Hazel. "Are you ready?"

She nodded. "Let's get this over with."

It looked like any other drab hospital building with modern grey concrete slabs and facias that many larger buildings consisted off. The dead had to be processed somewhere and Will doubted they noticed the building they were refrigerated in. They entered the hospital itself and followed the signs, past the oncology centre where Louise would be busy working, past the blood taking unit, and then they were there. The mortuary with its viewing room stood straight in front of them. Will felt Hazel pause for a moment. When she eventually summoned the strength to move forward, he hung back a little to give her some space. He was there if she needed him. Up ahead, he spotted who he assumed was DC Flint and watched as the man stepped forward to greet Hazel. He offered his own hand and the two shook. Will explained where he fitted in and why he was there.

"After you," Detective Flint said, his outstretched arm holding the door for the two of them. Hazel went first, closely followed by Will, and then the detective. A glass window with a curtain pulled across it was all they'd look through, and Will wasn't sure if that was a good thing or not. It certainly made him feel detached from the process of identification, an impersonal way of performing such a task. DC Flint had a word with a technician before asking, "Are you ready?"

Hazel and Will nodded, and the curtain opened. A body covered in a sheet lay in front of them. When the sheet was pulled down away from the victim's face, Hazel sighed sadly. The amount of angry, visible bruising around his neck told Will all he needed to know. He felt a lump rise in his throat, and he struggled for a moment to swallow it.

It was indeed Clyde Mollineau.

THIRTEEN

Will and Hazel told the detective all they knew about Clyde – who he hung around with, where he stayed occasionally, that sort of thing. The truth was there wasn't a great deal of information to pass on and that saddened Will. He wished he could have been more helpful.

"What will happen now, to Clyde's body?" he asked the detective. "Are you personally involved in investigating his death or is that it now for you?"

The young DC didn't appear to be much older than Clyde himself and Will guessed around twenty-five years old. He'd have preferred someone a bit older, more seasoned perhaps, to investigate what had happened to Clyde. He hoped the man wasn't in charge of the case, that he was part of the team and someone else was running the show. Maybe DC Flint picked up on Will's reservation because he explained to them both what would happen next.

"I'll report back to my boss now you've formally identified the victim, and we'll wait for the post-mortem results before we make a call to investigate. I would, however, say that preliminary findings suggest suspicious circumstances that merit further investigation. Of course, an inquest will be opened. I'll be working the case along with other team members." He handed both Will and Hazel his card. DC Stephen Flint had put their minds at rest at least. If nothing else, the man was astute and pleasant with it. "If you think of anything else that might be of use, please call, anytime. It can be the small things that break a case open," he finished. Will wondered whether the DI would be the same one he saw at the exhumation.

"What is the name of your DI, may I ask?"

"DI Rochelle Mason."

Will nodded.

"Do you know her?" the detective asked.

"No, though we have been on a case together recently. She wouldn't know me, though."

"Oh?"

"I dig graves, for the council. She was at the exhumation, night before last."

"Ah. I heard about that. Still a mystery about the brass name-plate too." Hazel looked at Will, puzzled. Perhaps he'd fill her in on the way back. The story might bring a smile to her face. The trio moved towards the exit; it was time to leave.

"We'll be in touch," Flint said as they parted, and Will and Hazel watched him head back to where he'd come from at pace. Neither of them felt like rushing off anywhere, that their friend Clyde was likely now back in the refrigerator behind them was a sobering thought. Neither of them spoke, both deep in thought.

When Will pulled up at Refresh again, he asked, "I guess someone needs to make an announcement about Clyde, so everyone is aware?"

"Yes, though that's way over my pay grade. I'll inform the boss, he can do what's best, not that he would have known Clyde. There'll be publicity to manage too, the press. *Managing the cafeteria is more than enough for me.*"

"And you do it so well," he said, smiling, lightening the

moment. She let herself out of the passenger side and stuck her head in through the open window.

"Thanks for caring, Will. Many wouldn't."

"I could say the same right back at you." A beat passed, "I'll be there later on tonight, so I'll miss you but chin up, eh?"

"Chin up." He waited until she'd gone inside before making his car available for pickups and driving off. His next booking wasn't until 2 pm so he headed towards the cab office to wait. Birdie's offer of help seeped into his grey matter as did the DI with the bluish hair. Add that to the likely suspicious death of someone he knew and he had himself three reasons why he should get involved somehow. Three small instances that all pointed to one activity. It was a sign, surely? A sketch from Monty Python's *Life of Brian* made him smile: "The shoe is the sign!" he shouted inside the car, holding one arm in the air as if he too was holding up a shoe, like in the movie. He believed in fate and he believed in acting on opportunities as they arose. While it didn't feel like an opportunity, was this such an instance?

His phone pinged with a fare request. He looked at the address: police headquarters, Wootton Hall Park. What were the chances? He picked up speed and headed over to meet his next customer. Maybe it was the area commander needing a lift, car in for service perhaps. Surely a liveried vehicle and a constable would sort that out. Or a visitor needing a lift? Maybe someone had had a job interview? He hadn't bothered to look for the passenger-to-be's name, he'd do that on arrival.

It wasn't long before he pulled up outside the huge, imposing red-brick building. It reminded Will of an old hospital from days gone by, though a newer wing had been added, again in depressing red brick. A sign informed him there was a restaurant off to his left and huge stone – or were they marble? – pillars held up the front porch. Will stopped beneath them to collect his passenger. He knew who she was before he'd pulled to a standstill – her hair gave it away. Intent on studying her phone, she was either unaware of his arrival, or was happy for him to wait while she finished whatever she was doing. After a couple of beats, Will got out and walked around to open the rear passenger door for her. She still hadn't looked up. He felt stupid with the door open and no activity on her part, so he called, "DI Mason, calling DI Mason, do you read me? Over." She looked up, blank. Had he got her name wrong? He was about to double-check his phone when she rewarded him with a smile. She stepped forward and seated herself on the back seat. When Will was buckled up, she asked, "How do you know I'm a DI?" He caught her eyes in the rear-view mirror and said, "I was sitting in the cab of the digger when the coffin lid blew off the other night."

"That's right, you were, I remember now," she said, before turning her interest back to her phone.

Will thought fast. DI Rochelle Mason was sitting behind him. Clyde was laid in the mortuary. He couldn't let the opportunity go to waste.

FOURTEEN

HE FIGURED HE'D START OFF WITH A QUESTION ON COMMON GROUND before casually mentioning Clyde's death and the country park. Since their journey was only going to be a short one, back to the hospital again it appeared, he wasted no time. He took the plunge and hoped for the best. He had to get her talking.

"Any clue as to how that name plaque managed to get above ground? There weren't any obvious signs of the coffin being tampered with, not from my understanding anyway. Mighty odd."

"There doesn't seem to be a reasonable explanation, yet, no. It's a first for me, but since no crime appears to have been committed..." She let her words trail off as she gazed out of the window. The A45 was not that interesting.

"What made you decide to exhume the body in the first place, just the name plaque?"

"That and the son of the deceased. He was worried that she'd been buried alive and wanted her dug up again to be sure. The coroner had said no, obviously, she'd had a complete post-mortem after all, so there was no way she could have still been alive. Perhaps if she'd only had a minimal post-mortem there could have been a chance, though still highly unlikely. But the plaque found in the grass made it a mystery. Someone had surely tampered with the coffin. We were wrong."

"Is the son satisfied now, do you think?"

"No clue, but he's clearly got a mental issue to be so adamant and push like he did. No one survives a full post-mortem, no one." Will nodded his understanding. Having your main organs removed, weighed and then placed together in a plastic bag before being inserted back into your chest cavity was a sure sign the person was indeed dead. Will moved on to the more important questions he had for her.

"How's the investigation going, the poor individual found out at Hunsbury Hill?" It pained Will to sound so casual about it. The man had been eating stew and dumplings in the canteen in recent days. Will had chatted to him occasionally.

"Progressing," was all she said and went back to her phone.

He needed to push a bit harder if he was going to get anywhere. "Do you know how he died yet? I know knife attacks are more and more common these days, had he been stabbed?" He tried to catch her eye, but she was having none of it. It was obvious she didn't want to talk.

"I can't comment about an active case."

Desperate measures. "Would it help if I told you I'd just identified Clyde's body only this morning? I met DC Flint at the hospital earlier."

Finally, she raised her eyes to meet his in the mirror. "You knew Clyde, then. I'm sorry for the loss of your friend, but I really can't say anything more. I'm assuming you've told DC Flint everything you know?"

"Yes, I have. There wasn't much to tell really. He was a loner, like many of Refresh's users are. I volunteer there one night per week, that's how I knew Clyde." She nodded but refrained from any further comments. They were almost at the hospital when Will reluctantly had to change the subject. "Which department are we heading to?" He wondered if she was going to the mortuary, and was surprised when she said, "Oncology, please. It's not far from the mortuary, so just head there again if you want, it's only a short walk." A moment or two later and they pulled up in front of the building. "Do you have time to wait? I'll be about fifteen minutes, maybe twenty. If not, I'll call another ride back."

"I'll wait, it's not a problem. My wife works in there," he said, smiling and nodding towards the department where the DI was headed herself. "Shame I can't grab a cuppa with her." DI Mason didn't return the smile, and it was only then that he wondered if she was going in for treatment herself, that maybe it had nothing to do with another investigation at all. He'd assumed her visit was work related, perhaps he was wrong. He drummed up a more fitting smile, one he hoped contained both concern and hope. He jumped out of his seat then opened her door just as she did so herself. "If I get moved on, don't worry, I'll be back here to meet you a moment later." He cut her some slack in the lack-of-return-smile department and made himself comfortable for the wait.

Last time he'd pulled into a parking space, it hadn't ended well, and he didn't want to mess up any further discussion opportunities with the detective. The return journey back to police headquarters was an added bonus. From his spot on the narrow street, he kept an eye open for a dreaded parking attendant ready to move him on.

Twenty minutes later, he could see her walking towards his car again, so he pulled forward to meet up with her. "Back to base or somewhere else, ma'am?"

The overly polite term raised a slight smile. "You make me sound like Patricia Carmichael in *Line of Duty*," she said, getting in. "It'll be a while before I'm a 'ma'am'. Always a 'boss', though. Is it all right if we make a detour first? I need a sandwich before I head back."

"That I can do. Anywhere in particular? Only there's a sandwich van I frequent quite a bit, it's run by the Refresh Centre and so the proceeds go back to it. They make the best rolls in town in my opinion, but then I am biased."

"That's fine," she said before resting her head back and closing her eyes. When he pulled up by the food van and she didn't open her eyes or stir, he made an educated guess what someone obviously tired, and perhaps feeling a bit under the weather, would like for lunch. He left her napping while he ordered a cheese and salad roll and a packet of ready salted. He added a bottle of water for good measure and grabbed a Twix for himself. With lunch packed away in a paper bag, and still no sign of her waking, Will retraced their journey back up to Wootton Hall Park and the police HQ. It seemed his luck, in terms of conversation about the case, had run out. He pulled up by the huge porchway and called out to her gently. It seemed a shame to wake her, but he couldn't drive around all afternoon with her sleeping in the back. Stanley Kipper, his regular twice-weekly 2 pm ride wouldn't be happy about that, he hated the police with a passion.

"Rochelle, we're here." Nothing. He didn't want to touch her and so tapped firmly on the headrest to make enough noise to bring her to. It worked. Sleepy eyes opened slowly and then, realising she'd been asleep, she gathered herself in a hurry and sat up straight. She groaned at the realisation she'd drifted off. "I won't tell a living soul," he said kindly and handed her the paper bag containing her lunch. "I went with plain cheese salad in case you felt rough. I hope I did right?" The smallest of smiles appeared on her mouth before she alighted from his car. Once out, she leaned in through the open passenger window and looked him straight in the eyes. "You're a perceptive individual, thank you. Cheese is about all I fancy," she added, before heading off.

Will wondered about her treatment and the effect it was undoubtedly having on her. He hoped his sandwich offering had helped a little.

FIFTEEN

He must have a trusting face, Will mused as he opened his Twix and bit into the chocolatey stick. A takeaway coffee sat in the cup holder, steam drifting upwards through the small hole in the lid, and he fought to retrieve a flake of chocolate that had fallen into his lap. A small brown mark on his trousers he could do without, so he stepped out of the car and brushed himself down. With the offending piece on the breeze, he climbed back in to finish his drink. What a morning he'd had. First identifying Clyde's thin body, and then ferrying the DI back to the hospital and her own treatment. He knew from his wife's work what went on in the oncology unit. Chemotherapy could take a while to drip into the veins of its recipient, but radiotherapy was over in only a handful of minutes. Louise had joked it took longer to put the gown on then get changed back into regular clothes again than it did to actually administer the radiation itself. Will figured that was what the DI had been doing for those twenty minutes, it made perfect sense. Where in her body the treatment was targeted, he'd never know, and Louise would never tell him and he wasn't sure it even mattered. He just hoped her prognosis was a positive one. Perhaps he'd drive her again, for further treatment. If only he'd thought to give her his card.

He finished the last of his Twix and turned his mind to the fact that Clyde had likely been strangled. That felt personal to him. A stabbing he could understand, perhaps in the course of a robbery gone wrong, though for what reward? His old coat? No, that couldn't be it. A random killing, maybe: did Clyde get into a fight, was it accidental? Strangulation seemed odd, a bit too organised perhaps, as if someone had planned to take Clyde's life. A random stabbing in the street was more commonplace, though would thugs move a body to the country park? Surely they'd leave him where he fell. He grabbed his phone, googled 'strangulation' and read the articles that caught his attention. Most were to do with either strangulation and its part in domestic abuse, or with a sexual angle – erotic asphyxiation. He couldn't be sure, but he didn't think Clyde's death was anything to do with the latter. Domestic abuse didn't fit either. Strangulation took about three minutes to achieve said a Wiki page. That meant someone was willing to hold on, hard, for that length of time. Someone who felt passionately enough that Clyde should die. For what reason? Was it more satisfying for the killer? There was no blood with a strangulation, unless piano wire was used, but that was garrotted. He wondered about the post-mortem; would it show the killer was in front of Clyde, someone watching life drain from his body and extremely personal, or behind him? He'd no idea how he was going to be able to find out, but he'd try. DI Mason was his only hope.

He checked the time – 1.30 pm, almost time to pick Stanley Kipper up. He was one person that certainly wouldn't contemplate courting the police.

SIXTEEN

The Crescent was a mixture of three-storey-plus-basement Victorian properties and an array of generally huge houses. A handful of smaller red-brick houses belonging to the not-quite-so-rich peppered the street in between. Stanley Kipper lived in one of the smaller houses and, like Birdie's, it was more than ample for an elderly person living on their own. While Birdie kept her place immaculate, the same couldn't be said for Stanley. Will regularly had the unfortunate experience of helping him in with his grocery shopping and had had his eyes well and truly opened. Stanley, it seemed, liked to keep each and every newspaper he'd ever read, and they were piled high in every room, like paper pillars holding the house up. Since the downstairs was almost entirely full, Will had wondered about the first floor and if it was the same. Perhaps the loft matched the rest of the house, in which case capacity would soon be reached. Will pulled up outside and waited for his elderly passenger. The front door opened immediately, and Stanley, a couple of books and magazines tucked neatly under his arm, slowly made his way down the front path, one slippered foot in front of the other. Will groaned and left his seat;

the man had forgotten his shoes again. When he was close enough, he called out to him, "No shoes today, Stanley?" He pointed down at the man's feet as a hint and waited for realisation to dawn.

"Couldn't be arsed," he said firmly. "These'll do. No one will notice."

Will doubted that very much but let him be. If Stanley wanted to wear his underpants on the outside of his trousers, he wasn't going to risk the man's wrath by suggesting he shouldn't. The same with his slippers. "Right you are," he said and walked alongside him to the car. He opened the rear passenger door and Stanley took his time getting settled, books and magazines beside him. "Today's reading material?" Will enquired.

"Well, they're not for toilet paper," he grumbled at Will's question. "Of course they're for reading, I didn't think they needed fresh air."

That told him. Will returned to the driver's seat and set off back towards town and the hospital campus yet again. This time it was the orthopaedic wing where Stanley read to some of the longer-term patients, who lay flat on their backs for days on end, a couple of afternoons per week. Will had mused to Louise that he wouldn't know which was worse, Stanley's literature choice or sheer boredom itself.

"What's today's entertainment you've picked?" Will watched as Stanley found the correct book to show him first, though he already knew the topic. He held it up so Will could see the front cover in his rear-view mirror. Will smiled. Someone was going to be fed up later on. It was a book by an ex Labour leader.

"Michael Foot's *The Pen and the Sword*, 1957. One of my favourites," Stanley said, smiling. "I never get bored of reading it. None of his books, to be fair, a remarkable man in my opinion, not to mention one of the best journalistic writers of our time. The envy of many politicians I believe."

Will watched two-day grey stubble bob up and down on the man's chin. Louise would have wanted to shave it off.

"Your hero."

"The working man's man. When I was on the picket line at Wapping…" Will had heard it all before and tuned out while the elderly man recalled stories from his time on strike at the famous printworks. Wapping was as famous for its workers' dispute history as Greenham Common's women's peace camp was for its nuclear missile protest history. Around 6,000 printworkers had gone on strike and it had lasted for fifty-four weeks in total, three weeks longer than the miners' strike that had only finished the previous year. With over 1,200 arrests and 400 police officers injured, the dispute had made history for being a particularly violent one. Stanley himself had been arrested and had spent time in a police cell on more than one occasion. He told his stories of those weeks of combat, as he termed them, as if he were a local hero. While Will could understand fighting for something you believed in, he drew the line at actual violence. The police had come off badly, being accused of heavy-handedness and Stanley had his scar to prove it. There wouldn't be many people he hadn't shown it to, and Stanley had already reserved a spot in Golders Green crematorium, where his hero was now. It was safe to say Stanley Kipper was a diehard Labour supporter. Will was grateful the journey into town was a quick one, traffic being light, since Stanley was on top form. The unfortunate, confined patients he'd be reading to later on would not be so lucky.

"Bloody Margaret Thatcher," Stanley grumbled. The words penetrated Will's ears and he resurfaced back into the one-sided conversation.

"Has anyone ever told you to get lost?" Will asked. "Conservative supporters, perhaps?" He was intrigued to know. Maybe a nurse had turfed him off a ward.

"Some, yes. Doesn't bother me." The man had skin like a rhino.

"Is that why you dislike the police, then? The strike, I mean."

"Useless, all of them."

"Haven't you ever needed them, maybe had something stolen, or reported a crime happening? I bet you've seen all sorts of things during your life."

"Not with my own experience of them. I stay well clear now. They can all do one for all I care."

Will pulled up outside the correct unit and opened the rear door for Stanley. When his passenger had finally shuffled out of the car, Will watched him gather his books and magazines, and noted one was in fact a western. Maybe someone would get lucky, the subject matter somewhat more palatable than politics. "I'll be back to pick you up in two hours then," Will called as Stanley made his way inside without another word, leaving him standing there shaking his head at the man.

SEVENTEEN

By the time Will had returned Stanley back to his house, it was almost time for his shift at Refresh. With another thirty minutes before his official start time, he was about to call Louise at home when his phone rang. It was Birdie. Did she need a ride? Because if she did, there wasn't much time to do so and be in his apron in the kitchen on time. He accepted the call. "Hello Birdie, what can I do for you?"

"I thought I'd see how you're getting on finding out who the boy in the woods is. What have you discovered?" He'd forgotten all about telling her it, that he knew it was Clyde Mollineau.

"Unfortunately, Birdie, Hazel and I identified Clyde's body earlier this morning. Sadly, it was someone known to us at the centre."

"Oh Will, I am so sorry to hear that. Do the police have much to go on?"

"Not that I'm aware of, though I think he's been strangled." The line stayed silent. Had she heard him? "Birdie?"

"Just thinking. From the front or behind, do you know?"

"No clue. I'm guessing you're also wondering about the killer's mindset?"

"Certainly am. From the front is much more personal, a real enemy. Not that someone strangling your friend from the rear isn't also an enemy, but you understand my meaning."

"The post-mortem was this afternoon sometime, I guess they'll know a little more by now. Maybe the killer left some DNA or Clyde fought and scratched them. We can only hope he took something from his attacker, something for them to work with."

"Have you found a contact at the police yet? That's the only real way you'll learn much, get one on your side somehow. Eventually they'll let something slip, that's what reporters rely on happening, for their stories."

"Working on it, early stages." He thought back to DI Mason and DC Flint. He needed to work on them more, build some sort of relationship and get them talking.

"I don't suppose you know what pub they drink in?" she asked.

"No idea. We're certainly not on drinking terms that's for sure."

"I'd start at the Old Bank," she said, "at least it's near a local station, of sorts." It was only a local desk, but hey, it was town centre and a start. "Maybe you'll get lucky?"

Will thought about his plans. He could call in for a pint after his shift, but he'd better let Louise know he'd be home a bit later than normal.

"I'll give it a go later. I've a shift to do now and I won't finish until nine, so they could be long gone by then."

"Where are you now?"

"In town, I'm heading to the Refresh Centre a bit earlier. Why?"

"Come and pick me up, and I'll babysit a spot at the bar for you, just in case. My ears can flap just as much as yours can. I can get a ride back from someone else." Will calculated the timings quickly in his head. It would work. He was about to say he was on his way when he realised the line was empty. She'd gone and he smiled at her style. He turned the car in the direction of Timken Way North and marvelled at the older woman's spirit. Most her age would be contemplating a night in with a hot cocoa and their slippers, not eavesdropping off-duty police officers in a town centre bar for an hour or two.

He hoped she would be ready when he arrived outside, he hated getting anywhere late, volunteer or not. He needn't have worried; Birdie was pulling the door closed behind her as he stopped out the front. She gave him a light wave as usual, and he held the rear door open for her.

"Better step on the gas back if you're to be on time," she said as they moved off, bright red lips catching his eye in the mirror. The car slowly filled with the scent of roses as they sped towards St Giles Street and the relevant pub, and Will dropped her off with a few moments to spare.

"Good luck, enjoy yourself," he said, smiling.

"You can count on it," she said, followed by a finger wave that told him she was a grown woman and could take care of herself. He watched her casually enter the bar before pulling away.

Once inside Refresh, he headed for the kitchen and Hazel, hoping she was still there. She often worked longer hours than was required of her and had already done the early shift before they'd gone to the mortuary. He needn't have worried; her short dark hair was clearly visible at the back of the kitchen and he could see she wasn't alone. As he made his way over, he could tell from her body language that the conversation was a serious one. Standing with her was one of the regulars, an older man called George, which was odd because Refresh's users didn't generally enter the kitchen itself. The whole situation seemed out of kilter. Will bided his time and waited until they'd finished, nodding in greeting to George as he passed him by. Hazel wore a look of concern and Will enquired if everything was okay.

"George was telling me he hasn't seen Jonesy for more than

twenty-four hours. With all the kerfuffle that has gone on with Clyde, I hadn't noticed. George is a bit worried, he's his buddy-up and has taken the youngster under his wing." It wasn't hard to detect what Hazel was thinking – was Jonesy missing?

"Shall I inform the police, do you think? How long since George last saw him, any idea?"

"Yesterday morning. At breakfast. He's not heard from him since and the lad's not as streetwise as some of the others. I'm starting to worry, Will. What should we do?"

"In light of Clyde, I say we err on the side of caution and report him as missing. At least the police will be aware, and if he comes strolling in for dinner later, then great, no harm done. Any idea what he was wearing?" Will knew it was a pointless question, the homeless all wore the same dark and often dirty clothes, it came with the territory. Clyde's red jacket had been an anomaly, an identifying feature almost.

"Dark clothes, like…"

"Yeah, I know, everyone else on the street," he finished.

"Shall I go and report it now?" he said, looking at his watch. It was gone 5 pm, the local desk closed. He thought of Birdie sat in a bar not far away and wondered if she'd even seen an officer to eavesdrop on as yet.

"Would you? I'll stay on here and cover. You'll need a photo," she said. "I'll grab one from the office." The admin team took a snapshot of their users so they had a record of who frequented the facilities. It came in handy in situations like this one, and with often no family members to fall back on, it made sense. A moment later she was back, George by her side. "I thought George might be able to supply more info, take him with you," she instructed. Rich dark eyes, filled with sadness, fixed on Will's own and he nodded his agreement.

"I've nothing to hide from the police," George said, as if Will had asked.

"Let's go."

It was nearly an hour later before a report was completed and filed, though from the desk sergeant's demeanour, both Will and George knew just how much effort would be given to finding Jonesy. He lived on the streets and certainly wouldn't be a priority. Will drove George back to Refresh and got to work in the kitchen. The change in pace gave him time to think.

EIGHTEEN

It was 9.30 pm when Will finally left Refresh, exhausted, and so there was no way he was going to the pub. On top of the physical side of feeding and clearing up after so many, with such an emotional day, he was done in mentally too. He was glad the village of Moulton and his bed were only a short drive back, and he hoped Louise hadn't gone to sleep as yet, though she was on earlies this week and would be as bushed as he was. He asked Siri to dial her number, hoping he wasn't disturbing her but at the same time desperate to hear her voice. She sounded wide awake as she filled the car through the speakers and he took a second to let it warm his heart before saying anything.

"Are you in bed?"

"Yes, but reading and hoping I can stay awake long enough to say hello to you in the flesh. Are you on your way back?"

"Not far off, heading north now so maybe ten minutes away. Can I ask you a work question?"

"Fire away."

"Someone having radiotherapy, do they have it weekly or what?"

"Strange question coming from you, Will, everything okay?"

"Of course. A customer going through it is all."

"Then they will be getting a dose each day except weekends, and it can be either three weeks or up to maybe five weeks, depending on dose rates and where the cancer is situated and a couple of other factors."

"That must be hard to fit into their schedule then – every day, I mean?"

"Not as much as you'd think. We have many that visit really early, before work, some at the other end of the day, and lunchtime is popular too. The quietest times are during the working day itself. Does that answer your question?"

"Thanks, yes. So, what I'm also hearing is that the person would likely stick to a regular routine then, if they were working and having treatment at the same time?"

"Almost certainly." Will was thinking about Rochelle. His plan might just work.

"Thanks for that. Look, I'm nearly home now, so if you can stay awake, I'd love to see you."

"I'll make you a cuppa, then." He could hear the change in her voice as she struggled to untangle her legs from the bedclothes. In his mind's eye, her foot would be chasing a slipper again and he smiled at the image.

"Thanks, it's been a long and eventful day. I'll tell you about the rest of it when I see you."

A few minutes later, Will pulled into their driveway. A lamp glowed in the upstairs front bedroom window, the rest of the house he knew would be fast asleep. He opened the front door and was greeted with a peck on the cheek from a sleepy Louise. As she was about to turn towards the kitchen, he gently pulled her back and took her in his arms. He squeezed her, tightly enough to say he needed to feel the contact between them, but not as tight as a bear hug. Louise let him, sensing he was upset about something and waited until he loosened his grip to speak.

"What's on your mind, hun?" They walked towards the kitchen and his waiting cuppa. There was a slice of toast sat with it and Will picked it up hungrily and began to chew. Even though he'd eaten at Refresh, tiredness made him crave carbs and the slice disappeared in seconds. Louise raised an eyebrow in question and Will shook his head 'no'. He flopped down on a kitchen chair and took a sip of his hot drink before letting out a long sigh. Louise waited.

"The body at Hunsbury Hill was known to us at Refresh, a young man called Clyde. Hazel knew him better than me and we identified him at the mortuary, as you know. He was only eighteen and judging by the bruises around his neck, he'd been strangled. The post-mortem was to be later this afternoon, so I don't know any more."

"I'm sorry to hear that, Will." She reached out and placed a hand on his shoulder, kneading it therapeutically.

"There's more. Another lad might be missing, Jonesy, similar age. He's not been seen since yesterday morning and of course could be absolutely anywhere by now. To be on the safe side, I've filed a missing person report, but I don't hold much hope of any action. He's of legal age to do what he wants, and homeless so a double 'inactivity' if you like. Hazel is worried it might be connected somehow, and I'm starting to wonder too."

Louise sat down next to him and leaned in to give him another hug, it was obvious he was hurting inside.

"Well, all we can do is hope Jonesy is doing his own thing somewhere, oblivious. I can see why you're worried, but there really could be a simple answer to his not being seen for a while."

Will knew she was right, but it didn't change the feeling in the pit of his stomach.

"Come on," she encouraged. "Let's get some rest, there might be news in the morning. Talking of which, you're taking the girls in early aren't you, from memory?"

"Yes, I'm on the digger first thing, then in the car from about eleven." He stood, ready to head upstairs to bed. "You know, it'll be a little easier once they all go to the same school, won't it? Poppy will be a little older and could escort the triplets by herself, don't you think?"

Louise chuckled at the notion. "Only if they were each on a lead like a dog. It would be like herding cats otherwise. You know what their minds are like – they see any shiny object and suddenly they've lost interest in what they were doing to follow it. They take after their dad with that one." She took his fingers in her own and led him upstairs, still chuckling.

"Just the one grave tomorrow, is it?" she asked.

"Yes, and that's enough. Graves needed means someone is waiting to be buried." It was then that Will wondered what would now happen to Clyde's remains. With no family to locate or fall back on for funeral arrangements, it would be a pauper's funeral. Still, at least he'd get a proper send-off, even if there wouldn't be any mourners other than Hazel and himself. Louise would put a wild wreath together with help from the girls, they could pick flowers and greenery from the back garden. It would be something at least.

NINETEEN

It was a beautiful though crisp morning as Will reached for his can of marker paint and measured out *an 86-by-34-inch rectangle*. The white paint contrasted starkly with the green grass and always reminded Will of the school caretaker putting the markings around the football pitch with his push-along line marker. It was one of the few pleasant school memories he had. He got to work with his spade, cutting around the line to ensure the edges of the final hole were nice and even. Once he was happy the earth had been loosened properly, Will fired up the small digger and carefully scraped a shallow layer of turf off the top, stacking it neatly on pieces of ply nearby. When the grave had been filled in later, long after the last mourner had gone, Will would carefully rearrange the turf pieces on the surface once again. Will took pride in digging a hole with edges so straight that even Sanjeev would have been happy with his efforts. It took skill to get the hole even and just right, and when Will was satisfied he'd done so, he jumped down from the small cab and slipped into the hole to double-check it was deep enough. He knew from his instructions it was to be a double grave; in the past someone had dug the same hole to seven feet, and underneath where he was standing were the remains of a loved one. His tape measure confirmed five feet, he'd dug down enough. With everything in order, he climbed back out and set about levelling the sides of the hole with a long-armed spade made specially for the job. Loose earth lay scattered in the base of the hole and he slipped back inside to finish off and make sure the base was even. Happy with his efforts, he climbed out for the final time. No mourner liked to see the cold bare soil of an empty grave before their loved one was lowered into it so Will liked to lay a bed of fresh leaves, or wild flowers if they were available, along the bottom. It seemed more respectful somehow, a little nicer. He got to work filling his wheelbarrow with a mixture of old and fresh leaves from the line of nearby bushes and tipped them into the hole. His long-armed spade evened them out easily. His last tasks were to add planks either side for the pall-bearers to stand on, and to drape the artificial grass to cover the sides of the earthy hole. Finally, planks at the front and the rear of the hole were placed ready to take the weight of the coffin later. Webbing straps alongside would ease the casket down when the pall-bearers finalised their mission. Will stood back to look. Everything was in order, the open grave ready to receive person number two. The headstone gone, he wondered who it was for, the husband or wife of the first deceased?

Having tidied away his tools, he covered the nearby pile of earth and slices of turf with green tarpaulin before returning the small digger to its parking place. It had taken him three hours and he'd return later to fill the hole in once again. His work here, for now, was done. Preparing the grave was one of the most satisfying activities of his day, and he enjoyed every moment of it. Exhumations, though, were a bit different…

Will changed into clean jeans and replaced heavy boots with casual shoes before stuffing his work gear into a large holdall he kept in the boot. Happy with his transformation to taxi driver, he checked his phone, then headed further into town for something to eat.

"Siri, call Birdie Fox," he instructed as he drove.

"Calling–Birdie–Fox," said the mechanical woman's voice. Will was anxious to hear if Birdie had any news about the previous night. He always set his phone to silent while digging in the cemetery, and on returning to his car he'd seen she'd called but hadn't left a message. He waited for the line to connect and hoped she wasn't sitting under the dryer at the hairdressers. An enthusiastic voice greeted him.

"Will!" she exclaimed. "I didn't want to leave a message, but first, how are you feeling today, better?"

"Thanks for asking, and yes, better. Sleep is a wonderful thing."

"Good. Now, I've a little news. I didn't overhear anything in the pub last night, nothing doing, but I did get lucky."

"Well, that proves you're never too old," he said before laughing at his own joke.

"Ha ha, very funny. Be serious for a moment, will you? Guess who was having a quiet drink in there?"

How was he ever likely to know the answer to that one?

"I give up," he said, playing her game.

"DS Peter Willow, though he was known as 'Windy' to his colleagues back then. Still would be, I'd expect."

"And who is 'Windy' Willow? Oh, I get it," he said, immediately understanding the reference.

"'Windy' was my arresting officer."

Will did a quick calculation – the man must be about as old as Birdie herself, surely? A working DS? Still? No chance.

"He's not still working, though. He can't be?"

"Retired now, of course, but what do a lot of detectives do when they retire?"

"Pass. No clue. What do they do?"

"Cold cases! For something to do." Will could see where she

was going with it. Could Willow be a way in for information? Had Birdie already something to report?

"Excellent, a contact. But was he receptive to you? I mean from what you've just told me, he arrested you and you went down for murder. He hardly sounds like your best buddy."

"True, but I went down because I stabbed Derek, which he deserved by the way. But that aside, Windy was kind to me back then and was simply doing his job. He'd have been in his mid-twenties, still a bit wet behind the ears, my case likely helped his career. Anyway, I'm sure you don't need all the history. I asked him about Clyde's case and at first he stayed shtum. He's retired, not in the same offices, remember. Plus, murder is investigated by the East Midlands Special Operations Unit, so not just the local lads and lasses, but I'm sure you already know that." It was news to Will; he'd find out more about EMSOU later. Birdie moved on: "That aside, I got him talking, and drinking," she said, laughing. "But get this: apparently there was writing scrawled across Clyde's chest, in blue ink."

"A message? What did it say?"

"'Your move'. Now, I swore I wouldn't repeat what he told me so you can't divulge your source," she warned. "Else I'd have to kill you too."

Will nodded, as if she could see him agreeing. He wondered if she still had it in her. Either way, the message was something to work with, but what did 'your move' mean exactly?

TWENTY

It was always a pleasure chatting to Birdie, she had such a way about her, always finding the funny side where others failed to raise a smile. It was refreshing to speak with someone so direct, someone who had no qualms about offending, though rarely did. There was never any malice and Will had a lot of time for the woman.

It was coming up to 11.30 am by the time he'd parked his car in a town-centre side street, bought the local newspaper and headed for the sandwich van. He ordered the same as he'd bought for DI Mason the day before and wondered about getting her lunch while he was there. He was about to change his order to two cheese salad rolls when he thought better of it. She might find it a bit creepy, a random taxi driver buying her lunch two days in a row, it was hardly the norm. He added a Twix again instead, he would eat it later. The warming sun was light on his shoulders as he waited, retracing the events of the last forty-eight hours or so in his head. So much had gone on: the chilly night in the graveyard and the flying undertaker, Clyde's body being found and identifying him at the mortuary, Birdie being so carefree about the murder of her husband, meeting the DI with blue hair once again, and now news of Jonesy going AWOL – at least he hoped that was all he'd gone. The message of 'your move' found on Clyde's body unnerved him a little, and he hoped it would light a fire under the police's investigation. East Midlands Special Operations Unit nudged at his grey matter. Where did DC Flint and DI Mason fit in with that? His sandwich order ready, he headed for a bench further along the street and sat down for a moment while he used his phone to look up EMSOU. There were several units within the set-up, but the crux of it was that five neighbouring counties had pulled police resources together to form a special operations programme to fight serious crime. It made perfect sense and encompassed Derbyshire, Leicestershire, Nottinghamshire, Northamptonshire and Lincolnshire. It was the East Midlands version of the London Metropolitan police, maybe even better. Clyde, a suspicious death, would fall under EMSOU-MC – major crimes. Maybe DI Rochelle Mason wouldn't be investigating after all? He wondered about DC Flint – would he be able to tell him who would now investigate if it wasn't DI Mason? He pulled the man's card from his wallet, dialled and waited for him to answer. After six rings, Will was about to end the call when DC Flint came on the line. After introducing himself, Will got straight to the point.

"Are you and DI Mason still on Clyde's team now that EMSOU are involved? I'm assuming they are involved since his death is considered suspicious?" Will was trying his luck with the tiny bit of case information he possessed. He waited for DC Stephen Flint to respond, and favourably.

"How do you know it's suspicious?" the detective asked.

"I would have thought most dead bodies found in the woods would be." DI Mason had taken a risk sharing what she had about the cause of death, and he wasn't going to break her confidence.

"So, are you? Are you and DI Mason still on the team?" Will pushed again and crossed his fingers.

"Yes, we are, though EMSOU take the lead, that's why they were set up. They have access to more resources than our small team here, but we provide the local knowledge angle, so we all win. Murders are not that common in our county."

Will clenched his fist and did a mini air punch with it. He wanted to shout 'yes!' but refrained.

"Was there a reason for your call, Mr Peters?" the detective asked. "Or is that it?"

Will thought for a moment then added, "I filed a missing person's report last night. Another one of the centre's users, a young man called Jonesy, hasn't been seen since two mornings ago, and after Clyde's body was found, there's a number of people feeling concerned about his whereabouts, including myself. Has anyone noticed the link – two homeless young men, one town?" Silence. Will realised DC Flint knew nothing of Jonesy being reported missing – his case would have been filed away in a drawer along with the other 'missing' adults of the town. They were free to go their own way, and some did. "You weren't aware, I'm assuming, hence your silence."

"I'll look into it. But don't put two and two together, he may well be hanging out with mates somewhere, unaware of being missed, and be back for dinner when he gets hungry."

Will wanted to ask about the cryptic message, 'your move', but couldn't push his luck or reveal Birdie's source. Realising there was nothing left to say, he finished with, "I'd appreciate you doing that, and of course if Jonesy does return, I'll let you know immediately. You have my number on your phone now, if you have any news."

The conversation over, Will finished his sandwich and people-watched from his bench. He checked the time; he had an hour before he planned to be one street over from police headquarters in the hope of driving DI Mason to the hospital for her daily treatment.

Enjoying the sun warming his shoulders, he unfolded his newspaper and flipped through it quickly, eyes searching for any mention of Clyde and the case. A single column containing a couple of short paragraphs was all he found. There was nothing new to report. It seemed the mayor's re-election campaign was still important news.

TWENTY-ONE

Daring himself, Colin Hayhurst glanced down at the text, the image and the message. Two words, 'your move', in what looked like blue ink scrawled on the chest of a young man's body. It could have been tattooed there. Not that it mattered since he knew the body was no longer breathing to care. Angry red bruises around the neck glared at him as if to say, 'you did this, you're responsible.' Perhaps he should have gone to the police right at the beginning, maybe they could have stopped it, but that would have meant his own involvement and his own secret floating to the surface like cream on milk, though it would have been sour. He couldn't have risked it, and whoever it was that had killed the youngster had tested him. The text had landed yesterday and yet he still hadn't deleted it, and certainly hadn't mentioned it to anyone, not at home or work, and certainly not to the police. It would have come from a burner phone anyway, that was how things worked these days. Why risk adding your DNA to a note or cut out letters from a newspaper and stick them in order to create words like criminals did in the past. There was no need to take the risk, modern forensics saw to that. Plus, he'd called the number from a payphone in town, it had been dead.

He felt the intense heat as it surfaced from somewhere around his middle and floated upwards, covering his chest, tightening it until he almost gasped out loud. Raising a hand to his forehead, he wasn't surprised to find it was bathed in a fine film of sweat. His trousers made a convenient place to dry his hand and he rubbed his leg vigorously before attempting to slow his breathing down. Was he having a heart attack? Was this what it felt like, no real pain but immense discomfort?

There was a knock at his door, which immediately opened, and he slipped the phone away as nonchalantly as he could. No one would be any the wiser to what he'd been looking at; it was just a phone after all. A woman with long dark hair tied in a tight ponytail entered the room – it was Katherine Spencer, his deputy. She carried a folder filled with papers as she headed for his desk. By the look on her face, she didn't look happy about something and he wondered if the woman knew of his intense dislike for her. It would have been hard for her to not know. He caught her eye as she placed the file down on his desk in front of him and, as was habit of hers, took two paces back before speaking. Perhaps she'd been military trained overseas in a previous life and been reincarnated with the sole purpose of grating on his nerves.

"Yes, Katherine?"

"For your signature, if you would, please." Colin looked down at the file in front of him and wondered about its contents. Katherine must have read his mind because she added, "Contractor's invoices, for the development." He nodded his approval and refrained from letting the smile on his lips develop any further.

"Leave them with me, would you." Katherine turned and was about to leave when he said. "If anyone is brewing up, mine's a tea." Without replying, she walked away. The sound of the door clicking shut was the sign he could raise a bigger smile, and he opened the folder and started to read, calculating the figures in his head.

His phone buzzed, and as he looked at the screen, it wasn't a number he recognised. That was common enough for him, but in light of the image text he'd been looking at before Katherine had barged in, he was cautious. Tentatively, he opened the message and immediately wished he hadn't bothered. Another naked chest, another message in blue. 'Touch move'. And so soon? More red welts around a young man's neck. Colin tossed his phone across his desk, hoping it would dislodge the image forever. He struggled to control his breathing again as pain shot into his chest like molten hot wires piercing his heart. He held on, waiting for it to pass, for the feeling of normality to resume once again. The attacks were coming more regularly than of recent and he suspected he knew the reason why. Perhaps now it was time to go to the police, put a stop to it all and forget his longer-term plans before someone else got killed. Or the stress killed him. He knew the picture was of a different young man, and that worried him. Colin leaned forward out of his chair and, with one swift movement, grabbed his waste-paper basket as his stomach projected his lunch straight into it. When the spasm finally receded, he wiped his mouth with the back of his hand and tried to steady himself.

He didn't notice the sound of the door gently closing once again. Someone had been in the room watching.

TWENTY-TWO

Will was driving along the A45 towards Wootton Hall Park in the hope that DI Mason would stick to her treatment time at the hospital. He'd given himself twenty-five minutes spare, just in case she decided to leave a little earlier than she had yesterday, and since he had no idea if that had been her normal time, had no clue if today's would be the same. He could only hope. He was about to make the turn for headquarters when his phone pinged with a fare request. It had to be her! He slowed a little, looked at the address and saw it was Newport Pagnell Road. It hadn't been what was expected or hoped for, and he was about to decline the fare when something told him to double-check the details. Eleanor House, Newport Pagnell Road. Pickup for the hospital. Rochelle. Will's spirit jumped a notch as he increased his speed and headed for the alternative address he'd been given. Rochelle must have been working from another location; he wasn't even aware the police had another office, but then he remembered his Google search of the EMSOU. A special task force wouldn't work out of a local station, it made sense. They'd have a designated space available for such operations, and he was heading there right now. As he turned into the car park, he could see her standing waiting, head in her phone again. Perhaps she was watching the app, and his particular dot heading towards her, but since she didn't look up at his arrival, he assumed it was something more important, a report maybe. He got out as usual and headed for the rear door as she finally lifted her head. The blue appeared to be fading slightly, he noted. As she recognised him, he smiled brightly her way.

"Hello again, DI Mason," he beamed. "What are the chances, eh?"

Did he detect a slight eye roll?

"Indeed," she said, getting into the back seat. "Let me guess, you just happened to be in the area?"

There was no point in lying, she was a detective for good reason. "Got me there," he said, keeping things upbeat, "though I'd no clue you'd be over this side. Is there an office over here, then?" He started the engine and pulled away, destination the general hospital.

"I'm sure you've already done your homework. And yes, the task force is here. We have a couple of satellite locations, depending on what is needed for what crime." He watched her in his mirror and said, "And you're seconded to the task force, I'm assuming?"

"As the local DI, yes."

"I spoke to DC Flint not long ago and told him about a missing person I reported yesterday, another Refresh user. He wasn't aware of it. Will it get investigated more now, since there could be a link with Clyde's initial disappearance?"

"If the team think there is a link, then yes, but it is likely he's gone off of his own accord, which in this case is the best outcome. I know you're putting two and two together and coming up with a neat four, but there could be a more favourable explanation."

Will nodded his understanding, she wasn't telling him anything he didn't already know. But still, Jonesy was missing, and he wanted to make sure his case was being given the attention it deserved. It didn't feel like it was.

Reading her signal, Will could tell she wasn't happy talking about it and so stayed silent as they approached the hospital. Perhaps she felt guilty about informing Will of the preliminary cause of death when they both knew she had taken a momentous risk in saying something. He pulled up outside the hospital entrance, and she let out a long sigh before speaking.

"THANKS. I'll be twenty minutes or so." She was about to walk away when she added, "You know, I don't know your name."

"It's Will, Will Peters. At your service, madame," he said, bowing and then removed a card from his wallet and handed it to her. This time, he wasn't going to forget it. He watched as she headed inside and then returned to his car to wait, keeping an eye out for a pesky traffic warden. As usual, the hospital grounds were a constant flow of people coming and going, many in scrubs and others in street clothes. Tiredness appeared to be a common look for both workers and the worried, those with friends or relatives inside receiving treatment. With the warm sun streaming into the car, Will was tempted to snatch forty winks, but after the last time, he rearranged himself into a more alert, upright position to stop himself drifting off. He remembered his Twix he'd bought from the van earlier and retrieved it from the glovebox before biting into a stick. He was just about to start on the second biscuit when he spotted a head of hair that he thought he recognised. Ambling along and walking straight towards his car, the dishevelled person looked a lot like Jonesy. Will stopped chewing. Were his eyes deceiving him? He took another look as the young man got closer before leaping out of his vehicle.

"Jonesy?" he called out.

The individual lifted his chin and searched for where the voice had come from.

Will called again as he approached, sure this time of who it was. "It is you!"

Jonesy's pimply face broke into a smile, "Hi Will, of course it's me, who did you think it was?" Will noticed the purple bruising around one eye, the dried blood of a deep cut on his upper lip. He'd taken a beating, and recently.

"What happened to your face?" he asked.

Jonesy lifted his hand to his eye, touching it softly with dirty fingers. "I got jumped, knocked me out. When I came to, I was out on the Towcester Road on the other side of town. Funny thing is I don't know how I got there – I certainly didn't walk." He grinned and Will watched as grimy fingers moved to the deep cut; it must have stung at being stretched into a smile.

"Did you see who did it?"

"Well, that's the funny thing. Who jumps a scruffy guy like me? It's not like I'm worth much, I don't have any cash and apart from my black eye and split lip, I've not been touched. Someone thought it would be fun, I suppose."

Will understood what the lad was telling him, he hadn't been sexually assaulted, something those that lived on the streets were often subjected to. That and being urinated on for fun, usually by groups of men after having had a skinful in the pub. Will did some quick calculations in his head and realised that Towcester Road ran towards Hunsbury Hill. Coincidence? Not likely. Will could feel the presence of another person standing close by and turned to see that DI Mason had returned.

TWENTY-THREE

"DI Mason, let me introduce our missing person, Jonesy," Will started, aware the lad's presence needed explaining and that the police needed to know Jonesy was no longer AWOL. They could then close the case, if it had even been open.

Having glanced at his grubby state, she refrained from offering to shake his hand, and instead said, "You're back, that's good news." She turned to Will, a question in her eyes.

"It seems Jonesy here was jumped, hence the black eye and split lip," Will said resignedly. It happened a lot. "But the part you might be interested in is that it sounds like he could have been taken, abducted if you like, since he woke up on Towcester Road, out of town, and he didn't walk there himself." He let her do the geography. She was a smart woman, but would she come to the same conclusion? After a moment or two of silence, Will almost heard the penny drop. Jonesy picked at a fingernail.

"Let's get in," she said firmly, heading for the back seat. Jonesy followed and Will instructed him to sit up front with him, catching her look of discomfort in his mirror. She'd just had her radiotherapy treatment, and if the previous day was anything to go by, would need a nap, though he doubted with Jonesy in the car she would even try. Will wondered about her lunch and regretted not getting a sandwich for her.

"Back to Eleanor House, then?" Will enquired. "Or Wootton Hall Park?"

"Eleanor House, please. The task force will want to hear this," she said, reaching for her phone and choosing a contact. Phoning ahead, Will assumed. He was right. As he listened to one side of a conversation, he wondered if Jonesy had twigged about what had almost certainly happened to him. Did he even know about Clyde's death? When her call finished, he turned to Jonesy and asked, "Did you hear the news about Clyde, Jonesy?"

"News? Clyde?"

"Unfortunately, Clyde was found dead a couple of days ago. Hazel and I identified his body. It's all very sad."

"Shit! What happened?" Jonesy stared at Will, shock all over his face. Will decided he'd said enough, especially as he'd already shared the information with Birdie, which was precisely what he'd promised he wouldn't do. DI Mason could decide what to say. Will caught her eye in the mirror.

If looks could kill, he would have been lying next to Clyde in the refrigerated storage in the bowels of the hospital.

"I can't say, I'm afraid. Not yet. The super will be issuing a statement to the press sometime soon. It's an active investigation, and I can't comment."

"But he was murdered, though, I'm guessing?" Jonesy asked. "He wasn't ill or something, then?"

"I can tell you a team are looking into his death. I'm sorry." Her final comments told them the discussion was over, about Clyde anyway.

Jonesy was busy putting two and two together in his head. "Wait a minute. Where did they find his body?"

Will took it. "Hunsbury Hill Country Park." He figured he knew where the thinking was going.

"And you get there down Towcester Road… where I found myself."

"There are other ways to get there," Rochelle said, "but yes."

Jonesy turned round to face DI Mason and said, "You think I was kidnapped?"

"That's what we'll want to ascertain, when we talk to you properly. You may have valuable information about what happened to you, so we need to gather everything you remember down on paper."

He turned back to Will. "I've only ever got grief from the police, and now you want me to help them?" It was hard not to notice the raise in pitch as the lad spoke. There was also a trace of something else. Will detected panic.

"Help Clyde, not the police. Plus, I'm sure DI Mason here is not interested in anything minor you may have done in your past. This is a murder investigation, and far more serious than nicking a packet of bread rolls."

He turned up Newport Pagnell Road and towards the task force building. This time, he pulled into a parking space properly, and the three of them stepped out of the vehicle. DI Mason led the way. Will checked the time. He had to be back at the cemetery before 5 pm to fill the grave in that he'd dug that morning. He hoped he wouldn't be too long with Jonesy, but finding Clyde's killer was important. He also hoped whatever Jonesy remembered was worth something to the investigation. At eighteen, Clyde been far too young to die.

"Am I in trouble?" Jonesy asked Will when DI Mason was out of earshot and talking to a colleague. Will could feel the lad's nerves jittering and hoped he wasn't using.

"Not in this instance, no. Unless you've done something more than shoplifting of recent?" Will searched the lad's eyes for a clue;

the whites weren't as bright as they should be, but he didn't see anything else there but a little fear.

"Just trying to live."

When DI Mason returned, Will asked, "Can I accompany him? It might make things a bit easier."

"Well, it's a little unusual, but I see your point." She turned to Jonesy and added, "It is, however, an informal interview, and you're free to leave at any time. Just so you're aware."

He nodded his understanding.

"Follow me, there's an interview room just down the corridor. Would anyone like a tea, coffee?" Two 'no thank you's as they followed dutifully, and she held the relevant door open for them both. Jonesy took a seat, but Will stayed standing. He'd been sitting down for most of the day and his long legs were beginning to grumble.

Will listened with interest as the conversation got under way, about how Jonesy had been minding his own business, walking along St Giles Street in the dark, near the post office. He'd estimated it being around 11 pm, the town centre fairly quiet at that hour during the week. He'd remembered stopping briefly to light a cigarette in a nearby doorway, out of the breeze that had been blowing. There was a cut-through near there, Fish Street. There'd been a male voice, asking for a light and he'd obliged. All he remembered was he was scruffily dressed like himself, was of average height and build, and had been white. That was all he remembered. When he came to, he was a way out of town, in the cemetery. It had been dark still and he'd no idea how long he'd been knocked out. He'd felt drowsy, so had curled up in a corner of the yard where he'd woken the following day with a splitting headache, split lip and still no clue how he'd got there.

By the end of the interview, Will could tell DI Mason wasn't exactly jumping with joy at the information. With no clear description of the man or any possible accomplices, it was a long shot finding them.

TWENTY-FOUR

The killer should have finished the job earlier. Getting him to the cemetery had been risky, a feat in itself since things hadn't turned out quite the way they were supposed to. Another unsuspecting, naive volunteer had helped, knocked the lad to the ground then watched as chloroform had been applied to lad's mouth. While killing him was to be the endgame, it would have made the rest of the plan too difficult to pull off. No, they needed their victim alive at a certain point, needed control at every stage. Otherwise, mistakes would be made, and that could leave a trail back to them.

The cemetery seemed the most obvious place under the circumstances. Few frequented them by night, and those that did, that hid their elicit acts behind the taller headstones, had other things on their minds. By the time they'd dropped the lad behind the wall at the cemetery, his body was already in distress, his breathing a giveaway as to what was happening inside of him. It was easy to overdose with chloroform, applying too much too quickly, but in the heat of the moment, there had been so much fumbling, nerves shot, that accuracy had gone out the window. There had been no foreseeable way to get him into the tunnel, or up to Hunsbury Hill, not like that, and so there'd been no choice but to leave him and hope he woke up without any knowledge of what had happened. The whole escapade had been one giant cock-up.

The killer had dropped the hired help a little way out of town and watched him flee into the night like a rocket. The killer knew he wouldn't tell a soul, and who would believe him anyway? Ketamine could do that to a person, make them hallucinate; it was a useful drug to know about. The killer had wondered if he'd survive the night. The extra loss of life would have been a waste without delivering the important message. It would have been pointless all round and not something they wanted attributed to them.

Now, watching what was going on just two cars over, the killer knew there was going to be a problem. Why was the lad now talking to a man and a woman in the hospital car park, a woman the killer knew to be with the police, and a man they'd seen countless times before, though it was doubtful he knew they existed? The killer was good at blending in, used to it, had done so for most of their life.

Jonesy – that's what he was called – talked animatedly to the two and it was obvious from the killer's spot what they were discussing, the split lip and black eye the centre of attention. The paid help had gone a little too far roughing him up that night, before running off themselves. Another disposable homeless person and no cause for concern. They did anything for a bit of cash. The three got into the tall one's car and pulled away. Was there time to pull in behind and follow, see where they were heading? It was a split-second decision as the killer jumped in their car and made a beeline for the hospital exit as the other car turned left onto the main road, towards the ring road. They had an inkling what their destination was going to be.

As both cars turned onto Newport Pagnell Road, the killer watched their target turn into the satellite police office before carrying on past themselves. Having driven on a hundred yards or so, they pulled up to the kerb and turned their engine off. What now? How much did he remember from that night? How much would he tell the police? This was not what was supposed to happen, far from it. There were still messages to be delivered, ransom demands to be paid. With the money spoken for, the plan had to work. There was nothing to be done right there and then, but there was one thing for sure, they couldn't chance whatever information he was giving up being linked back to them.

This changed things, it created a loose end, one that needed tying off. They pulled away, their brain frantically sifting through how to kill two birds with one proverbial stone, because that's what it amounted to.

No, Jonesy had to go too.

TWENTY-FIVE

As DI Mason got up from the interview table, Will quickly followed her out. A glance over her shoulder as he did so told him she hadn't been expecting to find him behind her. As soon as they were out in the corridor, Will dived in with his own thoughts and observations.

"If you're going to jump someone and abduct them, you whack them from behind, don't you? And he said he has no recollection of anything but woke up drowsy, not sleepy. Do you think he was drugged?" The words came out in a rush, like he was trying to force a large amount of information into a tiny space of time. Maybe he was, since he wasn't a police officer and needed to take advantage of the opportunity to be involved in the case, if only on the periphery of it.

Rochelle Mason stayed silent for a moment before saying, "Believe it or not, Will, I've done this before." Will's excited face crumbled at her sarcastic words. He knew there was more to come. "And to answer your questions, yes, I agree with you, in part at any rate. Now, can I suggest you take Jonesy back to wherever it is he hangs out, and if we have any more questions for him, I'll get in touch with you, shall I? I'm assuming he doesn't have a mobile phone?" Her tone told him everything he needed to know, she wasn't interested in his help, and he watched as she turned back to the interview room to call inside to let Jonesy know he could leave. Will felt like he'd been kicked in the stomach. What had happened to the pleasant woman he'd been getting to know? The one he'd bought lunch for, the one he'd waited at the oncology unit for and made sure she got back to work safely? Maybe she was tired, or hungry. Or both. As Jonesy caught up with him in the corridor, Will stayed silent and the two headed for the door.

"I'll take you back to Refresh, get you cleaned up," he said as they both got in his car. If the DI wasn't going to ask about Jonesy's facial wounds, he might as well.

"How did you get a split lip and black eye then, any idea?"

"No clue about that either. I sure as hell didn't have them before someone tried to kidnap me!"

"It must have happened around that time then, because if you were spark out in the cemetery, no one would beat a man as he lay asleep. I'm assuming you weren't robbed?"

"Nope. My bit of cash was still in my pocket and I don't own much else."

It didn't fit. Will remembered Jonesy's reaction to helping the police and circled back to it.

"Now the DI has gone, and it's just the two of us, why don't you tell me the story all over again? Without leaving any bits out this time."

Jonesy turned to Will and he met his gaze as they headed up the A508 back into the town centre.

"It was just as I said it was."

Will wasn't buying it. "Come on, it's me you're talking to. You weren't keen on going in there and helping them, and I of all people know what it's like living on the streets. I've been there, remember? You don't get a split lip while you're asleep. Urinated on, yes. Split lip? No." He stayed silent and waited for a response. It was a long time in coming. They were almost back at the Refresh Centre when Jonesy finally spoke. Will knew he would eventually.

"There's no point kidding a kidder, right?"

"No point at all, so spill." Will pulled into a space and turned off the engine. "I'm all ears," he said, turning to his friend.

"It all happened the way I said it had, everything I told her was true."

"But?"

"But I got my black eye and split lip because after I lit his cigarette, he laid into me. Two quick smacks and he was done. I wasn't fast enough to punch him back and the next thing I knew there was someone coming at me from behind and they put a cloth over my mouth. Then lights out."

"So why didn't you tell the detective that?"

"Because for a moment, I wondered if I knew him, from the streets, you know? There's a couple of nasty headcases knocking around, blokes high on Special K or something. And I reckon the other one was a woman," he mumbled. Will knew Special K was the nickname for Ketamine, and that it made users hallucinate, among other things.

"And you didn't want to be thought of as weak, is that it?"

"Something like that. Sounds silly, I know, but that's how it was." He was almost sullen, embarrassed even.

Clyde had gone now, and Will was conscious that if Jonesy had been abducted, someone else could be next. What was perplexing him was why they'd let him go. Jonesy stayed silent and Will wondered if he'd lost the moment. He nudged him gently.

"You were lucky in being let go."

"I've been thinking about that. Why do you think they dumped me?"

Will brightened, at least Jonesy was talking again.

"I could have been next, two bodies up at Hunsbury Hill."

It was true. "You say you didn't fight back when you got hit?"

"They were too quick, so no."

Will played with his top lip as he thought for a possible reason. To his knowledge, there hadn't been a sexual element to Clyde's death, but there could have been something he wasn't privy to. Was that it?

"Do you think you were undressed at all? Were your clothes as you put them yourself?"

"What, you think I was assaulted in that way? No, I'd know if I had been and I wasn't, for sure." Jonesy sounded certain on that. Almost casually he added, "But actually, my shirt was buttoned up wrongly, now you mention it. There was an empty buttonhole on one side, so I undid them and straightened the buttons out." Realisation dropped. "So I was undressed!" Jonesy's eyes couldn't have stretched any wider as he realised someone had undressed him without his knowledge. "But I know I'm not hurt, everything there is quite normal!" Will was as confused as Jonesy was. Someone had taken the lad's shirt off, but why? Will remembered the message on Clyde's body. Had that been their intention, and somehow the plan had changed?

TWENTY-SIX

Colin Hayhurst's stomach failed to recover enough for him to concentrate on anything useful, and by 3 pm he needed fresh air. Glancing out of his modern window to the street below, it wasn't exactly what he'd term a beautiful day, but at least it wasn't wet. The latest photo had disturbed him immensely, as had the first one, but he'd brushed that one off as a hoax at the time. That had been before the police found a body – their threat carried out just as they'd promised, the whole thing far from a hoax. His stomach roiled again, and he wondered if his lunch had been off. He'd only had a sandwich from the café round the corner, his usual chicken and brie, and he'd had the same most days of the week without a problem. He let a belch escape, feeling the gas force its way into his mouth and out. It tasted of onion, though he didn't remember eating any. He needed to get out, leave the office and think, so he dialled the mayoral chauffeur to call around the front and pick him up. It always looked good, the flash car gleaming black, the man in a cap up front. The public liked a bit of pomp and ceremony, even if he was only going to Sainsbury's for antacid and a decent bottle of wine for later.

He thought about his wife, Barbara, or Babs as he liked to call her, and her part in his scheme. She'd no clue at all what was going on in his world, her only concern spending his hard-earned money and being a true trophy wife, the mayoress. She wasn't in bad shape for a fifty-five-year-old and had kept herself trim, but the injections and fillers and regular hair appointments ensured her good looks, and she enjoyed the more glamorous side of being married to the town mayor. The various functions were right up her street, particularly when footballers were involved. As the mayor, it was commonplace to be given tickets to peripheral events, and Colin knew all too well the importance of mixing in the right circles. Networking and favours were what made the council economics go round.

It was time to leave, the car would be waiting downstairs for him, so he made his way to the glass expanse of the front entrance without a word to anyone. Plenty noticed him leave, but no one asked if he'd be back. Once out on Angel Square, Colin took his time getting into the rear seat before the car moved off. He smiled at a random passer-by and gave a little 'tinkle' of a wave as though he were the Queen Mother herself. Colin sat back and enjoyed the feeling of someone else driving for a change, even if it was only for a short distance. Perhaps he'd ask the driver to carry on someplace afterwards, give him time to think things through a little, away from annoying staff members, particularly that Katherine woman. He shook his head in dismay before mumbling about staffing quotas and getting the right balance of ethnicity, not to mention having the right number of women or LGBTQ or disabled or… In his day, the right person for the job was the right person for the job, no matter who they were. As long as they were male. He shook his head and kept his thoughts to himself. Ten minutes later, they pulled up outside the main entrance of Sainsbury's. Once again, he took his time getting out, catching the eye of several people who all stopped to watch the gleaming vehicle, no doubt wondering who was so important and had turned up to shop where they were. Colin repeated his 'tinkle' wave to no one in particular and sauntered inside as if on a royal visit. The car stayed put in the disabled parking spaces and waited. It was almost thirty minutes later when Colin emerged with his few provisions. Antacid was accompanied by wine, blue cheese, crackers, olives and a small box of Belgium chocolates for his Babs though, he'd eat them himself after she'd had her token one. With a bigger wave and a forced smile to match, he left the building and headed for the back seat of his waiting car.

"Take me to Hunsbury Hill Country Park, would you?"

"Certainly, sir," came the reply as Colin took a long glug of the antacid and winced at its taste. He wiped his mouth on the back of his hand and remembered the vomit from earlier.

"Do you have some of those wet tissues, by chance?" he asked the driver.

Colin watched as the man checked the glovebox and passed a packet of wet wipes over his shoulder. "It seems I do, sir." He took the packet and wiped his hands and, satisfied all traces of his earlier upset were gone, he slipped the packet into his bag of groceries and relaxed back until they reached his chosen destination.

The car park was heaving with late-afternoon dog walkers when they arrived, all out for exercise before being shut indoors until toileting just before bedtime.

"As close to the woods as you can get, if you would," he ordered, and the driver cruised on a little further into the park before pulling over. Heads turned at the sleek black car, but most *were more interested in their own activity than his arrival.* Colin stepped out and instructed the driver to wait. He didn't know how long he'd be. Gathering his grocery bag, he set out to find a peaceful spot to sit and watch the world go by. He found an empty park bench almost immediately that he rejected, intent on finding something a little more secluded further into the park. He spotted one in the distance and made a beeline for it before finally sitting down with a sigh. The woods weren't very deep, and Colin knew the body wouldn't have been found too far away from where he was sitting. He glanced around. When he was sure there was no one to observe him, he unwrapped the cheese, breaking small pieces off, and opened the box of crackers, which he laid out on the bag itself. He added cheese to a cracker and slipped the whole thing into his mouth and closed his eyes while he chewed. Maybe the homeless lad hadn't a family to notice him gone anyway. And if no one missed him, did it really matter he was dead? It wasn't as if the lad contributed much to civilisation or the economy even. Not like the work he was doing. No, he was building something for the elderly, for his and Babs' retirement and beyond, something that would hold a brass plaque for the rest of time. His name would be remembered all right – 'Colin Hayhurst House'. It had a splendid ring to it. He opened the wine and took a long mouthful directly from the bottle, past caring if anyone saw him. It wasn't what he'd intended it for, but there were plenty of bottles at home to choose another for later.

TWENTY-SEVEN

WILL PULLED UP OUTSIDE REFRESH AND TURNED TO THE young man.

"Jonesy, I can't come in with you. I've got to get back to the cemetery to my other job, but there'll be someone inside to get you some clean clothes and, if you're lucky, a meal." Will looked at the time on his phone. It was a little early yet, but there was always bread and jam in one of the big industrial fridges, if nothing else. "I'll try and catch up with you later. But I've got to go now so just promise me you'll think about telling them the rest, okay?"

"Will do," Jonesy said. He undid his side door and gave a light wave as thanks as he trundled off. Will watched him go. Once the lad had entered the building, he pulled away and headed back to the graveyard where that morning he'd been digging a hole for someone's partner. His job, now everybody had left the ceremony, the tears dried for now at least, was to fill in the hole and make it look good. Sometime in the near future, a headstone would be erected, but not until the ground had settled a little. In the meantime, it would be an unmarked grave, though family and friends of the deceased knew whom was buried there.

As he drove, he pondered why anybody would abduct someone, remove at least a shirt, not sexually assault them, in any obvious way at least, and then drop them back to a quiet location in the middle of the night to let them sleep off whatever drug they'd used to get them with. It didn't make any sense. Or maybe Jonesy had in fact been assaulted and was too proud or too scared to say anything. Either way, he was pleased that the lad had got back relatively unscathed. It was all rather unusual.

Fifteen minutes later, Will was changing back into his work boots and jeans, and climbing aboard his small excavator which was parked up behind a shed. It didn't do for mourners to see the mechanics of what went on prior to their loved one being buried, the lumbering yellow machine not particularly attractive or even necessary to proceedings. He steered the digger into place then left the small cab for a moment to take a look at the coffin. Flowers had been laid on the polished wood surface by mourners, while his own bed of leaves, which the coffin rested on, was nowhere to be seen. The pink roses and lilies told him the person he was about to cover was probably a female, most likely the wife of the first occupant of the space. It often happened that way, the men went first. Might he go before Louise? Statistically, he would.

Satisfied that everything was just so, he jumped back into the cab and began filling in the hole with the earth that was piled neatly nearby. He'd never found anything in the grave that shouldn't have been there, but knew of tales that others had found unusual contents, added long after the mourners had left. Pets, a book, even a flask and biscuits had all been found by his colleagues over the years. Over a pint one lunchtime, one of the same had recalled finding a stuffed cat in the hole, and he'd had to climb in to double-check it was in fact deceased and not a live one taking a nap in the sunshine on a warm surface. He hadn't decided if he was relieved at it not being real, or not. It had made interesting conversation and raised a smile or two. There were no such additions to this particular grave.

When the hole was finally filled in, he took care to smooth the soil evenly but with a slight mound for settlement to occur. The turf that he'd carefully removed earlier was placed over the top like a giant green jigsaw and finally the job was complete. It didn't take long. Will returned the excavator back to the shed and changed into his driving clothes for a second time. He wondered about Jonesy's near miss, and who the pair were. Were they just tasked with the abduction – the hired muscle, as it were – or were they more involved? Did the same thing happen to Clyde or was his situation different? Were they even connected at all? So many questions, and not much chance of finding the answers. DI Mason had made it clear he shouldn't involve himself; they'd take care of it. What had her words been? 'I've done this before.'

He placed his work gear back in the holdall and set off towards home. Louise and the girls would be back by now, and something tasty would be cooking in the oven. With the exhumation one night and then a longer shift at Refresh the next, he felt like he hadn't put his feet up and caught his breath with his young family in days. He hoped there was a bottle of wine on the go, preferably red, school night or not.

TWENTY-EIGHT

IT WAS STEPHEN FLINT THAT TOOK THE CALL WHEN ANOTHER BODY was found. Curiously, it was at Hunsbury Hill Country Park, though it wasn't the exact same spot as where Clyde Mollineau's body had been discovered only three days ago. He almost ran into the office, shouting to get DI Mason's attention. He succeeded.

"Boss! We've got another one," he said, sounding disheartened but excited all at the same time, if that was even possible.

"Another one?" she said. "Where?"

"Hunsbury Hill, near the woods. Same as the last."

"Who called in?" she asked.

"Someone walking their dog. Uniform are already on their way to secure the scene." He watched as she grabbed her bag and jacket and walked towards him with urgent purpose.

"Let's go over there then," she said. "You're driving." Stephen grabbed his car keys and caught her up. "Have the crime scene investigators been advised?"

"Yes, I believe they're en route. They might be there before us."

They quickened their pace as they headed for the staff car park where DC Flint slipped in behind the wheel of his own vehicle. It wasn't long until they were out on the main road and heading west over to Hunsbury Hill. Traffic was heavy around the ring road as usual, but they made good time and arrived just before the crime scene investigators. Once he had parked up as close as he could, they both leapt from the vehicle. Uniformed officers were milling around securing the area, and though it wasn't exactly the same place as where Clyde had been found, it wasn't far off. Curiously, it was further forward, rather than deeper into the woods, and in a more open area. The killer was obviously getting more confident in disposing of his victims. Or her. Blue-and-white crime scene tape flickered in the wind as they approached, and DI Mason wondered exactly what they would find this time. Would there be a message written on this one also, and what might it say?

"It's not even dark, still dusk," said Stephen. "Who would risk placing a body out here now, why not wait another hour or two?"

"A confident or stupid individual," said Mason. "There's plenty of them around. But I get what you're saying, why not wait until the full cover of darkness? Why risk it?"

"Perhaps they wanted to be seen?" said Stephen. "Though what would be the point in that? I read somewhere that some criminals *want* to be caught so they are put away for their own safety. They want to live in prison."

"Well, only a nutter would want to live in prison."

"You don't think you'd need to be a nutter to kill someone?" asked Flint. He wasn't being facetious, but quite serious. Rochelle grumbled anyway.

"Maybe you're right," she said hurriedly. A van door closing loudly behind them made her turn. The crime scene investigators had parked in the car park before following the track that they had just walked up themselves. It would be difficult to get much closer with their vehicle, but they would no doubt try once they'd seen the terrain they were dealing with. Lights would be set up and a canopy placed over the body to protect it from the elements. Even though the weather forecast hadn't suggested rain, it could never be counted on and all evidence needed preserving. It also helped with prying eyes. There were always dog walkers in the park, and when it came to respect for the dead, the general public had more of a morbid interest than a respectful interest. Rochelle approach one of the uniformed officers and showed her warrant card, as did Stephen, and asked for what was known so far, which turned out to be precious little.

A spotty individual who looked like he'd left Hendon Police College only last week seemed nervous in her presence, but that didn't bother Rochelle.

"Who called it in then, are they still here?" she asked rather gruffly. Tiredness was catching up with her. She hadn't had time to snatch forty winks this afternoon and it was beginning to show.

"A female dog walker called it in. She's sitting just over there," he said, pointing to his right.

Rochelle glanced across to see a woman bent over, sitting on an old tree stump. Her shoulders appeared to be moving up and down as though she was crying.

DC Stephen Flint glanced across at the same woman and said, "I'll go," sensing that his boss was not the woman for the job, not right then, not today anyway. Rochelle watched him go and was thankful for his intuition, she didn't feel much like being compassionate and her temper seemed to be wearing thin these days. That wasn't a good thing, she'd have to work harder to keep it in check before the team became suspicious. She just needed some sleep, the radiotherapy making it tough to operate without a nap after her appointment. Now, with another body found, there would be fat chance of getting an early night. She stifled a yawn as she slipped under the police tape and approached the spot where yet another young man's body lay, roughly covered over with a few leaves. It couldn't be termed buried. Apart from the jacket, he was dressed in a similar way to Clyde – bland thrift-shop clothing that hadn't been laundered in some time. Porcelain skin covering his ribs gleamed white, his shirt undone and hanging loose by his side. His hands were grubby, hair greasy and lank. It wasn't hard to assume the young man laid in front of her was another homeless person. Rochelle found a Sharpie in her bag and used it to lift the corner of the victim's shirt a little. Blue ink stared back at her, another message: Touch move.

While it didn't fit the dictionary definition of a serial killer, DI Rochelle Mason knew they were dealing with one.

TWENTY-NINE

IT WAS WILL'S TURN TO GET THE KIDS READY FOR SCHOOL SINCE Louise had swapped her shift with a colleague in need. When he was on duty, he set the clock on his phone so that he could wake before the rest of the family and sneak out of bed and have some quiet time with his coffee, toast and the *Mirror* newspaper alone at the breakfast bar. While he got plenty of time on his own during the day, it didn't compare to the time when the morning sun poured through the kitchen windows, and all was peaceful in the Peters' household. He liked to feel that, with his family safe and asleep upstairs, he was somehow watching over them. It made him feel good. Life was full of small pleasures. He poured a second mug from the cafetière and carried on through the newspaper, scanning the articles for something of interest and finding nothing of note. He wondered, not for the first time, why he bothered with the newspaper at all – it was yesterday's news anyway. He ought to cancel it and read it online instead. At least that was more up to date. With that thought, he pushed the newspaper to one side and grabbed his smartphone to check the online version. Will clicked on the yellow banner tickertape at the bottom of the screen – Breaking news:

Another body found in Hunsbury Hill Country Park. Will quickly read the short report. There wasn't much of note apart from the fact that there was another body. There was mention, however, that it looked like another homeless person. Will's heart sank to the bottom of his stomach. He hadn't realised that anybody else was missing; Jonesy was back, thank goodness. Who could it be? Another body? Was someone clearing up the streets, didn't like them loitering in their doorways, or was it something else? He closed the page down and sat back in his chair, pondering. Obviously, DI Mason would know by now, though there was little point in ringing in her. He wondered if it was the same cause of death as Clyde, strangulation. He needed to find out more. Maybe it was someone that visited the centre for the services they provided? Was it someone he knew? Perhaps, if he did know them, he could identify the body. Unless they carried ID of their own. But few homeless people had a driving licence or a credit card, and most were estranged from their families, if they had them in the first place. They didn't carry next of kin notification or useful information that would help if their body was ever discovered.

Will tossed back the remaining coffee and headed upstairs to the shower. He wasn't sure what he could do, but he knew that he needed to do something and getting a head start on his day was the best thing he could think of while he processed what he'd just learned. After he'd dropped the girls off, his first pickup wasn't till nine o'clock, so there was plenty of time. He could even pop in and see if DI Mason had got some news for him. Though would she even share? Maybe a phone call would be better. She'd looked tired when he'd left after the interview with Jonesy. A murder investigation would mean longer hours, and if she'd worked late, she could well be cranky this morning. That's what lack of sleep did to you. He only needed to look at Poppy to know that one. Whenever they let her stay up a bit later than normal to watch a movie, she was always the same the following day, a dinosaur to live with. The thought made him smile, a welcome reprieve in light of the news. It had only been a couple of days ago that she'd wanted to go to school dressed as one. He wondered what she'd want to be today.

Will dried himself quickly and popped his head into the bedroom to see if Louise was awake yet. He didn't want to disturb her, but he liked to take her a cup of tea in the morning if he had time. Swapping her shift at least meant a lie in. As he looked down at his beautiful wife, she started to stir at his presence, her eyes half-open, a smile beginning to creep across her mouth. He bent down and delivered a light peck to her lips. She tasted of sleep.

"Morning, sunshine," he said. "Would you like a cuppa?"

She rubbed her eyes and said, "Yes, please," so Will trundled back downstairs to make it. He put two slices of bread in the toaster then put the mug of tea on a tray and waited. When the toast was golden brown, he added butter and marmalade, taking care to remove the strands of rind, then took it upstairs to the bedroom. Louise, noticing the tray in his hands, sat up in bed as he put it down in front of her.

"What's all this?" she asked.

"Well, I thought as you're not in a rush this morning, breakfast in bed you deserve." He sat down on the mattress. "I've got some news," he said. "There's been another body found in the woods."

She stopped chewing for a moment and looked enquiringly at him. "Oh."

"From the description online, it sounds like another from Refresh, or someone homeless at least."

"What can you do?" she asked, resuming her chewing.

"Not a lot, I don't think, but I will call the DI in charge, see if she's got any news, if she'll tell me anything. I'll offer to identify the body, though I hope it's not someone we know. That said, I also hope I can be helpful."

Louise leaned forward and touched Will's hand gently. "I'm

sorry to hear that, Will. I know how much your work, the whole centre, means to you. You're such a good sort."

He raised a smile in reply. "Let's see what the day brings."

Glancing at the bedside clock, he noted it was not even 7 am. If DI Mason was still asleep, he didn't want to be the one that woke her. He'd call just before he picked Birdie up.

THIRTY

Will made himself useful and called the centre, hoping Hazel was on a shift. Breakfast started early and lingered until almost mid-morning since those that lived on the streets weren't exactly in a rush to get on with their day. Any early birds tended to be people that were struggling to make ends meet on the little income that they did have and perhaps did have an early shift to start. If Hazel wasn't there, it didn't really matter; there'd be someone he could talk to to see if the drums had been beating with word that somebody else hadn't been seen for a while. He'd only heard about Jonesy, who thankfully was now safely back on the streets, if 'safely' was the word he could use. Some people enjoyed the lifestyle, some couldn't wait to get away from it, and Jonesy fitted into the former. He was in luck, though. Hazel was on duty. He waited patiently for her to come to the phone.

"Hey Will," she said. "What can I do for you?"

"Have you seen the news?"

"Not yet, what's happened?"

"They've found another body at Hunsbury Hill Park. They seem to think it's a homeless person again and I wondered if anybody else had been reported missing."

There was a silence on the other end of the line, Hazel was obviously thinking. He heard a deep sigh before she responded. "I've not heard anything, no, but that doesn't mean…"

"I know, I thought the same. I'm going to ring the DI that is investigating Clyde's case and see if she'll tell me anything, though I doubt she'll say much."

"I am guessing you're thinking the same as me, it could be anyone?"

"Afraid so," he said. "I'll let you know if I find anything out. Keep your own ears open."

"I will. I'd better go," said Hazel before hanging up.

Will took his chance to risk the wrath of a tired Rochelle Mason. He dialled her number and waited.

"DI Mason," she said formally.

He could hear a mixture of tiredness and busy in the way she answered. With two victims, she and her team would have their work cut out for them, particularly with the deaths occurring in such close proximity of time. If both were left in Hunsbury Hill Park, there was an obvious link that any layperson would understand.

"Sorry to disturb you, DI Mason," Will said. "It's Will Peters."

"Yes, Will, what can I do for you now?"

"I heard the news about another body found in Hunsbury Hill Park, likely a homeless person again."

"What can you tell me?" she said gruffly.

"I was hoping you could tell me something actually," he said, trying to sound light-hearted and failing terribly.

"Do you have information that somebody is missing from the centre?"

"Not that we know of, no, but that doesn't mean much with the community we help. But I wondered if you needed me to come along and perhaps take a look at the victim, see if I recognise them?" Rochelle Mason stayed silent, obviously pondering what to do, and Will instantly knew that the victim hadn't been carrying any ID.

"Okay," she said with a sigh. "What time can you be at the mortuary?"

"I can be there about half nine actually, if that would help?"

"I'll meet you there then."

And she was gone. As Will placed his phone back on the kitchen worktop, he looked out at the green grass of the postage-stamp-sized garden, bright sunlight flooding into the room. A beautiful day for most people, but a terrible day for somebody that had lost their life. Rochelle Mason sounded a mixture of tired, overwhelmed and distracted, and he felt sorry for her, but he felt even more sorry for the latest victim and any family yet to find out.

He grabbed his car keys and set off to Birdie's house. She'd lift his spirits, she did every time they met, and he always enjoyed spending time with her. If ever he was feeling low or disgruntled with something, no matter what it was, she had a habit of lifting them in an instant, even though she was a feisty individual he'd never want to cross, particularly now that he knew she'd stabbed her husband to death. He'd find out the reason why one day, but it wasn't important, he simply enjoyed her company. Today, she'd be dressed in black Lycra ready for her Pilates class. She said it kept her supple. He smiled at the bright red lips that would complete the look. Yes, Birdie would lift his spirits for sure.

THIRTY-ONE

Will pulled up outside Birdie's big house as she was closing the door behind her. Just as he'd suspected, she was dressed head to foot in black Lycra, her red exercise shoes and small sports bag identical in colour to her lips, her grey hair tied up in a neat French plait. She cut a sharp figure and he wondered if she'd always been in such good shape all her life. As Birdie turned towards him, she waved lightly, a smile stretched across her face as per usual. He loved her mood – she only had the one and that was upbeat. He jumped out and opened the rear passenger door for her and waited until she'd set herself comfortable and fastened the seat belt before getting back in himself.

"And how is Birdie today?" he asked as he prepared to pull away from the kerb.

"Perfect as a usual. Every day I'm alive, I'm perfect," she added by way of explanation.

"Well, I'm glad that you're perfect every day, Birdie," Will said with a smile. "I must say I always enjoy your positivity. Not many of my customers, or should I say none of my customers, are anything like you."

"I should think not!" she said, sounding almost indignant, but Will knew he hadn't offended.

"What's the plan for today, Birdie, after you've done your stretching?"

She patted the bag that was on the seat next to her and said, "I'm going to get changed and I'm going to give you a hand." She caught his eye in the rear-view mirror.

"You're going to give me a hand?" he asked. "At what exactly?"

"What do you think, silly?" she said. "You're going to the mortuary, I bet." That stumped Will. He hadn't told anyone since he'd only made the appointment just prior to setting off.

"How do you know whether I'm going to the mortuary or not?"

"Because there's been a second body found and you'll have been on the phone this morning if you had any sense, and since you're a bright lad, you'll have offered to go and take a look, see if you know him. Am I right?"

There was no fooling Birdie, quick witted and quick thinking.

"Well, you've got me there, but the thing is I'm going at nine-thirty and you won't have finished your class. I'm meeting DI Mason there and I don't think she'd let you in either."

"I know that, Will. I don't expect her to, and I certainly don't need to view the body. I'd have no clue as to who it might be. But I'm here to bounce things off when you get back in the car. Plus, if it is somebody else you know, you may just need a bit of a chat, maybe a coffee afterwards." He watched as she turned to watch through the side window. Traffic was building and the journey slowed a little. She seemed intent on watching a woman push a buggy along the pavement, a toddler on foot beside her.

"That is thoughtful of you, Birdie, but I don't want to keep you." He didn't want to turn her generosity away, though he didn't feel the need for any comfort either, not yet anyway.

"You're not keeping me from anything, and so what if my class is cut a little short. I can always carry on with my stretches at home later. Not that I will, though. It's more important to lend you a hand. So, if you've got time, if you don't mind waiting for me, obviously I'll pay, then we can go on together."

Will couldn't help smiling. "It sounds like you've already organised everything, Birdie," he said. "I'd better go along with it – now I know your secret history, I'm very conscious of not upsetting you. You've already threatened to kill me once, if I reveal my source."

She winked at Will furtively, and he returned it with a light laugh. "Anyway," she went on, "on that note, remember I mentioned to you I'd kept in touch with one of my fellow inmates, the one that was a little meek and mild? Killed her bloke with rat poison?"

"I remember that well." How could he not?

"Well, I've tracked her down. Facebook is a marvellous tool you know."

"Really? Was she pleased to hear from you?"

"Yes, she was actually. I thought it would be fun to catch up and see what she's been doing, it's been some years, and you'll never guess what."

"What's that?" he asked, playing along.

"It turns out she doesn't live far from here actually. She's only in Leicester, so I thought I'd pay her a visit."

"That's nice for you. Will you be going on the train?"

"Lord, no. I thought I might get you to take me," she said, "if you're up for it. It would be a decent fare."

"It would be my pleasure. When are you going?"

"We haven't actually arranged a firm date yet, but I suspect it will be early next week. Neither of us are working now so there's no point in waiting too long."

"Well, you let me know what day when you know. I'm sure I can squeeze you in."

It was only a few minutes into town and Will soon pulled up outside the Pilates studio.

"What time do I need to be changed and ready for?" Birdie asked.

Will checked the clock on the dashboard and made a quick calculation. "If you could be ready for, say, quarter past? The hard part is getting the parking space, hospitals are not renowned for having surplus."

"Right you are," she said and proceeded to gather her things.

Will, having forgotten his manners, hurriedly jumped out of his driver's seat and went round to undo the rear door, but she was already out. "You don't need to fuss with me," she said. "I'll see you shortly." And with that he watched the black-Lycra-clad woman enter through the front door and head off for her shortened class.

THIRTY-TWO

AS LUCK WOULD HAVE IT, IT REALLY DIDN'T TAKE TOO LONG TO *find a parking space when Will visited the mortuary for the second time that week..* Will helped Birdie, who had thankfully changed and instead wore stylish drainpipe jeans and thick boots, out of the car. Aviator sunglasses perched on the end of her nose. He could never imagine her in elasticated waist trousers and a flowery shirt from a catalogue. He closed the door behind her and the two of them set off to a building Will was beginning to know quite well. He could see DI Mason talking on her phone and loitering by the door. She glanced their way and drew her call to a close.

"Is that her?" asked Birdie.

"That's my contact, yes, DI Rochelle Mason."

"And what's she like?"

"Hard case is how I'd describe her," said Will. "It's not that she's unpleasant or anything, she just keeps her cards close to her chest, a true poker player. But I can understand why. A real professional."

"You need someone that's a bit looser around the mouth, don't you, someone that will tell you a little bit more," said Birdie.

"Beggars can't be choosers, though," said Will. "She's all I've got to work with. I'm sure she'll come round. When she gets to know me."

As Will and Birdie reached the spot where Rochelle was standing, the DI finally looked up and acknowledged their arrival properly. She was wearing what appeared to be motorbike leathers, though Will couldn't see a helmet.

"Hello Will," she said.

"Hello Rochelle," he said, nodding politely, "or should I call you DI Mason?"

"I answer to both, from you," she said and gave a half-smile which Will took as a good sign. "But who is this, aren't you going to introduce us?" Rochelle looked quizzically at Birdie and nodded approvingly at her boots. They looked like they'd been buffed for hours.

"I'm sorry," he said. "This is my friend Birdie, Birdie Fox."

Something flickered in Rochelle's eyes and was gone in an instant. "And is Birdie in any way connected to Refresh?" she asked.

Will, not in the habit of lying, couldn't exactly say she was, and the look on his face told Rochelle all she needed to know.

"In that case, I'm going to have to ask you to wait outside," she said, turning to Birdie.

"No problem," Birdie said brightly and hung back as the two headed off.

Will knew what to expect. There would be a viewing room and he would see the victim's face as the sheet was slowly pulled down, but he'd got an idea this morning. He just hoped it worked.

"I'll just see if they're ready for us," Rochelle said and headed off into a nearby room leaving Will to pace slowly in the corridor in his own. It wasn't long before she came back and said, "They're bringing him through now, you know the drill."

"Sadly, I do," he said as a trolley was wheeled into the small room, the victim covered with a sheet.

"Ready?" Rochelle asked.

"Let's get it over with," he said, and she nodded to the mortuary assistant on the other side of the glass to come closer to the viewing window. Will stared for a moment, a little unsure, before saying, "I need a closer look. Can I go inside?"

It was unusual but not unheard of and so Rochelle led the way and the two of them slipped inside and stood beside the body laid out on the trolley. Will peered closer. There was a lot of bruising around the upper part of his neck, and an odour he couldn't quite place, damp almost, rather than stale or unwashed.

"What is that smell?"

DI Mason stayed non-committal; she wasn't going to tell him anything. He stood silently for a moment longer then removed a pen from his inside jacket pocket like he'd seen detectives do on TV. Quick as a flash he flicked the sheet down, exposing the victim's bare chest and terrible neck injuries. DI Mason was powerless to do anything in the moment, but as soon as she realised what had happened and what Will had now seen, she made her displeasure known.

"What the—" she half-yelled.

"I had to make sure it was who I thought it was," he said, pointing to a small scar, thankful for obvious evidence he could use in his defence. The mortuary assistant hastily pulled the sheet back up, visibly shocked at Will's actions, and Rochelle bustled him out of the viewing room and back out into the corridor. He could tell she was steaming mad at him, but it was too late now, he'd seen the message written on the lad's young chest. To deflect the reprimand he knew was coming, he said, "It's Bowie Marks. I haven't seen him for a while, but that's definitely Bowie." Will locked eyes with Rochelle and waited for any more wrath to subside. By the time it had sunk in that he had given her a name, probably saved hours and hours of searching missing person records and done the police a huge favour, her anger deflated somewhat. She still had to say her piece, though it wasn't as bad as it could have been.

"Don't you ever try something stupid like that again, do you hear me?" she said in a low, even voice. It told Will in no uncertain terms that she was pissed with him. "What good does that do you, now you've seen it?"

"I don't know yet," he said, "but when someone is purposely killing disadvantaged people and leaving them like rubbish in Hunsbury Hill Park, I make it my business to help find out what's going on."

"It's not your business, Will. I appreciate the thought but leave it to us, leave it to the professionals. We've got the resources and the know-how, it's what we do all day every day. You may have compromised an investigation now."

"My lips are sealed. You can trust me, Rochelle. It won't be a problem, but now I know what you're dealing with, I can listen to the gossip, I can be eyes and ears, I can find out what's going on with the people living in our community, see if they know anything, if they've seen anything. People that won't open up to the police. Like Jonesy for instance. You know as well as I do that he didn't tell you the full story, but I got him to open up to me a bit." It came out in one long stream, without even the tiniest gap for her to get a word in. Rochelle had to concede that what he was saying was true. Not everyone liked the police, particularly those that had been in trouble in the past, as she suspected Jonesy had. At least he'd got away from his ordeal safely. Whatever they were involved in, two victims now lay in the mortuary behind them.

"Let's get some air," she said, trying to defuse the tension, and the two headed outside. "Tell me what he told you."

Will had no choice now, but it meant breaking Jonesy's confidence – he just hoped his friend never found out. He told her about the nutjob on Ketamine and Jonesy's suspicions of a woman being involved. DI Mason filed it away for later.

"Thanks, that could be useful," she conceded.

Birdie was waiting. And watching. "Can I give you a lift back?" he asked Rochelle.

"I'm good, thanks. I've got my bike today, hence the leathers," she said, pointing to her legs.

Will could see Birdie approaching as they slowly walked. He raised his hand in greeting and the pair stopped.

"Birdie Fox, eh? You don't half mix with some characters, Will," Rochelle said before picking up her pace and heading off back to her motorbike, which was parked not far away.

"You don't know the half of it," he called after her, then smiled as his new partner in crime stopped alongside him.

"Went okay, then?"

"Perfectly. Any clue what 'touch move' means?"

"You obviously don't play chess," she said, linking an arm through his. "I knew I'd come in handy. Come on, I'll explain on the way. Coffee time."

THIRTY-THREE

Mayor Colin Hayhurst almost lost the contents of his stomach again when he heard it on the morning news. He'd only been sitting up at Hunsbury Hill the previous afternoon, eating cheese and crackers and drinking red wine from a bottle like a wino. He wondered about the timing – had somebody seen him there? Maybe the person that was blackmailing him knew his every move. Could they have been tailing him? It seemed a coincidence that not long after he'd left the park the second body was discovered. He wondered about the message, delivered by text, written on another victim: 'Touch move'.

He didn't feel like going into the office and debated taking a detour again, though not to the woodlands this time. But there was no chance of that, he couldn't keep skiving off like he had yesterday afternoon, there was work to be done. This latest death troubled him even more than the first, and he knew now that things were only going to escalate unless he took action. He could hardly go to the police – they'd warned him against it – so there had to be another way. Colin tossed the situation through in his mind yet again, like he'd done so many times of recent, the lack of sleep beginning to show both in his eyes and in his mood. Babs had commented on it only last night when he'd finally arrived home half-drunk. She hadn't been best pleased, and he'd made his excuses for an early night. Thankfully, she hadn't wanted to join him. With so much time spent cogitating, he'd come to only one conclusion: his latest development. Somebody knew what he was up to. How though, he'd no clue. He debated calling an emergency meeting with the other two investors. Maybe they would have some advice or know what to do or who to turn to if the police were out of bounds. Was it worth a try? In doing so, he'd risk letting them in on his being blackmailed and not reporting it to the authorities, and then they themselves would become part of a bigger issue. If the police ever found out they all knew about the deaths, had been contacted by the kidnapper, they'd all go down for sure. Plus, he didn't know how much he could trust them in this kind of situation. Did he have the confidence they wouldn't overreact? Colin laid his head back on the headrest and closed his eyes while the driver made his way to Angel Square. When he felt the car finally pull up by the kerb, he resisted opening them for a moment longer. It was only when the driver prompted him and said, "Sir, we're here," that he knew he must leave.

"Thank you," he said finally and climbed out, but he waited for the car to pull away before heading inside to his office.

It was a bright and airy modern building, so very different from the one they used to work in on George Row, which was both ornate and old, and had character. Now its original chamber was only ever used by the council as a meeting place. The new building felt like a modern university or Google headquarters. All it needed was a pinball in reception and a machine dispensing gobstoppers and you would never know the difference. He preferred the old office with its ancient leather chairs and polished wood desks.

Colin climbed the stairs up to his office, taking each one slowly so as not to put any further pressure on his heart and lungs. By the time he reached the top, he'd made the decision to call his business partners and explain the situation. The stress was killing him, he had to do something. If things went downhill from there, so be it, but he couldn't carry on the way he was. The worry and anxiety and missed sleep was getting him nowhere, and he certainly didn't want any more dead bodies because of him. His conscience couldn't cope.

Once at his desk, he called Rodney first and told him he needed to meet urgently that evening at the usual location. He then called Brian, who agreed to meet him later too. In Colin's head, it was a start to putting things right – he hoped. But what to tell them? Too much and it could backfire. Too little and he might as well not bother. A knock on the door broke into his thinking and he looked across to see the familiar ponytail bobbing towards him. It was Katherine, and in her hands she had yet another folder which she placed down in front of him.

"For your signature," she said without feeling or a 'good morning'.

"Thanks," he managed before adding, "mine is a coffee when you make it."

Katherine left the room as quickly as she had entered, leaving him to attend to the documents. She never did deliver his requested cup of coffee and Colin never reminded her.

THIRTY-FOUR

Birdie and Will chatted in the coffee shop in the hospital's main building. They could have chosen any café in the town, but it seemed silly when they were on the premises not to use the one that was nearby, and a coffee was a coffee in Will's book, though Birdie would disagree. The location suited them both and a steady flow of doctors, nurses, porters and hospital visitors sipped on hot drinks. It looked like any coffee shop in any hospital in any town. The two sat together in the back of the room, for privacy more than anything, not wanting anybody to overhear their conversation about dead bodies. Will had run through what had happened in the mortuary and Birdie hadn't flinched when he'd explained what he'd done. In fact, she'd said she was impressed with him for doing such a thing in front of the detective inspector. He had some balls.

"So, what do you think it means then, 'touch move'?" Will asked. "Why would somebody write that on a dead body?"

"Let me explain," said Birdie, leaning forward conspiratorially. "It's a term when you play chess, and it really means if a player deliberately touches the piece on the board when it's their turn to do something, then they must move that piece once they've touched it.

You have to move it if it's legal to do so. So, what the killer could be saying is 'I've done this because you made me, I touched the body therefore I have to kill it.' That's what I think anyway," she said, shrugging her shoulders and sitting back in her chair. "I don't know what else it could mean, and that seems the obvious answer to me."

Will thought about the rule for a moment. It sounded plausible.

"A forced move," he said.

"Kind of, yes. You touched, so you move, or in this case, you force my hand to do what I did."

"The first message said 'your move', so they were perhaps waiting for somebody to do something? If that's the case, we just have to figure out what and who that someone is."

"Got it in one," said Birdie. "I assume the police will have come to the same conclusion, put the connection together. It appears obvious."

"So, what's *our* next move, then?"

"Well, I'd say from what you you've told me this morning you've got access to eyes and ears on the streets that these people live in, and that gives you an advantage. Heavens, you've lived their lives, Will. You know how these people operate, who they trust, how they survive."

Will sat thoughtful for a moment and then asked, "Do you think there will be more deaths?"

"How can we possibly know?" said Birdie.

"There were two in quick succession, both with messages."

"Then someone obviously didn't respond to the first message in time," Birdie added. She leaned forward again, into Will's space, and asked, "Do you know something you're not telling me?"

Will met her stare. "What makes you think that?"

"I'm just reading you, and I think you're holding something back, keeping somebody's confidence perhaps, and from what my gut is telling me, I suspect it is that other character, the one that had a lucky escape, your friend Jonesy." She sat back again and waited.

She was, of course, correct.

"I didn't want to say anything, he's taken me into his confidence and I've already broken it with Rochelle. Not that he told me much to be fair."

"Well, out with it. One more knowing won't hurt," urged Birdie sitting forward again.

A couple of beats passed before Will gave in. "Okay. He wonders if there were two people that night. The one that smacked him a couple of times and then another that placed a cloth over his mouth and nose before he down he went. He thought it might have been a woman."

"He feels embarrassed going to the police, is that it? Really? Hell, some of the world's most notorious criminals are women, I should know. The lad shouldn't be so soft, silly bugger, and I'm surprised at you, Will Peters." Birdie shook her head at him. "Now, back to that cloth. Might it have been chloroform?"

"It would explain the drowsy part."

A notification flashed up on Birdie's phone, and Will watched as she picked it up and read it, her red lips smiling slightly as she pressed to open and read the message fully. He waited, not wishing to pry, but intrigued as to what was amusing her. He watched while she tapped a response and then looked up at him.

"It's Cynthia," she said, "did her husband in with rat poison."

"How could I forget. When are you meeting?" asked Will.

"She's suggested tomorrow. What's your diary like, fancy a drive up?"

Will knew exactly what his diary was like. He didn't have any regular customers the following day, so it was all casual pickups, and since he hadn't got any graves to dig for the rest of the week, he knew his diary was clear.

"What time do you want to go," he asked, "morning?"

"How long is it to Leicester, would you say? An hour?"

"About that, yes. You just pick a time."

"Excellent," she said, and he watched while she tapped a message, her red lips grinning as she concentrated. She put the phone down. "We're on. We leave here at nine o'clock and we'll be there for morning coffee," she said triumphantly. "It'll be fun to see her again. I wonder what she's doing with herself. I wonder if she's remarried," she said slyly. "Hell, I wonder if he knows her past! What a hoot!"

THIRTY-FIVE

O_NCE_ W_ILL_ HAD DELIVERED B_IRDIE_ BACK TO HER HOUSE, HE hadn't much else planned for the rest of the day except for Stanley Kipper at 2 pm. The rest would be casual pickups, as tomorrow would have been had Birdie not organised a chunk of his time. He didn't mind, he liked spending time with her, and since she was paying it didn't matter whether it was a casual pickup or a delightful regular. He made himself comfortable in a town-centre parking space, ready for anyone that needed a lift. He rested his head back, closed his eyes and thought about Bowie and his injuries before his thoughts drifted to why the abductors had decided to let Jonesy go. Didn't he fit the mould? He had to assume the cases were connected.

His phone pinged, someone needed him. He looked at the address and started the engine before navigating the lunchtime traffic around the town centre. A minute or two later, he pulled up outside the appropriate house and waited while a young woman made her way down the very short front path to the pavement. She was pushing a buggy, a young child sitting comfortably inside. He noticed she had a small bunch of flowers in her hands, and he wondered who lay in Towcester Road Cemetery that she was going to visit. Knowing where she was going but not knowing how close she was to the deceased made conversation a little difficult. Normally he'd be bright and chirpy, ask about her day, general chitchat, but she looked in no mood for conversation with a stranger. Will respected her need for privacy and stayed quiet. Maybe on another occasion. They drove in silence for the relatively short journey to the same cemetery where Jonesy had been dropped and pulled up out the front. Will retrieved the buggy from the boot then waited while she placed the child in it and set off with her flowers. At least it was sunny, if a little overcast, but no rain on the horizon would make standing at someone's graveside a little more bearable.

When she was finally out of sight, he locked the car up and made his own way into the cemetery, walking slowly to stretch his legs more than anything. He'd be ready when she wanted to leave, but in the meantime he ambled along through the mixture of headstones and plaques in the sacred ground. A small gathering over to his left told him a committal was in progress, one of his colleagues responsible for digging the grave today. He'd seen the hearse parked up nearby, with the same undertakers as at the exhumation and Will tried not to smile. A woman and a burly man, both dressed in funeral black, waited in the wings. The man he instantly recognised from him landing in the dirt by his digger. Was she the woman he'd noticed that night too? Not wanting to pry, Will headed back towards the entrance again.

Jonesy had described the place where he'd finally woken up that morning – just to the right and not far from the gate, he'd said. There was little point carrying someone further into a cemetery when you could dump them not far from the front wall. Will made his way over to the spot, though he wasn't sure what he was going to be able to see. The grass was newly mown and there were no signs of a struggle, no plants bending over where they'd been snapped by someone's foot, nothing out of the ordinary whatsoever. It was all nice and neat, there was nothing to suggest anyone had lain there overnight. Will looked around at the headstones. Many had stood proud for years, and nobody had been added to the space for a good long while. The whole area was nicely tended to, either by the sexton or by the dead's visitors. Small, neat bunches of flowers sat at a handful of graves. In the distance he could see his fare was slowly making her way back towards the entrance herself. Not everyone stayed at the cemetery for long – a quick tidy or replacement of flowers, a few words and it was often time to leave. It appeared the young woman was the same. Will was about to head back to his car ready when something in the grass caught his eye and he bent down for a closer look.

It was a marker pen – a blue one.

THIRTY-SIX

THINKING OF THE MESSAGES WRITTEN ON THE TWO BODIES, WILL wondered about the blue marker pen in front of him. Could it be the one used? Was Jonesy the next intended, and had he had a lucky escape? He took his phone from his pocket and photographed the pen where it lay, incorporating the nearest headstone for location. He needed to get it into his pocket without touching it; there could be valuable prints if it was anything to do with the murders. Since he never carried a handkerchief, he took his jacket off and gently used the edge of the cloth to pick the pen up then wrapped it within the fabric itself, hoping he didn't smudge anything. It could well be evidence left by the killer. Of course it could be a random blue pen tossed into the grass, it was hardly a sinister item, it wasn't like finding a bloodied knife or some such, and there could be a million simple explanations as to why it lay where it did. He wondered if the police had even been over the area where Jonesy had been found, but why would they really? Was Jonesy's experience even connected to the other two cases? Whatever the reason, the pen was safely wrapped up and he'd take it in. They could get lucky.

Will could see the young woman returning, and not wishing to intrude on any possible grief, not wanting to witness any tears that may be lingering in her eyes, he stayed by the car ready to receive the buggy for the boot. Her eyes averted, she gratefully thanked him and slipped inside on the rear seat.

"Straight home, please," the woman's voice said over his shoulder. "Thank you for waiting, it makes things a little easier, particularly with the little one," she said and stroked the boy's fringe on his forehead lightly – not that it was in his eyes, but more of an affectionate move by his mother. Will glanced across at the passenger seat and its tiny cargo and debated dropping the pen off with DI Mason and experiencing her wrath for a third time in one day. If she was still mad with him from earlier, hopefully this would appease her if there was any value in it.

A few short minutes later and parked outside the terraced house once again, he watched the young woman push the empty buggy up the short path, a toddler waddling very slowly at her side, hand held tightly in his mum's.

His latest passenger delivered safely home, he figured he'd got just enough time to drop the pen with DI Mason before going on to pick Stanley up and observe his choice of reading material for the orthopaedic patients that afternoon. He hoped for their sake it was time for a western and not more Labour Party politics, though what was on the menu depended on Stanley's mood.

Will made his way back across to Newport Pagnell Road in the hope that Rochelle had forgiven him and was in a better mood. Maybe he should have brought her lunch? Maybe she'd still be down at the hospital receiving treatment, or maybe she wasn't even in the building and he would give it to somebody else. That could be the best option. He entered through the front door and approached an officer.

"I'm afraid DI Mason is away from the building," he said.

"In that case is DC Flint available? He's part of the same investigation," added Will.

"I'll see if I can find him. Can I ask what it's regarding?"

"I've just found something I think both of them will be interested in, perhaps a piece of evidence. It was in the grass at Towcester Road Cemetery. I've not touched it," Will said, offering his wrapped jacket. "It's a blue marker pen."

The officer stared at the jacket as Will carefully unfolded it, revealing the pen in all its glory. It looked like any old pen from anyone's desk. Will proffered it to him and said, "It may be part of the case that they're working on. I spotted it by a grave only a few minutes ago." Will could tell by the look on the man's face he had no clue about the particular case, but that didn't surprise him. There could be several on the go that the task force was working on.

"I'll get an evidence bag in the meantime," he said and wandered off, leaving Will holding his jacket and pen. A moment later, the officer returned and placed the pen into the bag, sealed it and wrote something on it that Will couldn't decipher.

"Is DC Flint coming to take it?" Will asked.

"I'll just take this through to him now it's in a bag. Has he got your details?"

"He has, but please tell him Will found it at Towcester Cemetery. It's to do with Jonesy and or the recent deaths, he'll know."

"Righto, no doubt he'll be in touch if he needs anything else."

Will knew it was the end of the conversation, his time to leave. A quick glance at the clock on the wall said he needed to get over to Stanley's place quick smart or risk the old man's displeasure at him being late. He was getting tired of being told off, by anyone.

THIRTY-SEVEN

WILL NEEDN'T HAVE WORRIED BECAUSE BY THE TIME HE PULLED UP outside Stanley's house at the Crescent, he had two minutes to spare. After letting himself out of his car, he headed towards Stanley's front door in case the man needed help getting down the path. Why he didn't use some sort of walking frame, Will would never know, but the man was independent and preferred to go at his own pace, he wasn't ever in much of a rush. And who was Will to stop him? He was halfway up the path, and through the overgrown jungle that you could call the front garden, when the door opened and Stanley appeared. Will instinctively looked down to see if it was a good day or not and noted actual shoes for a change. It boded well. Instinctively, he raised his gaze to look at what was in Stanley's hands, but he couldn't see the titles of the books he held. Raising his gaze further, he met Stanley's eyes and broke into a smile. He hoped the elderly man would return one.

"Afternoon, Stanley," he said brightly. "How are you today?"

"Not bad," said Stanley somewhat gruffly, but Will knew 'not bad' was positive for him.

"Do you need a hand or are you flying solo this afternoon?"

"Bugger off, Will," he said. "I don't need any help. I'm quite stable on my own, just slow." Will suppressed a smile and watched, standing back slightly as Stanley made his way at a snail's pace towards the waiting vehicle. It was then he noticed Stanley had left the front door wide open. "Should I close the door for you?" Will called.

"What?"

"The front door, Stanley. It's wide open. Have you got your keys with you if I close it?"

"Of course I've got my keys, you idiot." The old man must have caught himself and what he'd just said because in a much softer tone he said, "Yes, thank you, you can close the door." Will watched as the man turned away and resumed his snail's pace, and wondered what he himself would be like when he reached his eighties. Would he be just as gruff? Were they all destined to be grumpy old men once they became octogenarian?

Will didn't need to hurry to catch the man up, several steps did it, and he walked slowly just behind him until they reached the car, where he opened the rear passenger door for him. Stanley grunted and groaned as he made himself comfortable, placing his handful of books alongside him on the seat. It was then that Will finally got to see the content. More Labour Party politics, more Michael Foot, though a different book from last time. There was no sign of a western, but there was something else peeking out that he couldn't quite see the title of.

"So, what's today's reading material, Stanley?" he asked, getting in behind the wheel.

"I thought I'd educate a bit more," he said.

"Just the Michael Foot, then?"

"Yes, and for a bit of colour I've brought a Jeffrey Archer. He was a Labour supporter, you know."

Will knew that was most definitely not the case, the old man was confused. "I thought Jeffrey Archer was a Conservative MP,

Stanley." Will knew from experience it was best to say there was a possibility of him being wrong to save an argument, even when he was one hundred per cent correct. Archer had later become a peer of the realm before going to prison for perjury and was most definitely *not* a Labour supporter.

"You're wrong, Will," said Stanley. "He certainly writes like one."

Will tried to imagine what a Labour novelist wrote like.

"You must mean one of his characters is a Labour supporter, do you think? What have you been reading?"

"*The Clifton Chronicles*," said Stanley. Will had read the first couple of books in the series, and yes, there was a lot of politics between the covers. He tried to be tactful with his correction.

"Jeffrey Archer was indeed a Conservative member of Parliament, Stanley, though some of his characters in the *Chronicles* were absolutely Labour. I've read them."

They drove in silence for a mile or two before Stanley spoke again. He must have been considering Will's information.

"Well, it's a good book anyway, and it talks about Labour so I'll stick with it, though if Archer himself isn't Labour, maybe I should reconsider."

"I think your patients this afternoon would much prefer the made-up tales of Sebastian Clifton to the real-life drama of Michael Foot." Will tried to catch the man's eye and smile, but Stanley wasn't for letting him. Silence reigned for another minute or two.

"Anyway," Stanley said, in an attempt to change the subject, "my daughter popped over yesterday afternoon and we went out. She drove us up to the country park. You know, where the woods used to be."

"You mean Hunsbury Hill?" said Will. "There are still plenty of trees up there these days, though you are right about 'used to be'. Anyway, what did you do up there?" With recent events at Hunsbury Hill Park, the words were fast becoming regular vocabulary.

"We went for a drive. Bought me an ice cream, she did. I don't get to see Janice very often, she's always too busy. But you'll never guess what I saw while I was there?"

Will glanced at the older man through his rear-view mirror and waited to see what Stanley knew. A beat of excitement hit his veins. Had he seen something to do with the case? The bodies?

"What was that?"

"That mayor of ours," he said. "Sat on a bench in broad daylight, swigging wine from a bottle. Can you believe it?"

"The mayor? Are you sure?"

"Of course I'm bloody sure, I know what the man looks like! Drinking like a wino he was, sitting there on his own."

"Whereabouts was he?"

"A little way from the car park. Seemed like we'd walked forever. I can only go slow on my legs, but I thought it was bad form, him being a public figure."

"What time was that?"

"I don't remember exactly. Afternoon, sometime later on, maybe five-ish. Must have been because Janice finished work early and came over."

"Did you see anything else?" asked Will.

"Birds. Dog shit."

Will took that as a 'no'.

THIRTY-EIGHT

Stanley must have been cogitating on the earlier conversation because as soon as he was back in the car and they were on their way home again, he blurted out what was obviously on his mind.

"The bloody football club," he started off with. Will was immediately confused since nothing had been mentioned previously and they weren't anywhere near a club.

"What was that, Stanley?" Will called enquiringly over a shoulder.

"Bloody Conservatives," said Stanley. "I was reading the newspaper this morning. You jogged my memory talking about politics earlier."

"Oh? What was that about?"

"Another council."

The statement landed as though it was meant to explain everything, but Will still had no clue.

"What about another council?"

"They've just lent millions to some football club is what. How is that right?" Stanley sounded incredulous. "It's public money. Why are they lending it to a private football club?"

"I've no idea," said Will. "Did the report not say?"

"It said something about interest payments, but I didn't read it all, I just saw the headline and thought that's out of order. My rates and fellow citizens' rates are going to a bloody football club, to prop it up no doubt!"

Will knew exactly what the council would be doing. If it was loaning money to a private company, it would be getting interest payments back as revenue, as a fundraiser. Lots of councils ran schemes to fund the shortfall since money was always needed for something and the government only handed out so much. Their own local would be no different.

"I'm sure it's all above board," said Will. "They'll be doing it for the interest payments so you can have your library or your hospital or you can have whatever else you want that funds are tight for."

"New bloody legs is what I want," mumbled Stanley.

"Maybe they can help with that too," said Will, trying not to sound exasperated. "Anyway," he said, "who's upset you? Did someone not like your choice of reading material this afternoon?"

"Didn't even get to Michael Foot. I only read Archer today."

"Well, our mayor is Conservative. Maybe our council does the same sort of things?"

"Their mayor is Labour."

"But you just said you didn't agree with them lending money to a private company." Will knew he was losing his battle and offered, "Isn't our deputy Labour?" It might appease the man.

Stanley harrumphed. "That's the only thing she's got going for. Not that she'll ever be our local leader."

"What makes you say that?" asked Will, trying not to get too riled up with the man's reasoning and political debate. It was time to change the subject if he could.

"She's too short," he said abruptly.

Will wanted to groan loudly and wished he'd never asked. It was hardly a legitimate reason for someone not to succeed in a role, but there was little point him saying anything further for fear of getting into an argument.

Soon enough they were back and parked outside Stanley's house and Will once again opened the rear door and helped the old man out. Once he had two feet on the ground, Stanley said, "I might need you again tomorrow. I might go to Sainsbury's, get something nice for the weekend." He almost sounded like a different person. They moved together, slowly, towards the house.

"Have you got visitors coming?"

"No, no visitors that I know of. Janice is the only one that pops in occasionally and she won't be back twice in one week. No, I've been fancying an apple pie so I might buy myself one as a treat." The elderly man gave a rare smile, revealing several badly stained teeth. "Small things in life," Stanley said. "And I deserve a pie if that's what I want."

Will waited while Stanley retrieved his front door key and slipped it into the lock. He'd learned not to interfere and help too much, the old man independent and liked to do his own thing at his own pace. Once he was safely across the threshold, Will said, "I'll wait to hear from you then, Stanley. I'm going up to Leicester in the morning but if it's the afternoon you want a lift for, you should be fine. Just call me when you know."

"Will do," said Stanley, and with a flick of his hand, Will was free to leave. He received the message loud and clear and headed back to his car, shaking his head slightly, knowing full well that Stanley wouldn't be watching his actions. Once the front door was closed it was as if Will didn't exist.

THIRTY-NINE

He was exhausted. Stanley hadn't been in the best of moods and the two journeys with him had been tantamount to mental torture. If ever he felt like a long cold beer, it was right now, but he still had work to do. He thought about his plan to do an extra shift at the shelter that evening and wondered if it would do any good. There was no point denying he wanted to get to the bottom of the two deaths at Hunsbury Hill Park and the abduction of Jonesy, and he knew that if he could eavesdrop on conversations, he'd pick something up. Even the smallest of titbit of word on the street could be useful. There were many eyes and ears that lived there. Somebody must've seen something, whether strange, sinister or unusual. Maybe Jonesy talking to the man that had asked for a light, or the person that had held a cloth to his face. He called Louise to make sure she'd got no other plans before committing himself for a couple of hours later on in the evening.

"Hi Will," she said, as breezy as a spring morning. From such a rough beginning during his younger years he was very fortunate to have met Louise, and when she'd agreed to marry him, he couldn't have been happier. It felt like only yesterday.

"I love the sound of your voice," he said simply, "I could listen to it all day. Maybe you should record it."

"What you need?" she said. Louise obviously understood that he was after something. It got Will thinking. Maybe he didn't pay her enough compliments, because when he did, it aroused suspicion. He'd been rumbled, he needed to work on that.

"I don't want anything. Can't I give you a compliment?" he enquired. "Though I wonder if you have any plans this evening?"

"On a school night? Will, are we going out?"

"No, we're not going out, I'm afraid," he said, "though we should at the weekend, but I thought if you hadn't, and you didn't mind…" He let it linger; she knew what was coming.

"So, you want to know if you can go down to the centre, is that what you're trying to ask me?"

"There's no fooling you, is there, and yes, would you mind awfully? I won't be too late I wouldn't have thought anyway. I'm tired actually but there's just a couple of things I need to check up on and the only way I can do that is to be there."

"Is it to do with the deaths?"

"Yes. I'm really not sure how much effort the police are putting into this. Then there's the fact those that live on the street don't exactly trust coppers, but they are a bit more trusting of me, so I might just be able to find out a bit more. That's the plan anyway."

"Then that's what you should do," said Louise. "Just try not to be home too late, you need your own rest too."

"I won't, I promise," he said. "But I'll pop home first anyway, have something to eat and get changed. Are you at home now?"

"I am. Just putting dinner on actually."

"I'll be there in fifteen minutes, I'll see you then."

"See you shortly."

The line went dead. Now all Will had to do was let Hazel know that he'd be in, though he didn't plan on working in the kitchen. He hadn't exactly publicised with the rest of the team at the centre what he'd been up to, instead keeping his involvement close to his chest. Hazel had done the same for her part. He dialled her number and waited for her voice to come on the airwaves.

"Will, what a nice surprise," she said. The other woman in his life was always bright and breezy too. He was very lucky.

"Hi Hazel," he said, trying to match her tone. "I just wanted to let you know that I'll be in later, although I wasn't planning on working in the kitchen but more out in the dining room, if that's okay?"

"The more the merrier," she said, "and since you're not actually rostered on, you can work where you like, I guess. It's not up to me."

"I just thought it would be good to see what I can find out myself. You know, listen in a little."

"I know what you mean," said Hazel. "I thought the same thing, though I am in the wrong spot like you say. Need to be out there where the chatter is, not where the pots and pans are clattering all the time. I can hardly hear myself think sometimes." Right on cue what sounded like a mixer cranked up in the background and Will struggled to hear Hazel's next few words.

"See what I mean," she said, raising her voice a little as if to prove a point.

"I'll be there about six," he said, thinking of what Louise had just told him about dinner. They often ate early if they were all home.

"Let's hope it's productive and someone has something worth listening to."

FORTY

He was almost ready to give up and felt the shift had been wasted, though those he'd helped and served during his time there would disagree. Will had heard nothing in the two hours he'd been working the dining room, chatting and eavesdropping as he went. Not a snippet, not even the tiniest piece to latch on to. With dinner service almost over, he wiped down tables and took dirty cutlery and crockery back to the kitchen ready for the next session the following morning. From the corner of his eye, he could see George, who seemed to be loitering in the doorway a little, not sure if he was coming or going. He wiped his hands on his apron and wandered over, catching George's eyes as he did so. Did he imagine it or did George look like he was about to leave, as if he'd changed his mind over something? He couldn't be sure, but carried on in his direction anyway. It was too late for the man to move on without appearing rude and Will put his hand out to shake. One of the things he'd learned being homeless himself was how much people crave human contact. People had assumed he was filthy all the time and they never wanted to touch or reach out in any way. A simple handshake made all the difference. The two sat down at a nearby table.

"How are you, George?" Will asked.

Chocolate-brown Labrador eyes searched his, unsure what to say, and George nodded his greeting, his eyes never leaving Will's. There was something on the man's mind, of that Will was certain. George's left knee jigged up and down nervously.

"Have you missed dinner? I can get you something."

"No, Will," he said. "I ate earlier, thank you."

"Is everything okay? Only you seem a little edgy."

"Just a busy mind at present."

"Right, yes. Have you seen Jonesy? Are you still buddying up with him?"

"Still his buddy, though I haven't seen Jonesy today, but that's not unusual. He often goes off on his own for a few hours, though after what happened to him, I'm surprised. He had a close call it seems."

"Yes, he did. I wonder why they let him go."

"I've been thinking the very same thing," said George. "Why or what did Jonesy do to be abducted in the first place too? Doesn't make sense really. I guess you heard about the ink on his chest?"

It was news to Will. "What did it say?" Will tried not to show his utter surprise at the news.

"It was only two letters, a T and an O, as if someone had started to write something then changed their mind." Will's head started to spin. Jonesy must have made the discovery when he'd taken a shower.

"Did Jonesy mention anything to you that perhaps he doesn't want mentioned to the police? I know you two are reasonably close, closer than anybody else is to him."

George simply shook his head 'no', he hadn't said anything apparently. Maybe there wasn't anything more to add.

"Just out of interest," Will asked, "where does he hang out to sleep these days?"

"Same as me most nights."

"Sorry, George, but I don't know where that is. Somewhere in the town centre?"

"Bottom of Bridge Street. You know, where the entrance to the old tunnels is. A few of us doss down there."

"I thought they were boarded up?" Will knew as soon as he'd said it anyone could dismantle the hoarding and gain access to the tunnels. The majority had been sealed up over thirty years ago, deemed dangerous, a health and safety hazard. It was said that the tunnels ran from All Saints' Church in the centre of town right out to the various churches and buildings in line with all eight compass points. There were many of them that ran under the town, created in medieval times apparently. It was said that Delapré Abbey was part of it and that the nuns had used the tunnels to get away from the war that raged on the other side of their wall and escape back into town. The abbey was still there, now with a golf course nearby. It made Will think for a moment. The tunnels would be a great place to take somebody after you'd kidnapped them, particularly if you knew the warrens well. The county club at the bottom of George Row was said to have tunnels and cellars underneath it, part of the original labyrinth, not that Will had ever been inside such a fancy place. Perhaps Stanley would know something thing about them; he'd been around the town a good deal longer than Will had.

"So, he sleeps there, does he? Do many people to go in and out?"

"Some of us, yes. You know what it's like, you get moved on, and with the seasons you need something different, but at least in winter it's reasonably dry, better than a doorway and being pissed on."

Will remembered such times and felt himself give an involuntary shiver at the memory. He was glad he'd managed to get his life sorted, but he'd wanted to and not everybody on the streets had the same goal.

"You've given me an idea though, George," said Will, standing. "Fancy a walk over there?"

FORTY-ONE

COLIN SAT IN HIS USUAL CHAIR IN THE COUNTY CLUB. IT HAD RICH, deep colours, leather-bound chairs, dark wood walls – everything surrounding him was steeped in history. He'd been a member for as long as he could remember, and it was one of the finest Grade II listed buildings in the town. It had the added bonus of being situated on George Row, so it wasn't that far away from the council offices. The club had been built after the great fire back in 1675 when a good deal of the town had been destroyed. One of his favourite parts of the building was the late-seventeenth-century staircase. Architecture inspired him and had been one of the reasons he'd been saddened to move to the new council offices from the old chambers, where he'd worked for many years, just around the corner. He'd liked the feel of history beneath his feet as he walked the halls, to feel the powerful presence of those who had walked there before him, or sat at the same desk he then sat at. It had all gone now, so he reminisced at the county club instead.

He dined alone, having called Babs ahead of time to say he was staying in town for a meeting and dinner – it wasn't a lie. He enjoyed the Regency-style dining room at the club and ate and drank like a king, even though his stomach was unsettled for the conversation ahead. A couple of brandies had helped calm the roiling, but it still felt heavy and not from the food. Colin glanced at his watch; he still had twenty minutes before the others were due to arrive, so he made his way out to the usually delightful garden at the back, though he barely noticed it this evening. He ambled along, thinking, rehearsing, choosing his words carefully in terms of what he would and wouldn't admit to during the meeting. He knew he couldn't afford to let too much slip, but he had to do something before anyone else lost their life because of him.

The night was cooling, the sun long gone as he made his way back inside just as the first of his business partners entered through the front door. It was bang on 8 pm as Rodney Walsh made his entrance. The man boasted a permanent suntan from his many trips to Spain, to his villa that he always seemed to be on holiday at. Colin knew he must be on the take since there was no way he'd be able to afford the lifestyle he so enjoyed on the salary for his position. As almost fluorescent-white teeth gleamed, the overly tanned man walked towards him. Colin grimaced inwardly at what were obviously new caps, each evenly shaped and sized, and at odds with the man's wrinkled skin. He held out his hand in greeting and felt soft fingers against his own. They didn't feel like they'd done much manual work in their time, but then Rodney would prefer to pay someone rather than do the job himself.

"How are you, Colin?" he asked, sounding somewhat sombre. Could he pick up on his mood?

"I'm fine, thanks," he said, dropping a heavy sigh at the end of it, indicating quite clearly that he indeed wasn't fine, he was worrying about something and that was the reason why he'd called the meeting. A moment later, another man, Brian Davenport, entered through the same front door. Colin didn't allow him quite as much attention since Rodney was occupying his mind. Brian joined the trio. He seemed a little harried himself, as if he'd been in a rush, and Colin greeted the man. Once pleasantries were over, the three sat down at the small table where he'd been mulling things over on his own moments ago. Colin looked around. The club was quiet, there was no one sat within earshot and he felt reasonably comfortable, but he wondered if they should perhaps move outside into the well-lit garden.

"We should have booked a private room," Rodney said, standing as if to leave. He must have read Colin's mind. "Follow me, I know somewhere." He led the way down a carpeted corridor and through doors that said 'staff only'. On they walked until they came to a staircase that carried on down and which Colin suspected led towards the cellar. He'd never been in this part of the club and wondered how Walsh knew about it since it was behind the scenes, an area the average customer would not be privy to.

Colin could feel the temperature dip the further down they went. At some point, the fabric underfoot changed to cold flags, or perhaps stone, it was difficult to see in the light. At the bottom was a huge wooden door that opened easily and without a sound and looked as old as the town itself. Rodney reached around the corner of the decrepit frame for a switch and the room exploded with light. Colin took a moment to steady himself and figure out where he was. It didn't look like a typical, white-washed, damp cellar with beer barrels and defunct equipment stored nearby, though it did smell like one. It looked as if he were inside some sort of crypt. The ceiling resembled that of a tiny church, and the stone-flagged floor, together with the cold steps they'd just ventured down, made him feel as if he was in some sort of chamber, deep underneath the town above. He tried not to shiver. Colin noticed another door, at the far end of the room, and wondered where it led to. The rest of the space held an old wooden table and four nondescript metal chairs you'd find in any office across town. A single light fitting with a high-wattage bulb hung from the ceiling.

"What is this place?"

"It's on a need-to-know basis, and you don't need to know," Rodney said. "Now take a seat."

FORTY-TWO

Colin could barely contain his nerves as he sat at the table with the other two men. It looked like they were expecting someone else – the one empty seat opposite looked at him almost accusingly, as if he'd missed someone out of the equation with his invites.

"So," said Rodney Walsh, "what's so urgent, what's upsetting you? Because quite clearly something is. I've never seen you so agitated, you're normally so calm."

Colin wasn't sure where to begin even though he'd spent the previous couple of hours or so rehearsing, thinking through everything he was going to say and what he wasn't.

"I'm not entirely sure where to begin," he said, mustering some energy from somewhere. He was pleased with his delivery, which settled his nerves – if only for a moment.

"Then why don't you start at the beginning," said Brian.

Colin was well aware of Brian's background. As an accountant at a high-powered local firm, the man was very clever, he just looked meek. His hairline had receded somewhat to the back of his head and his dome, which looked like it had been polished only this morning, had fair hair cropped short around its edges. At least he hadn't got a comb-over. Why Colin was even thinking about the man's hairstyle at such a moment he had no idea and put it down to nerves.

"I might as well start in the middle since that's the bit that's caused me so much aggravation," said Colin, once again pleased with the energy that he'd managed to put into his words, so he didn't show his true emotions.

"Go on then," said Rodney, prompting. "Time's marching on."

He took a deep breath and said, "I'm being blackmailed." He let it sit for a moment or two to watch their reaction and was surprised that all he got from Brian was a lifting of his brows and there wasn't much more from Rodney.

"Go on," Rodney urged. "Blackmailed about what exactly?"

That particular part Colin wasn't about to tell. He wasn't sure how much the other two in this joint business project knew about where he got his funds from, the fictitious invoices he submitted, and he needed to hedge his bets somewhat. Instead, he tried a lie. "I'm being blackmailed about the development. Obviously, somebody doesn't want it to go ahead."

"Bit late for that," said Brian, "it's halfway through. What do they expect to achieve from blackmailing you when it's already half-built?"

He had a point. Colin knew that but figured those that sent the ransom texts were not necessarily that bright anyway. "I don't know the reasons why," he said somewhat sarcastically, "but the truth is I am being blackmailed, and they want five hundred thousand pounds. I haven't got it and it's causing me grief!"

"Why don't you go to the police?" said Brian.

"I'm not likely to bring the police into anything around this, now am I? This development is already behind schedule, and in case you've forgotten, we don't want them sticking their noses in and uncovering the loan that I organised via the council," he said, pointing his finger at Rodney. "Not many folks know about that aspect, it's certainly not public record. If I go to the police and tell them I'm being blackmailed because of the development, they are going to ask all sorts of questions. So that means we all get investigated. Do you want that? I don't think any of us fancy corruption tagged on to our names."

Colin let that settle for a moment while the other two men thought about their responses. It was like passing a tennis ball back over the net and waiting for someone to serve back at you.

"That loan is all above board and you know it," Rodney said.

"It's above board and has a legitimate contract," said Colin. "But when people get wind that their local government is handing out loans of ten million to private companies, they are not necessarily going to respond favourably, because they don't understand the mechanics of it." Colin was very careful with his words, speaking slowly, making sure each one sunk in. "You and I know that our venture is paying the interest so the council get an income, but questions will be raised as to why our development is seen favourably to get the loan in the first place. Mates' rates and all that."

"But again, I say, it's all approved and above board," said Rodney.

"Come on," said Colin, "you know as well as I do it's creative accounting at best. There's deliberate favouritism and the company that got the loan, our company, wouldn't have without my help, my direct involvement from the council. We absolutely would not be getting the money at all, not to mention the miniscule interest repayment rate. I don't need to tell you we need that money to finish things off. So no, I don't want the police looking into why I'm being blackmailed!"

"What did you call this meeting for, then?" Rodney asked.

"I want to know what you think I should do about it, but if going to the police is the only thing you can think of, I might as well not have bothered."

"Okay, they want five hundred thousand pounds, half a mil," said Rodney, "or else what? What will they do?"

Colin had wondered about that question himself while he'd been tossing and turning earlier. He didn't want it to be about the two bodies that had been found at Hunsbury Hill.

"They say they will go to the press with knowledge of our deal and leak about the loan and the fact that I'm part of this business, that there is a conflict of interest, which of course we know is true."

"Then we should call their bluff," said Brian, pushing his chair back, preparing to stand up. Colin looked up at him from his seat. The contrast between Brian and Rodney was extreme, they were poles apart.

Rodney stood too and said, "I suggest the same, leave them be. I don't think we've got anything to worry about. Let them go to the press, and when it comes out, we just need to figure out what our response will be before then. We all know our names are not on the shell companies building this development, so we have nothing to trace directly back to us. Unless of course they get too close and see our spouses are named, but even that's doubtful on such a cleverly constructed shell."

Rodney and Brian were both standing. It was time to leave.

"Though it does concern me how someone can possibly know that you're involved to blackmail you in the first place," Brian finished.

This wasn't going as Colin had planned – what was he to say next?

"It has to be internal," said Brian. "It can only be internal; you've got a mole and you'd better find it quick."

Colin pushed his own chair away from the table and stood, he certainly didn't want to be left in the cold room on his own. They were ready to leave, the meeting over. He didn't feel any better than when he'd first walked in. It had been a complete waste of time.

FORTY-THREE

With the new information George had supplied Will about where Jonesy had been dossing down, and indeed where other people regularly slept, it was worth investigating and taking a look. Before he left the centre, he went in search of two torches and handed one to George. It was only a short walk for the two men, Bridge Street was in the middle of town, and on a clear night with plenty of street lights it was an easy journey there. Will and George chatted about life on the street in general conversation and soon enough they could see the entrance straight ahead. It had been boarded up at one stage, but the signs of tampering were obvious.

"I'll show you how to get in," said George and made adjustments to a couple of the planks so the two could enter easily. Once on the other side, he put the planks back in place and Will marvelled at how easy it had been. The first thing that hit him was the smell, like a damp cellar. The second thing was the cool air. He'd expected it to be warmer than it was, though didn't know why, but like George had said earlier, being inside at least they were away from the elements and away from those that wish to pee on people for the fun of it. Will let his eyes adjust to the semi darkness and the two set off further into the tunnel. They hadn't gone far when they could see the dim lights and makeshift homes of those that lived there. *For Will, it brought back memories that he didn't want to revisit.*

"Which one's Jonesy's place?"

"Here," said George, pointing to a corner that looked like any other homeless area, with the usual paraphernalia all present: shopping trolley, tarpaulin, cardboard, sleeping bag and a few clothes. Those that lived on the streets didn't own much and certainly nothing of any value, and what little cash they had, they kept hidden on themselves. There was nobody there. Will bent down to look through the lad's belongings, trying not to disturb them. There was very little to see. A voice called out to him, "What you doin'?"

Will didn't recognise it, but George did.

"It's okay," George called. "It's Will from the Refresh Centre."

"What you doin'?" the voice asked again.

Will stood up from his cramped position, walked over to the voice and asked, "Do you remember when Jonesy disappeared? We're just trying to help figure out what happened to him that day. Do you know anything about it?"

"Are you a pig?"

George stepped in. "I just told you, Hoppy, it's Will from Refresh."

"So," Will tried again. "Do you know anything about his disappearance?"

"He's back."

"I know he's back, which is great news, but do you know anything about when he went missing, were you there, did you see anything when he got attacked?"

"He was attacked, was he?"

Will was beginning to feel exasperation build up in his chest. He was getting nowhere with this particular person, who was likely high on something, alcoholic or chemical, perhaps another on Ketamine. Will tried one more time.

"Look, I used to live on the streets too some years ago," he said, hoping it would give him some empathy. "It can be hard, I know, but I also know that you see things, hear things. Two people have been killed now and we're trying to help find out what happened. We're not the police and we mean no harm to you, but since Jonesy is the only one that's come back safely, we need to find out as much as we can, stop anyone else getting hurt. Do you understand?"

There was a silence that lasted for several beats, but Will could see in the half-light that something registered with the man and he was thinking. He didn't want to be the one to speak first or walk away in case he missed something vital and so he waited.

Finally, the man said, "I've seen people, in another tunnel."

"Go on," encouraged Will. "Which tunnel?"

"Under the church in the town centre," said the man. "All Saints. I go in there occasionally for a cuppa. I know there's tunnels underneath and I went down once but got caught. Thought it was interesting, but they kicked me out."

"What did you see down there?"

"Two men was all I saw, don't know what they were doing."

"Maybe they were just looking like you were," said George.

"No, they weren't looking, not like I was." He sounded sure of himself.

"Can you describe the two men?" Will asked.

"Nah, just two men. Didn't really see much, but soon as they saw me, they made their excuses and left. Like they weren't supposed to be there either."

"When was this?" asked Will.

"Couple of weeks ago. I've not been back since."

"Would you recognise them again, have you seen them since, perhaps the night that Jonesy got attacked?"

"Doubt it, and no, not seen them."

"Well, if you think of anything, tell George here or Jonesy, they know how to reach me at the Refresh Centre, okay? Or you can call at the centre yourself. If I'm not there, ask for Hazel."

"Okay," said the man, but he'd lost interest. Will felt in his pocket for a couple of £2 coins and handed them over.

"Get yourself a hot drink or something to eat," he said, "and thanks for letting us know what you've seen. There's more if you can tell me anything else."

Will watched as the man pocketed the money and hoped it went on food. As they ventured further along, Will finally placed the odour he'd detected on Bowie's body.

FORTY-FOUR

Will and George spent a few minutes chatting to the remaining inhabitants, but nobody had seen or heard anything of relevance. It seemed there was nothing to add to the man's story. Will was intrigued about the tunnels that ran under All Saints' Church and part of him couldn't wait to get back home so he could research online and find out more, particularly since he thought he'd matched the odour he'd picked up on Bowie. He wasn't aware of such tunnels underneath the town and what George had shown him at the bottom of Bridge Street had opened his eyes somewhat.

"Do you fancy a detour?" Will asked as they left the Bridge Street entrance, heading back towards the centre.

"I wondered when you would ask," said George with a slight smile. Even in the half-light George's teeth were quite brilliant white, unusual for somebody that lived as he did. Will guessed he cared about his own dental hygiene, either that or he was naturally blessed with excellent teeth. Will was conscious of the time; it was coming up to 9 pm and he'd told Louise he wouldn't be late back. He needed his own sleep; he'd missed enough this week and it was beginning to catch up with him. But this was important, and with a new piece of information he needed to find out more, see if it was connected somehow. It could of course, like the blue pen he'd found, be just a random coincidence, people in the tunnel quite legitimately.

All Saints' Church stood proudly in front of them, and Will wondered if the door would even be unlocked at this hour, so many now closed at night because of thieves. While he wasn't an atheist, he couldn't think of the last time he'd been inside a church. The two men entered and Will glanced around at the handful of heads bowed, deep in their own prayer or thoughts and in silence.

"How can we find the entrance to the tunnel?" George whispered.

"I have no clue. Maybe there'll be somebody out back that we can ask?"

"Do you think they will tell you, let you go down there?"

"I don't know, but we've got to try." Just at that moment a man dressed in black entered through the side door. Will was momentarily frozen to the spot and wondered what to do next. It was obvious since they were right up front, and with George's dishevelled state, what the man would be thinking. Thieves.

Will walked forward, hand outstretched to introduce himself. "Hello father, it's not what you think," he said quickly. "I am Will Peters from the Refresh Centre and this is my friend George."

"What can I do for you?" he asked. While there was a smile on his face, there was concern in his eyes.

"We have just come from the tunnel at the bottom of Bridge Street, and I'm intrigued to know more about the ones that run underneath this church. Is there anything you can tell me about them, perhaps where the entrance is?" Will asked.

"There are tunnels, yes. What is it you would like to know of them?" He avoided the entrance question – was that deliberate?

"I'd like to know where they go, but what I'd really like is to have a look if I may."

"What's your business?"

Will took a moment to think about how he would answer, how much he would tell the father; he didn't want to frighten him off.

"I'm investigating what happened to the two bodies found at Hunsbury Hill Park. A friend of George's was abducted recently and he managed to escape, and we think that the tunnels may have some connection to the case."

"So, you're with the police?"

He couldn't lie. "No, not exactly, more a private investigation."

"Ah, in that case, I can't help you tonight," he said. "The tunnels below the church don't go far, and yes, there was a maze of them originally, but most of them have either since collapsed or been boarded up. I can't show them to you, sorry."

Will detected a finality in the man's words and wondered why he was reticent to let him explore further. Had George's acquaintance, Hoppy, in the Bridge Street tunnel, been telling the truth about seeing people down there? Will knew the conversation was over, it was time to leave.

Maybe they could find another entrance elsewhere.

FORTY-FIVE

Will dropped George back at the Bridge Street tunnel then drove himself home, hoping Louise hadn't stayed up waiting for him. By the time he got there it would be close to 10 pm, and she had an early shift the following morning. He felt bad for not texting her earlier to let her know what he was up to, but the excitement of finding the tunnels had meant time had got away from him.

The journey home was a quick one with hardly any traffic on the road, and soon he'd parked outside his house and let himself in the back door. He could see there was a single lamp on in the hall, so he knew everyone was upstairs, tucked in bed and likely fast asleep. He quietly tiptoed through the house, turning the lamp off as he went, then navigated the darkness from experience and feel. Once upstairs, he popped his head round the bedroom door, and with the little light that came in from the outside street lamp, he could see the top of Louise's head. He crept across and bent down to plant a light kiss on her temple. At his touch she started to stir, a tiny whimper escaping her mouth, making Will smile. She never fully woke or said anything, the whimper enough to acknowledge him, so he carried on to the bathroom for a quick shower. Once he was finished, he checked in on the girls, each one fast asleep, transported to their dreams as he again headed for the bedroom. Will gently lifted the duvet and slipped in beside his wife. In a whisper he said, "Goodnight". Not a sound escaped her lips and Will lay on his back gazing up at the ceiling while he dissected everything he'd learned during the evening. There was no way he was going off to his own dreams just yet; he needed to box up all of the new information and put each piece in the right compartment of his mental filing cabinet before sleep had any chance of finding him. Tomorrow, before he picked Birdie up to drive to Leicester, he'd call DI Mason and find out if there were any test results back yet from the pen. At some point in the afternoon, he'd go back to All Saints' Church and have another word with the father, and without George's presence this time and he himself dressed a little smarter. He could understand why the man had looked so alarmed, as if they were about to thieve something. It hadn't been the ideal situation to then ask a favour and hope he would oblige. If he went back dressed a little more appropriately and with a slightly different tale, he might get somewhere. It was worth a try.

Will finally closed his eyes, and let sleep take him to his own dreams just like his girls were in theirs. Tomorrow was another day. He'd take Birdie to Leicester then plan something nice for his family for the weekend coming. Louise had been right, he needed his own rest too, and with his extra shift at the centre and the exhumation at the beginning of the week, it would be nice to spend the day with them doing something silly. He'd figure something out tomorrow.

ON THE OTHER side of town, Colin Hayhurst lay in bed, staring at his own ceiling. The meeting had been pointless really, but that was because he hadn't told the whole truth. Had he mentioned the real reason for the blackmailing, that he was skimming public money for his own gain, he might have got a very different solution than 'ignore them'. With two deaths already, the last thing he wanted was a third on his hands, but he had no clue how to stop it and he couldn't possibly pay the ransom. He thought back to the latest text, 'touch move', and the hideous image. There hadn't been much time between each victim, and he hoped there wasn't a pattern, another body with another message tomorrow.

FORTY-SIX

The killer had been surprised at how easy it was to gain their trust. It was always interesting finding out what had happened in their often young lives, how the rails had come off their past, or not in some cases. Not everybody living on the street was trying to get off it, indeed some just liked the lifestyle, the freedom, no bills and no property to worry about, and some had been homeless for most of their days. As long as they had enough food to keep themselves going, that was fine by them. When it came down to the basic needs in life, as long as you had access to shelter and food there wasn't much else the human body actually needed, the rest superfluous.

The killer wasn't sure quite when it had started to form in their mind, but things quickly made sense. From there it had been relatively easy, though some parts of the plan had been more difficult than others. They'd focused on making new 'friends', and when they'd seen them again on the street, it was easy enough to entice them with the promise of food. They'd been trusting, expecting a friendly chat and not something to be alarmed by. And so the killer would take them to a local café for hot tea and a burger, and then would find some excuse of why they needed to pick up some heavy items from nearby – they wouldn't mind helping out, would they? They could finish their meal in the nice warm car, with the promise of being dropped back to wherever they wanted afterwards.

Like lambs to the slaughter, each of them agreed to lend a hand. It would have been rude not to. Once they found themselves down in the tunnel, the sedative that had been slipped in their tea back at the café was nicely at work and they soon found it hard to keep awake. No matter, there was a bed at the ready. It was all so simple, the body no defence to the powerful drug circulating in their system. That gave the killer all the time they needed to restrain hands and feet, and tie the thick belt around their neck. It would be uncomfortable when they woke, but the position of it stopped them straining hard against it, or else they'd strangle themselves. A gag across the mouth made sure they stayed quiet. The killer went back the following day, taking some food, and hoping by that time the stupid mayor would have succumbed to the demands, then they'd be able to let their captive go. It wasn't easy finishing the act at Hunsbury Hill Park.

Sending the photographs to the mayor had been a risk, but how else were they supposed to send proof that someone was being held prisoner without giving too much away? So far, the man hadn't responded favourably – that part of the plan hadn't worked at all.

The killer knew they needed to up their efforts. No, it wasn't over yet. Not by a long way.

FORTY-SEVEN

WILL HAD AGAIN STRUGGLED WITH POPPY, WHO HAD YET AGAIN
wanted to go to school dressed as a dinosaur. He knew the headmistress wouldn't allow it, otherwise she would have a classroom full of fairies, dinosaurs, Superman and any other character a child chose to be. He'd finally relented by letting her wear a dinosaur-themed T-shirt under her school uniform. It was the best he could do to avoid an early tantrum. Sometimes she could be harder work than all the triplets put together, but he wasn't complaining, he just needed to know how best to handle her on days when he hadn't time to spare. Today was one of those days. Had he not got an early appointment, the dinosaur issue would have been water off a duck's back, but he had things to do, people to see, places to go and thoughts he needed to allow to percolate.

He'd tossed and turned a lot during the night and hoped he hadn't disturbed Louise with his own restlessness, but the discovery of the tunnels and the handful of people that lived there had been exciting to say the least. What was even more so was the discovery that the tunnels ran under the church in the centre of town, and he wondered about the relevance of them to the case, if there was any at all. The fact that Hoppy had seen two men in another tunnel gave him a reason to ponder just how far the tunnels ran for. But was he off on a tangent? There was no actual link between the tunnels and the investigation or the deaths, apart from the strange damp odour he's picked up from Bowie. Had the police made the same connection? In reality the two lads could have been killed anywhere and taken to Hunsbury Hill Park, but the tunnels were the perfect place to hide someone before dumping them later.

Will had woken early to spend time searching online. He'd found an old map of the town, and although it hadn't got all the tunnels listed, it had suggested that there were several that ran across from the centre, at various angles, to the periphery of the town, but that they weren't connected. While many had been sealed off, or later used as the town's drains, many people had already found a way in. Given he and George had successfully entered the tunnel at Bridge Street, had others managed the same at other entrances? If so, how could he find out where they were?

While it was exciting, all he had was a hunch and an odour. He didn't even know if Jonesy's abduction was anything to do with the two bodies found, and the same went for the blue marker pen, though he would follow that up this morning. He could have a big fat nothing and just a whole load of wild ideas that didn't make sense, or he could have a lead. He wondered what the police themselves had got, what they were working with since they had access to forensic evidence, if there was any to be had.

Will thought back to the marks he'd seen on Bowie's neck after he'd flipped the sheet back. He was no pathologist, but he could rule out some causes of death. For instance, the skin around his neck wasn't cut, so it hadn't been wire. It was, however, terribly bruised and those bruises were wide in pattern, rather than narrow, so had to have been made by something wider than a standard belt, say. He could only assume Clyde's neck was the same, since he hadn't seen it. More was the pity. Will needed more to work with if he was ever going to get to the bottom of what had happened.

He closed the back door and locked it as he left for work. All family members were exactly where they should be for the rest of the day and Will set off towards his car. At least Birdie would be good for a laugh this morning. He was looking forward to spending an hour with the older lady. She hadn't asked him to wait in Leicester, having instead planned to travel home by train, so he would pick her up from the station, time to be confirmed.

As he pulled up outside her house, he felt much more positive about things. He hated dwelling on something, hated it taking his mental energy and sapping his time, but he'd found himself involved with the case and while a part of him enjoyed it, a large part of him was incredibly frustrated with what little knowledge he did have. Maybe a journey with Birdie would help put things into perspective.

FORTY-EIGHT

WILL HAD BEEN CORRECT, THE JOURNEY WAS JUST WHAT HE NEEDED, and by the time they hit the outskirts of Leicester, he felt a whole lot more upbeat. Birdie had been ecstatic at the revelation concerning the tunnels. She had heard about them as a youngster but had never actually seen one nor been anywhere near one and, like a lot of locals, assumed it was fable, folklore and they didn't really exist. Some said they were just a batch of interconnecting cellars where people stored things back in the seventeenth century, and others were adamant that the tunnels were linked and headed somewhere. From Will's research the previous night he knew there were underground rooms at the county club as well as quite a maze of chambers under Market Square itself. While in the car, Birdie had spent some time looking up what she could via her phone and came up with a story about St Thomas à Becket. It seemed the man's infamous escape from the Castle was a well-documented part of twelfth-century history, but how the then Archbishop of Canterbury managed to flee from the fortress still remained a mystery. Local myth said that he'd escaped from the clutches of Henry II thanks to a tunnel that linked the Castle to All Saints'

Church on George Row. How true it was, she had no idea; it was only a rumour and a hell of a long time ago. But it definitely seemed that there were several religious houses surrounding the town that might link back to All Saints' Church, and if you were to draw lines between them all, you'd uncover a starlike pattern. If there weren't tunnels underneath the town, there was certainly evidence of vaulted crypts. The church itself used one as a boiler room.

"Anyway," said Birdie excitedly as she put her phone back in her pocket, "it's exciting nonetheless. Who would know that under our old town was such history?"

"Agreed."

"Let me ask you this, Will," she said. "What makes you think tunnels or crypts, or empty old rooms or whatever they are, are linked to the deaths, just the odour you picked up?"

"Yes, unfortunately. I don't have anything else to link them at this stage," he said. "Just a gut feeling, which is nothing I know, and the police would laugh me out of the station."

"That they would," she said. "You need something more concrete don't you, excuse the pun."

"I thought if I could get into another of the tunnels, I could perhaps take a scraping off the wall and the floor. It's easy enough to get a little pot to put the particles in so forensics can compare them to what debris they took from Bowie's clothing. If they found anything, of course; they might not have. Same with Clyde. Plus, with so many tunnels and cellars and the like, they are bound to give varying results and they won't have the budget or resources to test them all. That's where we come in, is what I'm thinking."

"It's a good idea, but a long shot."

"I know. If the rooms and the tunnels are nothing to do with it, fine, but I don't suppose the police have got much more either, from an evidence point of view. Both lads lived on the street, remember, *so most of what's found on their clothing would likely be useless.*

Not like you and me where our clothes have been through the washing machine regularly."

"What about your friend, Jonesy? Wasn't he there last night to speak to you?"

"No, but he often goes walkabouts apparently, so he likely found friends somewhere else and will be hanging out with them."

"I don't suppose your policewoman with the blue hair has been in contact with anything?"

"No, she just thinks I'm a joke, I'm afraid – interfering. I'm going to give her a call later and see if they've got any results back off that blue pen I found, though probably nothing." Will sounded disheartened to his own ears, not the way he wanted to be. Birdie had picked him up when she'd first got in the car, but all the negative talk of the case was beginning to drag him down again. His phone ringing interrupted his thoughts and he debated answering it since he had a passenger. From glancing at the screen, he noted it was Sanjeev.

As if reading his mind, Birdie said, "Don't mind me."

"If you don't mind? Only, he's a regular." Will said, double-checking.

"Go for it," she said again, and Will clicked answer.

"Hi Sanjeev, what can I do for you?" The car filled with background noise, but nobody spoke. Will tried again. "Sanjeev? It's Will here, do you need a lift?"

A slight stutter and then finally the caller spoke. "It's Sanjeev, Will. Can I book a lift, please?"

Will smiled and wondered not for the first time about the man's lack of confidence; he assumed it went with his condition. It must be hard for him to form relationships, Sanjeev no doubt being the brunt of ridicule and hurtful jokes from his peers. It would be a patient individual that would get close to the man, that was if Sanjeev would even let them.

"You can, my friend. What time and where from?"

"The library, please. Two o'clock. Will you be there?"

"Of course, not a problem. See you later."

Sanjeev had already gone, and Will disconnected. Birdie leaned forward from her seat in the rear and said, "I'm guessing he's a handful, am I right?"

Will smiled and caught her eye. "How could you tell?"

"Life, Will. What's his story?"

Will wasn't comfortable talking about his somewhat taxing customer and went with, "Let's just say I'm extra patient with him, that I have to be. I can see the frustration in him some days and it makes me sad, but I can't do anything for him *but* be patient. It is a whole lot harder for him than for me." Will changed the subject back to his quandary at hand, the two murders.

"What do you suggest I do, Birdie? With the murders, I mean."

She adjusted herself back in her seat. "Have you any idea what either of them was strangled with?" she asked, picking up where they had left off.

"No, only that it was something fairly deep, I'd estimate three or four inches or more. It looked like something with more surface area pressure, maybe a sleeve off something or a rolled-up towel, something like that." He did his best to describe it, though he was no forensic expert. "What are you thinking, Birdie?"

"Fortunately, we're on our way to Cynthia's. I wonder if she remembers a couple of the old cons we were inside with. There's bound to be someone that strangled their victim, maybe she can shed some light on it. Worth asking."

It wasn't long until they pulled up outside Cynthia's address in Leicester. It was reasonable area, Will surmised, with the property a regular semi-detached box that looked out over fields at the front. Hers was one in a row of thirty or so, all fairly much the same, though some had different coloured trims or front gardens if they'd chosen to stay with grass rather than block paving. The majority had converted their gardens into parking spaces. Cynthia's front garden was paved and Will parked his car next to what he assumed was Cynthia's own. A net curtain in the living room window twitched slightly as Birdie opened the passenger door and Will helped her out. A moment later, another elderly lady was standing in the doorway with a smile as wide as a coat hanger. She looked trim in black cargo pants and a T-shirt that read 'game on' across her chest. Will had been expecting elasticated waist and a floral blouse, and the woman in front of them couldn't have been any further from it.

With open arms, the woman called out, "Well, if it isn't Birdie Fox!"

Will left the two women to it and wondered about their topics of conversation from times gone by. He would have liked to be a fly on that particular living room wall.

He also bet Cynthia was a dab hand with a fly swatter.

FORTY-NINE

The killer hated this part. Entering the tunnel, they ran through all that had to be taken care of for the plan to work. They'd done it twice before, but it was important that every last detail was executed correctly. There was no way they were going to get caught, doing time in prison was not an option. No, they didn't relish the prospect of sharing a cell with someone twice their size and not fussy about the gender when it came to sex.

There wasn't a sound as they approached the cellar doorway, but as the light from the torch lit up the room, they heard a familiar shuffling as he wakened and tried to orientate himself like others had before him. The killer shone the beam in his face and watched as he winced away from the light, eyes tightly closed and still unable to speak, the gag seeing to that. His neck looked red raw now, he'd obviously been struggling against its tension. It wouldn't be long now before he'd have to struggle no more, his end in sight. The killer perched on the end of the dingy bed, breakfast in a paper bag.

"I hope you slept okay. I brought you something to eat; I assume you're hungry?" There was little point in waiting for a reply.

"Right, here's the plan: just like we did yesterday, I'll take your neck restraint off and put the shock collar on, then take your gag off." At the sound of the collar, his eyes widened in terror. "It only hurts if you do something stupid. Now you're not going to do anything stupid today, are you?" Jonesy struggled to move his head from side to side, even the slightest movement causing him to wince. "And then you can have your breakfast." The killer took the neck restraint off then fitted the electronic dog collar before removing his gag, not wanting to chance him yelling out. One squeeze of the remote-control button and 6,000 volts would shoot into his neck. While the zap didn't feel much more than a sharp jolt from an electric fence, it hurt like hell on the tender flesh around the neck, particularly when the button was held down for any length of time. The threat had the desired effect, had made him think twice about yelling or running. Not that his bound ankles would take him very far. Once the collar was in place, the killer took the gag off and watched as Jonesy tried to moisten his mouth with his tongue. They then removed his hand restraints so he could sit upright. The killer handed over a bottle of water and watched as Jonesy drank greedily. It had been some time – yesterday, in fact – since he'd last been fed and watered.

Jonesy's eyes searched the killer's, likely wondering what he'd done to upset them enough to be doing what they were doing. He doubted he was a random find, the wrong person in the right place, not on this occasion at least. He'd got lucky on their first attempt, he suspected he wouldn't be so this. How long had he been down there? Maybe three days, maybe four? That's how many breakfasts he'd eaten. He assumed he'd been drugged – probably a blessing, being asleep and unaware of the cold, damp surroundings he was captive in.

"Anyway," the killer said, "we're going for a drive today," as if they were going to the funfair, perhaps for candyfloss and a hotdog.

"So, when you've finished your breakfast, I've brought a change of clothes for you."

At the mention of a drive, Jonesy stopped chewing. He knew a drive didn't mean fun and excitement, but at least he'd be out of the bone-chilling space that he'd been in for far too long. He gave an involuntary shiver. Perhaps it was the temperature getting to him and not the notion that something was changing, that he might be nearing the end of his ordeal. He knew that leaving the cellar didn't necessarily mean freedom and he tried not to think about it. He attempted to talk, but with his throat constricted, it came out a croak before the word finally came free.

"Why?"

"Why are we going out? Simple, it's time to move, time for the next part. As I said, I've brought you clean clothes, and we'll be going upstairs, out the back door, where the car is waiting." He watched as clothes from a holdall were laid on the bed. In the torch-light, he could see there was a black suit and a white shirt and what appeared to be some sort of cravat along with a long-haired wig. Even in the dim light it was obviously not a nylon one from a joke shop, but more likely a natural one. It shone in the glow from the beam.

"I guess you're wondering, 'why the get up?' Well, we're going to pose as funeral directors and I thought the wig was a nice touch. You'll look smart in those," the killer said, pointing to the collection of clothes. "So, as soon as you've finished, you'll get changed and we'll go. From there it really depends on your willingness to cooperate, because you'll be keeping the collar on – the cravat will come in handy to cover it and your bruises up. I don't need to remind you quite what it feels like when I hold the shock button down?"

Jonesy struggled to move his head, 'no', his neck sore and stiff from being shackled and him being constantly sedated. He finished his food as quickly as his throat would allow, grateful for the greasy burger and water. A packet of baby wipes was handed to him. "To wipe your face and your hands with. I'm sure you'll feel like freshening up."

"I need… toilet," he struggled.

"You'll have to wait, I'm afraid. Maybe when we get upstairs there'll be an opportunity. I suppose your nappy is full, is it?"

Jonesy nodded slowly. Getting it off would be a blessing. Lying in his own urine was not pleasant and it hadn't been changed since yesterday. Or had it?

"Now, I'll hold the torch, you take your clothes off and slip into these, and when we're upstairs, we'll see about that toilet visit properly." He did as he was told, though it wasn't easy, his hands and fingers fumbling awkwardly, and with the drugs still floating around in his bloodstream, it was almost impossible to even focus on the task, never mind complete it. To speed things up, the killer gave him a hand remove his filthy T-shirt, the message penned on his bare chest a stark reminder of his place in the cruel game. When he was finally fully dressed, the wig was arranged neatly over his own dirty hair.

"Well, if I say so myself, you look smart. You should grow your hair out a little, the length suits you."

Jonesy watched as his belongings and the linen from the mattress were placed into the holdall before the killer glanced around the room, as if checking it. It was obvious now he wasn't coming back. With only the few food wrappers left behind, they were ready to leave.

"No point taking rubbish with us, my fingers haven't touched it and anyone that finds it will blame kids anyway. Now, you go ahead of me, and just remember what's around your neck, I've got control of you each and every step you take."

FIFTY

With a plan to stick to, there was no time to waste, and the pair were soon sitting in the black Mercedes and heading out of town. The killer hadn't wanted to risk taking him to Hunsbury Hill like they had the others. The time between removing the victims from the cellar and taking them to their final destination in the country park had always been an issue, an unnecessary risk, but there was no way they could have left either of them underground. Jonesy was the third victim, which meant the police might be closing in, and since the mayor could well have reported the text messages at any stage, they couldn't take the risk of a repeat destination. As soon as the killer had taken the photograph of their latest victim, moving him had been the sensible thing to do. It wasn't worth heading out to Hunsbury Hill and finding out the police were already waiting for a third body, so another plan had been concocted. In hindsight, which was a wonderful thing, they should never have used the country park to dispose of both bodies in the first place. Today's chosen venue, however, would be perfect for what they needed.

The plan was a clever one. Who would suspect a funeral

director of being up to no good? Two smartly dressed people in a shiny black car wouldn't have looked out of place driving through the town centre, though the killer knew it might do at their final destination. The shock collar had come in extremely handy, keeping him under control without much effort on their part. The killer had taken no chances, though, and as soon as they'd got in the car, had restrained Jonesy's hands behind his back with cable ties, just in case.

"I suggest you slide down your seat a little, until we get through the traffic. I'll let you know when you can sit back up," they instructed. "I can't have the CCTV cameras picking you up, not that you even look like the young man they *might* be looking for. That's the beauty of all this, you know, that's why I picked your type – disposable almost. In fact, I picked you twice." Jonesy turned at the mention of twice. He had been correct in his assumption. "Yes, that was me too, and another street person, hired for a tenner. But the planets didn't align that night, a miscalculation we'll call it, and since I couldn't trust that you hadn't blabbed to the police, here we are again. It was an added bonus you hadn't noticed me from the first time, made things a lot easier."

Jonesy stared. The blue ink he'd discovered on his chest in the shower, the start of a word perhaps, explained a lot. It didn't matter now; it was all far too late as they made their way out of town.

Ransome Road was a dead end, – a fishing lake with plenty of trees and shrubs to hide away from prying eyes. It would be perfect. The killer again ran through the plan, the process to go through so they weren't disturbed and didn't hurt him too much. There had been enough pain of recent to last a lifetime, and they didn't want to inflict any more than was necessary, it wasn't the young man's fault.

Parking the car just off the road, the killer turned towards Jonesy. Terror filled his eyes. He must've known he was close to the end.

"Relax. We've a short walk ahead of us, and I've got a picnic basket in the boot, I'm sure you must still be hungry." Confusion added to fear, he had no clue what the killer intended. "Come on, I'll help you out." With his hands still fastened behind his back and legs wobbly from previous sedatives, he managed to swing his legs out and stand up. "It's not far, I thought you'd appreciate some privacy, and there's plenty of shrubs and bushes by the water." The killer grabbed the picnic basket from the boot and they walked slowly together. Once satisfied with their position, the killer spread a chequer blanket out on the grass and placed the basket on top of it.

"Sit down."

Jonesy remained standing for a moment, ignoring their request.

"Sit, I said. Unless you want me to persuade you via the collar?"

He struggled not to topple over, his legs weakened after being bound uncomfortably. The plastic cuffs were snipped away and he rubbed at his wrists.

"Why are you doing this?" he asked, his voice barely audible. "What have I done to deserve this?"

"You've done nothing. You're just the unfortunate person I happened to come across."

As if that explained his ordeal in its entirety.

They passed him an egg sandwich which he glanced at. "Take it, I know you're still hungry."

The killer watched as he ate then passed Jonesy the rest of the box before pouring out two mugs of coffee. It really was a peaceful spot, but there could well have been anglers fishing, hidden in the longer grass. They pulled a set of binoculars from the basket and scanned the area. It seemed they were alone. Perfect.

Jonesy finished the sandwiches as directed. It wouldn't be long now before he felt the effects of what they contained, and the killer waited patiently for the final sedative to get to work, enjoying the view in the distance at the same time. Jonesy struggled to stay awake but he was no match for the drug. Finally, he slumped to one side, his head thumping the ground awkwardly. The killer scanned the area again before completing the next part of the plan. Being out in the open during daylight now meant a change to the final assault. Smothering him could draw attention from someone unseen before.

The killer worked quickly, retrieving the small syringe from an inside jacket pocket and, on hands and knees, lifted Jonesy's hair to expose the back of his neck before slipping the needle into the skin. As the poison made its way into his system, the strong sedative meant he wouldn't feel a thing, his heart finally giving out as the fine balance of sodium and potassium ions was disrupted. His heart would race, then still.

The whole process took less than ten minutes and was peaceful. Without the sedative, though, it would have been sheer torture as fire raced to his heart and he thrashed and screamed in an attempt to put it out.

There was no need to do that to him.

It was time to leave, and quickly. This one had certainly been riskier; it was daylight for one and a new location for another, definitely not the place to smother someone. The killer worked rapidly to gather everything together before removing Jonesy's wig. Satisfied that nothing had been left behind, they rolled him off the blanket and left him exactly where he lay. In a perfect world, they'd have swapped his clothes back for his own, but it was far too risky to do so now, and the new ones had come from a charity shop anyway.

As the killer drove away, they wondered how long it would be before someone found the body.

FIFTY-ONE

Birdie followed her old friend inside as Cynthia turned back in the small front porch and said, "I have to say, Birdie, you look absolutely stunning, you've aged really well!"

Birdie gave a light chuckle and replied with, "I'll take that as a compliment, Cynthia, and I have to say you do too. I remember you when you first entered the cells, all mousey and drippy looking, but hell, look at you now," she said, standing back a little. "You have blossomed. And your confidence I can see a mile away. Prison, or something, has done you good."

"I know. I went inside a withered wallflower that wouldn't say boo to a goose and came out a prickly rose. Then I had to spend my time working on being a little less of a prickly rose, but I think I've turned out fine, don't you?"

"I'd say so." She followed her friend through to the kitchen at the back. The room was bright and airy with sunflower-yellow on one wall. With the sun shining in through a large window at the back, it was a very pleasant and inviting room indeed. "Well, you look like you've done okay for yourself," said Birdie, admiring her surroundings. "What a lovely view of your garden." Birdie made her way over to the huge window and looked out upon flowers down one side of the garden path and a vegetable patch in full production on the other. A tabby cat lay on the manicured grass washing behind its ears in the sunshine. It all looked very peaceful and rather tranquil. "Did you remarry?" Birdie asked, remembering an earlier conversation with Will.

"No, I never found anybody I wanted to spend the rest of my life with," Cynthia said. "But that's okay, I'm happy enough with my own company now, and the neighbours along here are all very good, quite sociable actually. I play cards once a week with the man next door and a couple of us get together to play dominoes. It's all very civilised." She turned to face her friend full on. "How about you, Birdie, is there a man in your life, or a woman?" she said, adding a wink.

"Neither," said Birdie. "I came to the conclusion that I don't need anybody. I'm happy in my own skin, and like you, I've got friends to keep me busy, so no. Had a fling or two. All males," she added.

Cynthia busied herself putting the kettle on to boil and dropped teabags into a pot. A variety pack of biscuits sat on the kitchen counter nearby. She put everything on a tray, poured the water when it had boiled and then carried everything through to the conservatory. It was another bright and sunny room, and the two women made themselves comfortable while they waited for the tea to brew.

"I'm guessing you're fully retired now, Birdie, or have you got a part-time job somewhere?"

"No, fully retired. In fact, I don't know how I'd find time to work now, there's always something to keep me amused and occupied. I'm not into gardening like you," she said. "Some days I wonder quite what I have done, but I'm not sitting around doing nothing that's for sure. I'm always out and about." Birdie reached for a biscuit and asked, "And you? You're a bit younger than me, are you still working?"

"Ah, I do a bit," she said. "In fact, I've got a small business now. I retrained."

"Oh?" said Birdie, leaning forward with interest. "I'm intrigued, go on."

"Well, when I came out of prison, I tried several things and I never really got on with anything and then I saw an advertisement for a night school class about computer programming and I thought I'd have a go. And do you know what? I absolutely love it," she said. "Now I write computer programs – mainly for small businesses that need something in particular, but I have written a couple of games of my own as well. Maybe I'll market them one day, I don't know."

Cynthia paused while she poured the tea and handed Birdie a full china mug.

"So, what sort of things do you make?"

"Well, as an example, I've just finished some work for a private investigating firm actually," she said. "It takes a lot of hours gathering relevant information and what have you for a case when someone's gone missing, and the police don't spend any time doing much at all if it's an adult. But people lose spouses and family members all the time, it appears. They just take off for whatever reason, and unless there's foul play… But anyway, I digress. I came up with a piece of software that scrapes various websites and collates everything together and saves hours of time. I've sold it to a couple of different PI agencies now. It's quite lucrative. Plus, like I mentioned, a couple of games," she said, pulling at the front of her T-shirt.

Birdie sat riveted in her chair as she bit into another biscuit. Her friend was clearly very clever.

"I must say I'm impressed," said Birdie.

Cynthia sat back and looked across at Birdie in amusement. "Look at us two now. Two old jailbirds back together, sipping tea and munching biscuits in my house. It's good to see you. You haven't changed one bit, Birdie Fox," she said.

"You've changed dramatically," said Birdie. "It's good that something positive came out of a miserable situation, don't you think?"

"Indeed. I should have knocked him off years before!" Cynthia said, throwing her head back laughing. Though Birdie laughed alongside her old friend, her mind was whirring.

When their laughter had died down a little, Birdie asked, "So, excuse my lack of knowledge on the subject, but as a programmer, does that mean you can hack into others' software as well?" She kept her face a friendly smile, as if she'd asked about the weather for the upcoming weekend. Cynthia saw straight through it.

"I was about to say I knew there was a reason you got in touch, but there is no way you'd know about my computer skills, so I won't. Tell me what you're thinking, and I'll tell you if I can do it. And I didn't say 'will do it'."

Birdie understood, and the two women locked eyes for a moment. The change of atmosphere in the room was palpable. It had gone from old-friend friendly to a covert business enquiry that wasn't exactly legal.

"Here's what I'm wondering," started Birdie.

FIFTY-TWO

BIRDIE HAD GIVEN CYNTHIA SOMETHING TO THINK ABOUT, AND from the way she'd taken in the request, Birdie knew the woman would be intrigued enough to carry it through. It wasn't legal at all, but Birdie figured her friend had the chance to either turn it down or see it through and see what happened. She also knew the secret would be safe with her, birds of a feather and all that. Without Cynthia's new-found skill, Birdie would have no way to complete the task, and it gave her a bit of a buzz to be thinking along the clandestine route again. She'd learned a lot during her time inside but hadn't put any of those learnings into practice, choosing to stay clear of crime, never wishing to go back to the slammer, and she still didn't want to. But now, in her late 'seventies, perhaps she could risk it in order to do some good. Tomorrow she could be dead. If there was some way of helping Will, she'd do it. It would be fun, though they just had to make sure they didn't get caught, and if Cynthia's skills were up to scratch, they'd be in the clear. After tea and biscuits and catching up on the more mundane areas of their lives, Cynthia had eventually dropped Birdie at Leicester Station for the journey home. She'd assumed it would be a straight run through and hadn't bothered to check the journey, but it seemed it was going to take a while longer than planned. There were two stops, one at Nuneaton and one at Rugby, and she had to change at both places. It didn't really matter, she didn't have too much to rush home for, but she did need to notify Will to pick her up at the other end. Since she had raced to get her ticket and get onto the relevant platform in time, she hadn't phoned him on the first part of the journey, and it was only after another change at Rugby that she finally picked up the phone and called him. She hoped he wasn't too busy.

WILL WAS SITTING stationary on the A45. A lorry had jackknifed some way ahead of him and one lane of the carriageway was completely closed off. Traffic was making its way through the only open lane at a snail's pace. He had been sitting there for an hour already, on his way back into town after another drop-off and was concerned about again being late to pick up Sanjeev. It would likely be the end of his contract if he missed him for a second time. Will looked at the clock for the umpteenth time and took a deep breath; he only had half an hour then he was officially late. Figuring that to ring Sanjeev directly would only send the lad into a flap unnecessarily, he decided to wait and see what happened traffic-wise. If he got back into the town centre bang on time there would be no issue and Sanjeev would be saved from getting distressed and worked up, but Will felt bad because leaving it to the last minute could also be detrimental to his mental state. It was a tough choice to make, though he finally settled on waiting and hoping they moved forward sometime soon.

When Birdie called and said she was on the train and heading in, he inwardly groaned, wondering how he could do both pickups at the same time. All he needed now was for Stanley to call, as he said he would, and add to the confusion. Heavy rain pelted his windscreen as he waited, and he turned the radio on to listen for any available updates. At least the chatter from the radio hosts would help ease the tension that was building rapidly in his head. No sooner had he flicked the radio on than his phone rang, and looking at the caller ID, he could see it was Stanley.

"Oh for heaven's sake!" he said in an exasperated voice before wondering whether to answer. Should he let it ring out? After all, he knew exactly what the man was going to say. He clicked to answer and forcibly changed his face to a smile.

"Hello Stanley," said Will as chirpily as he could muster.

"Where are you?" asked Stanley accusingly.

"What do you mean, where am I?"

"I organised a pickup and you're not here, and it's pissing down." Will knew that the man had not actually organised any time at all, that they had left it that Stanley would call to book sometime today.

"You said you would call me, Stanley, but to answer your question, I'm stuck on the A45 in the accident."

"You've had an accident?"

"No," said Will, "a lorry up ahead has had an accident, I'm stuck in the tailback. Where are you?"

"I said I was getting an apple pie and needed a lift home." Will refrained from rolling his eyes even though Stanley couldn't see him. There was no pleasing some, but Stanley did get confused, and often. The man's slippered feet came to mind.

"I can't get there right now, Stanley, I'm headed to the library once I get out of this traffic, to pick another customer up, then I have to swing by the station and pick another one up. I'm running terribly behind."

"But I need you," said Stanley. He sounded like a petulant seven-year-old.

"I can only advise you to get a lift elsewhere if you can," said Will. He hated turning business down, particularly regular customers, but he couldn't be in three places at once. It was bad enough as it was that he was now going to have Sanjeev and Birdie in the car at the same time.

Stanley either wasn't listening or was ignoring Will. "It's raining and there are no sodding taxis," said Stanley sternly. At that moment Will's lane started to move on – slowly, but at least he was moving again. He could see blue flashing lights up ahead now, likely from fire engines or whatever emergency services were needed for a jack-knifed lorry. There would be police up ahead no doubt. Will was conscious that Stanley was still waiting for him to appear as if by magic right there and then. He had another idea to try and appease the man. "Stanley, why don't you go back inside to the café and get a pot of tea, and as soon as I'm free, I'll come and get you, okay? But it won't be for a little while."

"I guess I haven't got a choice, have I?" said Stanley, clearly unimpressed.

"Well, you have actually. You could try and get another taxi home if you're in a rush. I just can't do everything all at once."

"You're my driver, Will, I'll wait."

"I'll be there as soon as I can, I can't say any more, okay?" The line went dead, but at least Will was moving now, and as he passed the scene of the accident, he tried not to rubberneck, as it was always tempting to do. There could well have been a fatality, and he didn't want to be disrespectful. As the traffic ahead of him increased its speed, the accident now behind them, the clock informed Will there was no need to ring Sanjeev and all that entailed, but he did have to figure out how he could persuade him that Birdie should share a ride. Maybe if he put Sanjeev up front next to him, so away from coming into physical contact with her, that might work. He didn't want to let the lad down again, but nor his friend Birdie. Not Stanley either for that matter.

With five minutes to spare, he waited for Sanjeev to appear, knowing full well he'd be bang on time. There was no need to make sure the door was secured behind him or that light switches were in the upright position. Sanjeev moved from other people's property a little freer than he did his own. When Will saw him heading towards his car, he opened the front passenger side for him. A look of confusion shrouded his face.

"I sit in the back," said Sanjeev when he was close enough to have a conversation.

"I know, but we have to make a detour today, if it's okay with you? I've been sitting in traffic on the motorway, an accident, and it's put me behind a little. I was really anxious to get here on time for you, which I've managed, but it does mean a double up."

"I'm not sure," said Sanjeev, hovering by the front door.

Will willed him to get in. "You'll like the other person, she's lovely, her name is Birdie, so why don't you get in and we'll go over to the station and pick her up? Then I can drop you straight home."

"I'm not sure," said Sanjeev, repeating himself like a broken record. Will was tempted to push him into the passenger seat and drive off but that would never do. "Please, Sanjeev, take a seat and we'll be there shortly. You don't have to touch anything, though you know my car is nice and clean, you've been in it many times before, and you don't have to sit next to anybody. I'll make sure Birdie sits behind my chair so she's away from you." Will stared into the deep brown eyes of the young man and hoped there wasn't going to be scene on the street. Poppy and her dinosaur outfit jumped before his eyes, as did the tantrum that followed. He couldn't cope with more raised voices and tantrums, not today. Reluctantly, Sanjeev climbed into the passenger seat and Will let out a long sigh of relief then closed the door before getting in himself. He figured he needed to keep the lad's mind off what was happening and any stress it might be causing internally, and so immediately started a conversation about his day. It seemed to work.

FIFTY-THREE

As Will rounded the corner to the train station, he could see Birdie waiting patiently outside the huge glass building. The overhang was doing a decent job of keeping most of the rain off her head and shoulders, and she waved lightly when she spotted him. He pulled up and she dashed across to the half-open door and slipped inside.

"The heavens just picked their right moment to open!" she said, catching her breath and rearranging herself on the seat. "Oh, we have a visitor, Will. Who is this?"

"This is Sanjeev, Birdie, a friend of mine and part of my calendar crisis this afternoon." Sanjeev looked over his shoulder at her before nodding to her quietly. Will wondered if she'd offer to shake hands and hoped she wouldn't.

"It's nice to meet you, Sanjeev," she said, beaming, keeping her hands to herself. "And what glorious long black hair you have, so shiny. Women would kill for that, let me tell you!" she added, then finished with a small chuckle at her own joke. Sanjeev turned back to the front and stayed focused forward as Will pulled into traffic that seemed to have doubled in size since the rain had started. He refrained from glancing back and smiling at Birdie and her killer comment.

It was only a short drive over to Greenwood Road and Sanjeev's home address, and Will amused himself listening to Birdie chatter on like a canary about the more mundane aspects of her day. It seemed to have gone well at her friend's place. His phone rang, and Will glanced at it. Stanley, again. He'd let it ring out, not wanting to talk to the cantankerous old man with two passengers on board.

"Don't mind us, answer it if you want to," said Birdie. "You don't mind, do you, Sanjeev?" she asked.

The lad shook his head, and Will could see the tension building at being in such close proximity with a stranger, Will present or not. Stanley, on the other end of the phone was not letting Will off the hook and the phone rang a few more times before Will finally hit the green. Any longer and it would have been embarrassing. He heard Birdie mumble in the back seat, "Thank goodness for that." Before Will could even say hello, Stanley filled the car with his now booming voice. Sanjeev visibly jumped a little in his seat.

"Where are you, Will?! I'm getting wet!" There was no mistaking his raised voice, the man was clearly unhappy at the delay. This was exasperating now, and Will wanted to tell the grumpy old sod he was being unreasonable, but held his tongue.

"I did tell you I would be a little late due to the accident, Stanley," he said calmly. "I also have two customers in my car, so please be careful what you say."

"I couldn't give a rat's arse who's in your car, young man. How long are you going to be?"

Birdie leaned forward, and not liking the way Stanley had spoken to her friend, bellowed back at him over Will's shoulder, not exactly sure where the microphone was to speak into. "I'd advise you you'd do better to show some manners if you're looking for a lift any time soon," she shouted towards the sun visor's direction. Sanjeev cowered down in his seat a little, and Will, taken by surprise at the shrieking from Birdie behind him, did the same. It wasn't conducive to driving in wet weather.

"Who the hell are you?" Stanley screamed back. Will was about to interrupt but Birdie beat him to it.

"I'm Birdie Fox, a friend and customer of Will's, and if you don't want to go the same way my late husband did, I suggest you pipe down and be civil." The airwaves stayed silent for a second, though Stanley still had the line open. Birdie again stepped into the gap: "Now, if you'll stop shouting for a damn millisecond, we'll swing by and pick you up. At least you'll be out of the rain. Does that suit?" Will could only wonder how this was all going to work and could only think of the possible fireworks to follow. All he needed now was for Sanjeev to start stressing big time and try to get out of a moving vehicle. He chanced a glance over to him and was relieved he appeared calm – on the outside at any rate. Birdie was waiting for an answer from Stanley. Quietly, Will spoke to the lad.

"Is that okay with you, if we pick Stanley up too?"

He nodded ever so slightly, and Will took it as a 'yes'. Stanley finally spoke, in a near to normal voice. He'd calmed himself down.

"Right, yes. Okay."

At that, Birdie sat back in her seat and puffed her cheeks out slowly.

"I'm looking forward to meeting him. He reminds me of that old git off the telly, Meldrew. He was full of bluster too. Does he always talk to you like that?"

"Occasionally, yes."

Will pointed the car in the direction of Sainsbury's. It wasn't far as the crow flies, but the back roads were chocka and he hoped they'd get there before the man made another call.

Finally, they pulled up outside and a dishevelled Stanley ambled over. Will got out into the rain to help him with his carrier bag. It wasn't the day to wear slippers, and Stanley's feet were soaked. A moment later, he was being helped into the rear seat, next to Birdie, and he eyed her suspiciously.

"You must be the mouthpiece," he said by way of introduction. Will closed the door after him and hurried round to his own seat.

"And you must be the ungrateful one. We didn't have to pick you up, you know, so do try and be pleasant while in our company."

Will smiled to himself at the pair on the back seat – Birdie's red lips pursed tight, Stanley trying not to care.

"Right! Drop off for Sanjeev coming right up!" Will said theatrically, trying to shift the mood between the three and stop another world war. He once again pointed the car in their original direction. Since there were no more seats available, they couldn't possibly pick anyone else up, and that suited him.

To his surprise, he heard Birdie ask Stanley, "Do you know anything about the tunnels under Market Square, the ones that go out and under the church?" Will watched with interest in his rear-view mirror. Stanley gave a chuckle, and with a smile on his lips, waited a beat before answering.

"I spent my teenage years smoking and drinking in the tunnels under Market Square. Best hiding place ever."

FIFTY-FOUR

Will finally pulled into Greenwood Road to let Sanjeev out at his house. He couldn't ever remember a journey being so fraught with so few in a car and hoped that one day he'd look back on it and have a good giggle. Right now, he was glad to deliver Sanjeev to the safety of his own home in one calm piece. He walked the few paces with the young man for his own peace of mind, to make sure that he was in fact okay.

"I'm sorry about that, Sanjeev," he said. "There was little I could do as events turned out."

Dark brown eyes locked on to his own and for the first time in a long time Sanjeev gave the beginnings of a smile.

"It's okay, Will," he said. "Some days it might not have been, but today is a good day and I'm fine, thank you for asking."

Will felt something pull at a heartstring and wondered about the lad's solitude and whether he ever got lonely. Maybe he should make more effort himself to engage in conversation or perhaps be a bit more sociable with him. He made a mental note to put more effort in.

"Well, I'm glad you're home safely. I'll see you next week as usual?"

"11 am, Monday morning," said Sanjeev. "11 am, Monday morning."

"I'll see you then. Have a good weekend." Will wanted to pat the lad gently on the shoulder, but knew he hated being touched and so refrained. It always felt as if something was missing when they parted or greeted – never a handshake, never a fist bump, never anything but words. But so be it, there was little he could do for the lad and Will would have to be content that once a week he got to take him to his therapy session. Sanjeev slipped the key in the door and went inside, leaving Will on the doorstep for a moment on his own. "See you on Monday," he said quietly to himself before turning back to his car and the two waiting elderly folks that were sitting in the back seats awaiting their trips home.

Things had quietened down considerably, and Birdie and Stanley were now chatting like old buddies. Considering the way they had first met one another a few short minutes ago, they'd simmered down pretty quickly. He'd had it all on to concentrate on his journey to Sanjeev's place and try to listen to the conversation going on in the back at the same time and so had missed a good deal of what had been said.

He slid back in behind the wheel and turned to catch the eye of Stanley, who was sitting directly behind the passenger seat. "Well, I suggest we take Stanley home first because he's soaking wet. Is that okay with you, Birdie?" he asked, straining his neck to face her.

"Change of plan," she said matter-of-factly. Will looked to Stanley, who confirmed it with a slight nod.

"Oh? What's the plan now?"

"Stanley's just been talking about the tunnels, and I think while we've still got him in the car, he could show us where the entrance is that he knows about, and if we call into a pharmacy on the way through, we can get some specimen pots and a nail file. Perhaps we can go down into the tunnel and take those samples that you wanted and then later on you can go and get a sample of the Bridge Street one. You know how to get in there, that's easy."

Will looked doubtful, purely because he didn't want Stanley to catch cold. "This is what I suggest," he said. "Stanley is considerably wetter than either of us and I'm sure you won't mind me saying it, Stanley, but you're old. Let's run back to your place so you can get changed, and if you still intend on coming and fancy bit of excitement for the afternoon, then you can show us where the entrances are that you know about. Deal?"

"You're on," said Stanley, sounding like a kid that was going to the circus for the afternoon. "I've not had such an exciting afternoon in a long time," he said. That, Will could believe.

"That's settled, then." Will started the engine and pointed the car in the direction of the Crescent and Stanley's address. He wondered if the man would be able to manage on his own to get his soggy clothes off and some decent footwear on without taking all day, but he needn't have worried. As they arrived outside his house, Birdie got out of her side of the car and was preparing to help him up the path.

"I'll help him," she said. "It will be quicker." Stanley never uttered a peep – maybe he was looking forward to a woman undressing him – and it tickled Will, but he too said nothing. He watched with amusement as the two ambled through the overgrown front garden and back up to Stanley's front door. He wondered how long he would have to wait for the pair to return.

Whatever Birdie had done, she'd somehow worked a miracle, because five minutes later a dry Stanley, complete with trainers, of all things, on his feet, emerged from the house and they made their way back to the car. Will waited until they'd both got in before asking, "Everything okay?"

"The inside of that house is like something off *Britain's Biggest Hoarders*," Birdie exclaimed as she fastened her seat belt.

"If you'd spent as much time with newspapers and picket lines as I have over the years, you might be as protective of them as I am!" Stanley offered by way of explanation.

"I very much doubt that," she said under her breath. Will caught it.

"Are we ready?" Will asked hopefully, changing the subject.

"Certainly are," said Birdie. "Let's get off before it gets much later. We don't want to be down there too late."

"So, where are we headed then, Stanley? I'm sure there'll be a chemist somewhere nearby."

"St Sep's on Sheep Street if you don't mind, driver," Stanley said like a Royal sitting in the back of a horse-drawn vehicle. "And don't mind the horses."

FIFTY-FIVE

THE OLD NORMAN ROUND CHURCH IN SHEEP STREET LOOKED uninviting and foreboding. It was a Grade II listed building, like so many of the older buildings in the town, and dated back to around 1100 AD. At that age, it was quite probably one of the oldest in the town, as well as only one of four medieval round churches still in use in England. It was Stanley that spoke first.

"Never bloody liked churches," he said. "Always give me the creeps."

"Then how did you know about these tunnels?" Birdie asked.

"Because it's pretty much the only way in now," said Stanley. "I used to get in from the Gold Street entrance, where the old Conservative club used to be, but it's not so easy now."

Birdie was intrigued. "When did you last try and get down there, then?"

"Not that long actually," said Stanley. "Probably only about ten years ago. Before my legs started jerking me around."

Ten years ago wasn't exactly what Will would call recent.

"Why then?" asked Will. "I hope you weren't drinking down there at that age?"

"No, though I can't remember the reason why. Somebody asked me, we got talking about it, but I can't for the life of me think who it was." Stanley's brow creased in concentration; it was going to take him the rest of the afternoon if he ever figured out whom he'd spoken to.

"So how do we get in?" said Will.

"Around the back," said Stanley, pointing to a pedestrian door. "You can get in the front, but probably safer the back way, less people to notice you. There's bound to be somebody in there praying."

Will detected a hint of disdain in his comment of somebody praying, but he let it go. Each to their own. Those that want to worship should be allowed to do so, and if Stanley didn't believe in such activities that was his prerogative. One shouldn't preach to the other, so to speak. Will gathered his bag of plastic specimen pots and nail file, which he'd purchased on the way in, ready to take scrapings from the wall and floor of the area.

"We'll follow you then," said Will, knowing full well that Stanley wouldn't exactly be flying across the grass to the entrance-way. He just hoped that they could get down there and be back out again before too much longer.

It took a good five minutes to reach the door and Will wondered if they were doing the right thing. Perhaps he should go down alone and not take the two old folks with him. It would be quicker and quite probably safer. Birdie must have read his mind because she said, "Oh no you don't, Will. We're coming too, or at least I am."

"I wouldn't have it it any other way," he said to Birdie, smirking. "Are you going to be all right on your feet though, Stanley? I suspect there will be steps."

"There are, but I'll get you in. I'll be lookout at the top, shall I? I can be of use there."

"What will you do to alert us of impending danger?" asked Birdie theatrically.

Stanley tapped his pocket with satisfaction. "I might be ancient, but I'm no T-Rex, I've got a mobile."

"Then we should swap numbers now," said Will. "Hand your phones over, it will be quicker if I add each of you for the other." They already had Will's.

Stanley and Birdie dutifully did so, and one by one Will exchanged numbers into their phones and then handed them back.

"There, we're all set," he said. "Now let's get going."

When everyone was ready, Will led the way, followed by Birdie and with Stanley bringing up the rear. Will had an idea that it wasn't going to be in the main part of the church, there was no point going in there, and thought it had to be out the back with the other rooms, including the offices. Somewhere in the back there would likely be a boiler room, as per his research, that had a hidden entranceway which led down and on from there. Hopefully Stanley's memory was still intact to locate it.

Like three church mice, they made their way forward. Stanley directed them silently so as not to be heard by the vicar or a church worker – it wouldn't do to let anyone know they were there. As they moved further and further into the old building, Will could feel the temperature drop slightly and the air change, a much cooler breeze emanating from somewhere. They were going in the right direction and eventually came to a doorway at the end of the corridor. It had to be the entranceway. Will turned to Stanley and said, "I think you'd better stay here now. Let us know if anyone comes, okay?"

"I doubt your phone will work down there," said Stanley.

"Not a lot of point in swapping numbers then really, was there?" said Birdie sarcastically.

"Either way, I'll think of something. I can always say I was lost. Who wouldn't believe me?" Stanley said with a sly grin.

"I don't doubt that," said Will in a hushed voice. Surprisingly, the door was unlocked, and he and Birdie slipped through then turned on the torches on their phones. All the pair could see was darkness onwards from about five feet in front of them. They made their way down a handful of stone steps and paused at the bottom. The tunnel felt like something *from an Indiana Jones movie*. All they needed now was for a huge stone boulder to roll towards them and it would be complete.

"Are you okay, Birdie?" he said in a loud whisper. He could feel her at his side, but wanted to make sure nonetheless.

"Of course I am," she said somewhat indignantly. "I went to prison, remember? This is nothing as bad as that. I'd rather be down here than locked up in a concrete box for hours on end."

"Then let's get this over with, we don't have to go far."

"Like hell we don't," said Birdie. "We're here now, let's get the scrapings and see how far this baby goes."

FIFTY-SIX

Colin had mulled it over all day while sitting at his ugly modern desk at Angel Square. He'd hardly done anything more than gaze out of his window at the street below or pace up and down in his office, wondering what to do next. Acid churned in his stomach, the little bit of toast he'd eaten at breakfast had been nowhere near enough to soak it up, and he was producing more and more with the stress he was under. He could almost taste it. At 2 pm he could take it no more and marched out of his office, speaking to no one as he left the building. Normally for a journey in the day, he'd take the mayoral vehicle, but he didn't want to go to the police station in such a grand affair; plus, he was in no mood for the formality of it all. What he was about to do didn't warrant fanfare, he just wanted it done with. It would be better all-round if he drove himself there. He just hoped he could summon the strength when he needed it and not chicken out of telling the police what he knew.

Once in the safety of his own car, he pulled out into the traffic and made his way to Campbell Square police station to report the incident. He thought about alerting his solicitor to his intentions; after all he would need one later on in the day, because no doubt they would arrest him and charge him with something. Withholding information concerning a murder investigation was going to warrant more punishment than a slap across the knuckles. He didn't care at that moment, all he wanted was to feel normal again, get rid of the stress and stop the blackmailing, let someone else take over, because he couldn't cope any longer. Whatever might have happened in terms of his retirement, his future, was probably lost now, though he hoped he'd still have Babs alongside him. The election, he really couldn't care about. He wondered how Babs would react when it all came out? Still, the money that he had squirrelled away over the years, which now sat offshore, would help, and he hoped and prayed that his life wouldn't be in tatters after the revelation he was about to make. He needed to be strong and right now he felt like a wimp, but as he made his way to the station, he began to feel a little more in control – it was the right thing to do.

Soon enough he pulled up outside the building and sat for a moment considering the consequences. Anyone looking in would say, 'absolutely, do the right thing', but he had so much to lose. Was he really prepared? It was several minutes later that he finally made a move.

"Come on, Colin," he said to himself sternly. "Let's get this over with."

Once inside the building, he stated that he needed to speak to someone, preferably the investigating officer in charge, about the recent deaths, the bodies found at Hunsbury Hill Country Park. He had information and he needed to get it off his chest. The uniformed man looked at him suspiciously. Was he another crackpot or the real thing?

"Please take a seat," the desk sergeant said. It was the last thing Colin wanted to do, and he hoped the wait wouldn't be too long. He ignored the officer's suggestion and instead paced up and down, much like he had in his own office not long ago. He'd been there only a couple of minutes when a voice called him from behind.

"Colin Hayhurst?" He turned to see a woman much taller than him with hair the shade of residue blue. He wondered about that for a second or two, but now was not the time to ask, he had more important things on his mind. "I'm DI Rochelle Mason, I'm on the team investigating the case. I believe you have some information to share with me?"

"Yes, I do. Quite a lot, actually," he said.

"Then follow me, if you don't mind, so I can take it down properly."

Colin followed the woman through an internal door and into an interview room where she offered him a seat and this time he took it.

"So, what is it you know?" she enquired.

"I guess the best place to start is at the beginning," he said.

She must have sensed his nerves because she smiled, which did help to relax him just a little.

"I find it the best place, but take your time." As a detective, she recognised that the man sitting in front of her had something of consequence on his mind and needed some persuasion to jerk it loose.

"It started at the beginning of the week…" Colin began to fill her in with the story of the first two text messages and then the bombshell from earlier today – he had received a third one. With the added message of 'checkmate', he hoped it was the last, the game over. Colin had lost and the blackmailers were now going to do their worst, as they'd promised. DI Rochelle Mason looked at Colin as if he was something stuck to the bottom of her shoe. By the vein that pulsed in her neck, he could tell she was struggling to contain her anger. If he had come forward earlier on, he could have saved a life, if not three. People had died because of his selfish actions, but as a professional, the detective didn't say a word.

Instead, she asked, "Is your phone with you?"

"Of course," he said, "But I'm afraid I've deleted the first two texts."

He could see her visibly groan, and wondered if there was any way to get those images back like they did on TV. Surely somebody could resurrect them, see what had been there?

"Have you still got the latest image?"

By the tone of her voice, he could tell there was an urgency in it.

"I do, yes." He pulled it up and handed his phone to her and watched while the detective looked at the image then tapped the screen several times. He had no idea what she was doing. She looked across at him. "Lucky for you that whoever's done this is a complete amateur." What did that mean exactly?

She jumped up from her chair and ran out the room, shouting as she went. A moment later, another police officer entered and positioned himself by the door, as if to guard him.

"What will happen now?" he asked the man.

"I am to watch over you until DI Mason gets back is all I know."

Colin hoped it wouldn't be long, he felt sick again.

FIFTY-SEVEN

It had been a stroke of luck for the investigation that DI Mason had been in the Campbell Square police station on another matter. So, when Colin Hayhurst had announced that he had information on the case, she was able to spring into action and meet with him instantly. What she hadn't been prepared for, however, was the fact that he was involved by being the recipient of certain images, he wasn't just another crackpot that thought he knew where the next body was – they thought they were doing the right thing, meant well, but ended up wasting police time. But Colin Hayhurst was the real McCoy, he had an image on his phone to prove it. Now it looked like there was a third body that they had yet to find.

There was no way to tell from the photo whether the person was alive or dead; it was a naked torso with yet another message, 'checkmate'. Rochelle had run from the room and hastily made a call to the SIO, DCI Karen Miller, back at Newport Pagnell Road for further instructions. Right now, Colin Hayhurst was being guarded by a constable and she knew she hadn't got much time. He wasn't under arrest, not yet, so she needed to make it snappy. Outside, Rochelle jumped on her motorbike and raced around the ring road as fast as she could safely drive. It didn't take long to get to the satellite office where the team were operating from, and she immediately handed the phone over to DCI Miller. Rochelle Mason was a smart woman and had promptly looked at the image information to see if it gave the time and date of where and when it had been taken. It was all there in front of her, at 8.06 that morning and the GPS coordinates were displayed at the bottom. It had been taken on an iPhone X. She recognised the latitude and longitude numbers for the town, so she knew it had been taken locally. What she didn't know was the exact spot until she looked them up online. It was now their call what to do next. Whatever the location turned out to be, they had to tread carefully, the victim could still be alive.

DCI Karen Miller wasted no time in organising the team and their roles. As men and women piled into vans to head out, nobody quite knew what to expect when they arrived at the coordinates given. DI Mason was among them. As adrenalin pumped through her veins, she hoped, like her colleagues, that the third victim was still alive, whoever they were. With no sirens and only flashing lights to clear the traffic, they headed north towards the Church of the Holy Sepulchre, which was frighteningly close to Campbell Square police station itself. In fact, it was just across the road. Who would think of committing such a crime right under the nose of the police?

As the van that Rochelle was in pulled up in the church car park, she looked around at the location and what they had to deal with. The coordinates were only feet from where they were right at that moment, yet there was nothing to see, only the church, the grave-yard and some other small buildings. It had to be in one of them, or the church itself, which didn't seem particularly realistic. Who would kill somebody in a church and then move the body to Huns-bury Hill at a later date? Surely, they'd just leave the body where they'd committed the original crime. Why risk moving it and someone seeing you? As the SIO gave orders, DI Mason scanned the area again and noticed a familiar vehicle parked up nearby.

"Now why is that minicab driver here? Why is his car parked in this car park at this time?" she said, almost to herself.

"What was that, boss?"

It was DC Flint. "I know that car over there," she said, nodding towards it. "It belongs to a local minicab driver. He volunteers at the Refresh Centre and has tried on several occasions to insert himself into this investigation. Name is Will Peters, you've met him."

"I have, yes. Could be inside praying? It is a church."

"I hate coincidences."

"You think he might be involved?"

"I'm beginning to wonder now," she said. "He works with the homeless, he wants to get involved, keep an eye on things, and as you well know, often those types turn out to be the culprits, that's their primary reason for keeping up with what's going on."

"I guess we'll find out soon enough. Have you seen him?"

"Not yet."

FIFTY-EIGHT

As Birdie and Will ventured further down the tunnel, Stanley made his own way slowly back towards the rear entrance to the church where they had first entered not long ago. There seemed little point waiting at the top of the steps, there was nothing he could do there, so he figured he may as well stay where it was a bit warmer and wait for them to reappear. If anybody saw him, he would go with his excuse of just having a look around, say he meant no harm, and hoped that that would suffice. When he reached the door, what greeted him on the other side was not what he expected. From his spot by a nearby window he could see the flashing lights of emergency services, but he couldn't hear sirens. That in itself was strange, but he ignored it and watched with interest as several van loads of uniformed police, and what looked like a forensics team by their white paper suits, stood around in conversation. He realised something was adrift. Will and Birdie were someway under foot, and he hurriedly tried to send a text to them both, alerting them that they had important visitors. His fingers didn't seem to want to work, and he fumbled to make a coherent message he could barely see, his reading glasses in their case back in his living room.

Not needing them to show his friends how to get into a tunnel, he hadn't thought to bring them.

"Dammit," he said as he struggled to see what he was typing. Deciding a phone call might be better, he pressed for Will and waited for it to connect. It went straight to voicemail. He did the same with Birdie and hoped that hers might give him better reception – maybe she was with a different provider – but hers went the same way, voicemail. "I might as well leave a message," he mumbled and waited for Birdie to stop talking. "Get back here and quickly," he blurted and ended the call. He glanced out of the window to see what was happening just as half the group set off towards the back door of the church.

"Shit!" he said to himself and pressed send on his rough typed message, hoping that something, message or voicemail, would get through to the tunnels below. From memory they ran in every direction, and he just hoped that Will and Birdie had had the good sense to stay on the main track and not go branching off and getting lost, that they could find their own way back easily enough. He had no sooner had the thought than the back door opened, and a woman with bluish hair was standing in front of him. Even though Stanley's hearing wasn't the best, there was no mistaking the sound of other police officers that were entering through the main door, all entrances covered. What the hell were they looking for? He waited to see what would happen next.

"DI Rochelle Mason. Who might you be?"

"Stanley Kipper," he said clearly.

"What are you doing back here, Stanley?" she asked.

"Just browsing." He hoped it sounded enough.

"Browsing? Browsing what exactly?" she said in order to clarify, obviously not convinced by his nonchalant comment.

"Always wanted to know what it was like at the back of the church," he said. At that moment the vicar came out of her office, having heard the police arrive, and raised voices in conversation.

"May I ask what's going on?" she asked. "I'm Joanna Cox, the vicar."

"Good afternoon, vicar," Rochelle said. "DI Mason. We have reason to believe that somebody is being kept on these premises against their will. We are here to search," she said.

"I can assure you there is nobody being kept on these premises," said the vicar, in a tone that relayed her displeasure, "but please feel free to confirm that." She opened her arms as if to invite them to search every crevice. "Any idea where this person is supposedly being held?"

"Our intelligence tells us this location, not exactly which room."

"Well, feel free to look around. If you need my help, I'll be right here."

Both the vicar and Stanley watched as the gathered police split into groups and went off in various directions. Stanley could hear a distant 'clear', followed by another distant 'clear', as each room in turn was searched. The crew that had entered through the front entrance of the church met up with the rear-entrance team and evidently all was 'clear' there too. DI Mason made her way over to Stanley and said, "You appear to be the only person here apart from the vicar. What is the reason for your visit and how did you get here?" she asked.

"I said, just browsing, and to answer your other question, by car," he said. "Like I could walk very far?"

Rochelle had to agree with that, the elderly man obviously doddery on his feet, but since he was wearing trainers, she had to be sure. She pointed to his feet, "You didn't run here, then?"

"What planet were you born on?" said Stanley. "Do I look like a bloody Olympic athlete?"

"I guess not," she said. She'd known the answer, but wanted to check anyway. Plenty of older people ran to keep fit. "Is that your car outside?"

"Not my car, no," said Stanley, starting to enjoy himself. He wasn't going to give the police anything. It wasn't his car, and if they'd bothered to look the registration up, she'd have known that it belonged to Will Peters. He'd let her wait until she did so. "Any chance of a cuppa?" he asked the vicar, before turning back to smile at the female detective. It had been a long time since he'd had so much fun with the police. He only hoped that when Will and Birdie returned, they weren't in any real trouble.

FIFTY-NINE

Some feet below where the police were now standing, Will and Birdie made their way along the tunnel in the dim light of their phone torches.

"We should get the samples," said Birdie, "then at least we've got what we came to get. Then we can carry on if we want to."

"I'm not sure I want to go all the way," said Will. "This could go on for miles, and I don't want to be down here at dark, although I know that sounds silly since it's dark down here anyway, but you know what I mean. Plus, we ought to get Stanley home and drop you back, and Louise will be wondering where I've got to. Nobody knows we're here, remember."

"Good points," said Birdie. "Then we should get the samples and make a date to come back. Maybe tomorrow morning? Although that's Saturday and you may have family commitments?"

Will tried not to work on a Saturday because Louise very often had shifts to cover at the weekend, though not in the outpatients. They did have plans, they were due to take the girls out to the theme park for the day, but if the weather turned to custard like it had this afternoon, they might have to change to indoors activities. He'd think about that later.

"Let's give it another five minutes," he said. "We'll get the samples and walk a little way further, and then yes, you're right, we should get back."

"I'll hold your torch while you get them then," she offered, and watched as Will scratched tiny particles off the walls and put them into one pot, then added scratchings from the floor to another pot. He pulled a pen out of his pocket and wrote on the labels which was which.

"I'll grab some more from further up before we turn around," he said, as if by explanation of what the other pots were for. He slipped the two used ones into his pocket and they slowly carried on down the tunnel. They'd only gone ten feet or so when Birdie noticed that it branched off to the right.

"This looks like a spot where we should turn back," she said.

"I agree, we don't want to get lost, though it is only the first branch we've come to so why don't we just go on for a couple more minutes and see where the right fork takes us? If we come to another fork, we won't take it. We know when we eventually turn around that we've just got to go left at the fork and walk straight back home. Agreed?"

"Sounds good to me," said Birdie. "I don't fancy getting lost and being down here all weekend. No one would notice me gone."

"Well, Louise would have no idea where to look for us, certainly not down here anyway. I've not told anybody where we are, although my car is parked back up above ground. Not that it means we're here."

"Come on, let's hurry," said Birdie, picking up speed, and the two carried on at a slightly faster pace to see where the right fork went to. Time was nearly up when Birdie exclaimed, "It forks off again, end of the line for today."

"I agree," he said, relieved the end had come, for today at least.

They couldn't go any further at that moment, it wouldn't have been wise. Both shone their torches in the same direction.

"You know, I don't think that is a tunnel," said Birdie. "It looks more like cellar, a room. Look," she said, pointing her light beam at the wall. "You can see the back wall; it doesn't go anywhere."

"I think you're right, Birdie," he said, "let's go the few more feet and have a snoop around. Then we'll definitely go?"

"Yes," she said. The two carried on just a few more steps to confirm their thoughts. It was, in fact, just a room and not another tunnel.

"Look at that," said Will. "Who would want to stay down here?" A single metal bed with a soiled mattress was the only thing in the room. "There's food wrappers," he added, pointing at them.

"And they look like McDonald's," said Birdie, having taken a closer look.

"Probably kids, like Stanley when he was younger, drinking beer. They probably come down here and smoke."

"It's a long way to come," said Birdie. "Not the nicest of places. I could think of easier places to go and smoke dope." Will had to agree about that one, it was unusual. "And unless they know another way in, they'd have to come in through the church."

Will shone his torch around the room. Yes, there were food wrappers, and there looked to be half a dozen or so all in one corner. He walked over and shone his light down at them. "Fresh ones too," he said, sniffing. "Curious there's nothing else here..." There were no cigarette butts littering the floor, no beer cans, no nothing. "Come on, let's get back. Stanley will be ready to get home. I know I am."

The two made their way, turned left at the junction, then headed back up the steps and into the rear passages of the church. It didn't take that long at all, and when they re-entered the storeroom, both were surprised that they could hear voices. There were quite a few. Birdie looked at Will and both wondered what was going on. As he opened the door, it all became clear. What he wasn't expecting was to again come face to face with DI Rochelle Mason. Over her shoulder, he could see Stanley with a half-smile on his face, and he wondered what had been said. His phone pinged with a text message and then again with a voice message. Birdie's phone did the same.

"Fancy seeing you here," Rochelle said.

SIXTY

He certainly hadn't been expecting to see DI Mason when he walked through the door and it was obvious she wasn't too pleased to see him either.

"What's going on?" he asked innocently. There must've been a dozen people, including the vicar and Stanley, in the small area.

"I'd like to ask you the same question," she said. "What were you doing down there?"

"Sightseeing," said Will. "I suppose that's what you'd call it. I only learned of the tunnels just recently and only today learned that there was a way in from this church. Why, what's wrong?"

"I don't believe in coincidences and you've got some explaining to do, so I suggest we do that down the station."

"What you mean?"

"We need to have a formal chat," she said.

"Am I under arrest?" asked Will, sounding incredulous.

"I'm not sure yet, but I think it's in your interest to explain exactly what you've been doing down there. I suggest you go with DC Flint. You too, Birdie Fox, and you'd better take your friend with you, not that he's been much help." She glared at Stanley. DI

Mason was too young to know of Stanley's involvement with the police from way back, which was probably to Stanley's advantage.

"All we went down there for was to get some samples," he said, pulling the two pots out of his pocket and handing them over. "One is off the floor and the other is off the wall. I thought you could compare them to any traces left on Clyde's or Bowie's body. I've no idea if they're connected to these tunnels or not, it was just a hunch, it seemed like a good place to hide somebody. Plus, it fits in with the damp odour I detected on Bowie at the mortuary." He was pleading his case as best he could. The last thing he wanted was to waste his time in an interview room.

"What did you find down there?"

"Tunnels. Cold and damp tunnels," he said. "But just as we were about to turn around, we came across what we thought was another tunnel, but it turned out to be some sort of chamber, like a cellar. A room, if you like. We went in, but I think it's just somewhere where kids probably hang out, because there was an old single metal bed that looked like it had been there since time began, and food wrappers, though those were recent. I could still see the grease on them – McDonald's. But as Birdie pointed out, why would kids hang around in a cold, damp tunnel just to smoke weed or whatever? That bit that doesn't fit. Plus, there were no cigarette butts or smoked joints in there, just the filthy bed and food wrappers."

Something glinted in DI Mason's eyes. Will knew he'd struck on something.

"How many, would you say? How many wrappers?"

"Probably half a dozen or so, we haven't touched them. Why?"

"Good," she said and turned to one of the forensic team and passed the message on. "Leave it to us now, Will, but if you had to go in again, could you remember the way? Could you tell one of the officers exactly where you found them?"

"Straight on, and at the first fork, take a right, and it's not far off there, on your right."

"Easy enough," she said. "Right, we'll take it from here now. Go with DC Flint, all three of you. I want to talk to you lot properly back at the station."

"How long will you be? Only I've got to get these two back, and I've got a family waiting for me."

"Then I suggest you ring your family and let them know you're going to be a little late. I don't know how long I'll be here."

Will thought for a moment. He wasn't happy with her suggestion. "If we are not under arrest, I'll meet you tomorrow morning, we can talk then. I want to get these two home. Stanley's already had a soaking today and the last thing I want is for him to catch a chill, or worse, pneumonia. We aren't going anywhere." It wasn't like she had any evidence against him, just because his car was parked outside, and being in the tunnel with Birdie didn't mean he had done anything wrong. DI Mason knew when she was beaten, he had a point. Still, she didn't believe in coincidence, and she still needed to find out where the person in the latest image was and if they were still alive. That was the priority now, not Will and his group. Knowing about the tunnels, it now made perfect sense. From the coordinates they had, the room must be off one of them. That meant a whole different search and she hadn't time to waste on the nosey trio.

"Go home, all of you. I'll be in touch later; it could be a late one here. But just don't go anywhere," she said sharply. "Stay close by."

"I'm not planning on going anywhere," he said. "I'm on your side, remember? I want to find Clyde and Bowie's killer just as much as you do, and make sure there's not another one." Something must've flashed across Rochelle's face and Will saw it immediately. "Oh lord, there's been another one, hasn't there? When?"

"I'm not going to talk to you about an ongoing investigation."

"Hunsbury Hill again?"

"I'm not telling you any more. Now, if you don't mind, let the professionals take over, we need to get down into the tunnels."

"I'll wait to hear from you then," he said. "Stanley, Birdie, let's get you two home. The DI knows where to find us if she needs us in the meantime," he said, catching Mason's eye.

Stanley was particularly glad to be getting back, he'd been on his feet far too long and cold was starting to settle into his bones. The three headed out to the car, though Will would be lucky if he could get it out with the amount of police and other vehicles that were parked around it. He was somewhat blocked in.

"Great," he said. "How the hell do I get out of this one?"

"Might be better to call a taxi," Birdie said helpfully. "Perhaps pick it up tomorrow. iIt'll be safe in the churchyard with all these police around. It sounds like these guys are going to be here a while."

"Maybe you're right," said Will resignedly. "I'll get Louise to drive me tomorrow, pick it up." He looked at the time on his phone. She'd be at home with the girls by now, so he couldn't even ask her for a lift back, there would be no one to mind the little ones.

"I can recommend a lovely taxi driver," Birdie said, winking. "Unfortunately, though, I hear his car's off the road currently."

SIXTY-ONE

IT HAD BEEN LUNCHTIME BY THE TIME THE KILLER HAD GOT BACK TO work. They'd been surprised at how calm they'd felt, though the first one in particular had been fraught, and they'd been on edge and upset afterwards. The second one had been somewhat easier, but the third? It had barely registered on their emotional scale. They wondered about the cellar location – the bed and the room had been so convenient. Most people didn't know the chambers existed so no one would even think to look down there.

On the way home from work that evening, they took a detour to drive past St Sep's, just out of interest to see if there was anything going on. They knew that each time they took a victim, they were surely another step closer to being found out, it was inevitable, but were the police on to them yet? Three victims would give them three sets of clues – how close were they? As the killer approached the church on Campbell Street, they felt a little disheartened to see so much activity in the church car park. Police cars and vans, with forensic teams and others that made up the entourage, could quite clearly be seen as they drove past. There was nothing in the room that could link them to the crimes; the bed stripped, there were only food wrappers left, if they even discovered the room in the first place. Nothing could be linked back – they'd worn gloves, of that they were grateful. Still, seeing the police activity gave a jolt of realisation as to how close the authorities were getting. Moving the last victim in time had been a stroke of luck, and the killer wondered for a moment what had led the cops to the church in the first place. Thoughts curdled in their stomach at the realisation of the close call. The money hadn't come through, the blackmail scheme hadn't worked, and three lives had been wasted for nothing. So far, the one person they did want to hurt hadn't been at all. If nothing else, the killer needed to fix that. He was the whole point of the exercise; the three unfortunate victims were collateral damage.

Pulling up outside their own neat property, they sat quietly, looking out at the building to their side. Inside was a normal life ready to envelope them – family, belongings, everything they cared about. Would these be hit by the fallout from their actions? If it was ever revealed what they'd done, prison would be the least of their woes. The living room curtain twitched slightly, and a slender hand waved. Somewhere deep inside the killer's chest, a heartstring pulled in several directions all at once, threatening to snap. What would happen to her and her needs if a parent was taken away? There was no doubt the girl would suffer. The killer forced a smile to their face, and headed indoors as if they'd had the same depressing day at work that they had every other day, that nothing had happened in their world and all was the same as usual. At least they wouldn't have to slip out to Hunsbury Hill in the middle of the night again, there was that.

It was done now, there was no going back. All the killer could do was act normal, stay relaxed and consider the next part. They hoped there'd be no more bodies, three was enough.

The message had been sent, loud and clear, but *had it simply been ignored?*

SIXTY-TWO

Darkness settled on the car park as DI Mason took a break from the cellar and tunnels below the church. Will had been right, it was cold and damp down there, and she felt an aching deep inside her bones. She wondered how the team on Hunsbury Hill were doing. DCI Karen Miller, the SIO on the case, had organised another group to watch the area for the evening, since they expected another body to be delivered, presumably to roughly the same place where the previous victims had been found. If the photograph was anything to go by, there would be a third, it was just a matter of time before somebody found it. The forensic team had set up shop and were busy working below ground, but by the look of the old stripey mattress, there could be a good deal of DNA to filter through. Goodness knows how many people had slept on the thing over the years. The only obvious recent addition to the cellar was the food wrappers and they'd gone off to be fingerprinted. If the prints were on file, she should have the results back very soon. If they were either Clyde's, Bowie's or both, that could be the deciding factor of whether a crime had in fact been committed below her feet. The location would fit with the coordinates of the image she'd seen.

She stared up at the dark sky, heavy clouds covering any moon. Perhaps it would rain again soon. Closing her eyes, she plunged herself into deep thought and blocked out the surrounding noise. Who else knew about the access tunnel from the church? It wasn't common knowledge, and apparently was a long way from other entry points that were known about. It made sense, then, that whoever had been using the room gained access from the inside. Did they have a key, or were they brazen enough to enter in broad daylight? She tossed Will and his two elderly friends and their involvement into the mix, though deep down she knew they weren't involved. She believed Will's explanation, he'd been down there to get samples for the CSIs to compare to, he was trying to help and his actions didn't fit with someone who had something to hide. It was purely gut instinct to link the tunnels to the deaths of those he was trying to serve, that and the odour he'd so intuitively picked up at the mortuary. It was only because of the GPS coordinates from the photo sent by the amateur that she'd become aware of the tunnels herself.

Colin Hayhurst was in a whole lot of trouble now. Why the hell he hadn't come forward at the beginning was beyond her imagination, save to say he was one selfish individual. She'd interview him properly in the morning – he could stew for a while first, safely retired in one of the cells until she was ready to get to him. Tomorrow was going to be a busy day. Her phone buzzed; it was DC Flint.

"Stephen. What do you have?" she asked, focusing.

"Three sets of prints on three sets of food wrappers, I'm afraid," he said.

She could detect his pause. "I have a feeling you're going to tell me who they belong to and I'm not going to like it."

"Two belong to our first two victims and the third belongs to someone we are already aware of. He's been collared for petty crime and was in the station recently. He goes by the name of Jonesy."

"Oh hell."

"You know him, then?"

"Yes," she said, letting out a heavy sigh. "We've already met Jonesy in the course of this case. Remember, he was left in Towcester Road Cemetery after being beaten up. What's he doing involved in this now? As a victim, or the perpetrator?"

"Do you think they'd tried again because he talked to us?"

"Possibility. Or he could be involved up to his neck and what he told us was a crock of shit."

"Victim?" he asked.

"More likely. There's no face on the photograph, just the torso, and we know from the coordinates it was taken here."

"The wrapper just means Jonesy was here and nothing more. We need to keep an open mind."

"I'm guessing you've not heard anything from Hunsbury Hill?" she said, changing the subject. "Maybe it's a bit early yet."

"I'd say so. If anything is going to happen up there tonight, it will be much later, too many people hanging around at this hour still walking dogs. If you're going to move the body, you're going to do it in the wee hours, surely."

"Agreed, though that wasn't the case with the first one, remember? For now, let's make sure all units are on the lookout for Jonesy – we need to speak to him urgently, assuming he's still with us. Send someone down to the shelter and see if he's been seen today, and I'll contact Will, he might know more."

"Righto."

Rochelle hung up and dialled Will's number. She needed his help after all and wasn't too proud to ask for it.

"Sorry to bother you, Will. I hope it's not too late?"

"Not at all. What can I help you with?"

"I need to know if you or anybody has seen your friend Jonesy recently. DC Flint is speaking to the shelter, but I know you know a little more about the man. Have you seen him recently?"

"No, I haven't actually. Why, what's happened? Surely you don't think he's involved in some way, do you?"

"I think I can trust you, Will. Can I?"

"Of course."

She could hear the indignation in his tone, but pushed it aside. He'd been thoughtful enough to look out for her after her treatment that day, and figured he was a decent sort. She had nothing to suggest otherwise. "Keep this to yourself, but one of the sets of prints on those food wrappers belongs to Jonesy."

"I hardly think he's involved in this – is that what you're thinking?" Will said, trying not to sound too incredulous.

"I don't know what to think at the moment, I'm keeping an open mind, but he's obviously been in that room. I'm also hoping he's not a victim we're about to find."

Will took a moment to digest what he had just been told. "What can I do?"

"You can find out if anyone has seen him, those close to where he has been hanging out, and who he's been with."

Will thought back to where the lad had been living, not far from the tunnel entrance at Bridge Street.

"I know where he's been staying of recent, another tunnel actually, just by the Bridge Street entrance. I'll go and check it out now."

"I'll have an officer meet you there, don't be going in on your own."

"Under the circumstances it's probably better if I do go on my own. Not everyone wants to see the police. They know me, most of them. I'll be fine." Will glanced at the clock over the mantelpiece. It was coming up to nine o'clock. Not the ideal time to be going into the tunnel again – on his own.

SIXTY-THREE

Louise had heard every word, at least Will's side of the telephone conversation. When the call ended, she said, "I guess you're going out?"

"Sorry, I'll try not to be long," he said. "It seems that Jonesy… Well, I'll fill you in later. I have to go and check again where he currently resides, if you could call it that, see if anybody has seen him recently. He might be in trouble, that's all I can say." He watched her face fall at the word 'trouble'. "I'll be fine. Now, just so you know where I am, there is an entrance to a tunnel just at the bottom of Bridge Street behind some boards. I've only got to check if Jonesy is at his place and then I'll be back, okay?"

"Why can't the police do it?"

"I need to talk to him, and he might run off if the police show up, I don't want to risk it."

"Okay. Take care of yourself, Will," she said. "Don't do anything silly. I know you're only trying to help in this investigation, but please just look after yourself." She gave him a quick hug and a light kiss on the side of his neck. "The sooner you go, the sooner you'll be back," she said, starting towards the door.

Will took the hint and grabbed his coat off the banister at the bottom of the stairs and checked his pockets for car keys before remembering where his was still parked. "Damn! I'll have to take your car, mine's still up at the church. Where are your keys?"

"I'll get them," she said, bending to retrieve them from inside her bag nearby.

"I'll be back as soon as I can."

Louise watched from the front step as he headed out into the night. The temperature had dropped considerably from the day and she pulled her cardigan tight around her body before going back inside. The girls were all tucked up in their beds, and she had the living room to herself but didn't feel much like finishing the movie they'd been watching together. She turned the TV off and headed up to read in bed, where she'd wait for him to arrive home later.

WILL PARKED as close to the tunnel entrance as he could. He hoped this wasn't going to take long, that Jonesy was sat with his mates by his makeshift home and all he had to do was have a quick chat and report back to DI Mason then go. He moved one of the boards that was covering the entrance, as George had shown him only a couple of days ago, and slipped inside, pulling the board back in place behind him. He waited until his eyes adjusted to the darkness. He could see the distant, shallow lighting up ahead, so turned on the torch on his phone and made his way down the short way to Jonesy's patch. It was obvious to Will, as soon as he got there, there was no sign of him. His crude bed didn't look like it had been slept in and his few belongings were piled neatly as they had been before. Something told Will that Jonesy hadn't been there for a while. A familiar voice called out to him, the same one from last time he'd been there, with George.

"He isn't there, not seen him." Will turned towards the voice and approached the man.

"Jonesy?" he asked.

"You asked about him last time, not seen him since."

It wasn't what Will wanted to hear. Had the lad just moved on again, like he had last time? Found new friends to hang out with? Will wasn't convinced, he'd have taken his stuff.

"Have you seen anybody else hanging around his place?"

"Nah."

There was nothing left for it but to head back out. DI Mason already said an officer was going to the centre to see if anybody had seen Jonesy, but Will knew that if he hadn't been back to his own place, he wouldn't be up at Refresh either. He called Hazel anyway, just for his own peace of mind. After a brief conversation to confirm what he already knew, Will could feel his heart sinking and just hoped that the lad hadn't gone the same way as Clyde and Bowie had.

It seemed strange, though. It didn't fit. They'd already had a go at him once, he'd woken up at the cemetery. Why hadn't they taken him then? Had they been disturbed? Why bother with him now? He'd had nothing to tell the police. Maybe that was it? Maybe they knew he'd been to the police and couldn't guarantee that he hadn't given evidence, hadn't seen something himself, and maybe someone had since decided to clear up a potentially loose end?

He called DI Mason and relayed to her that Jonesy hadn't been home for some time in his opinion. There was little more Will could do. He rang Louise to tell her that he was on his way back and tried not to dwell on the fact that the lad was missing – again. It wouldn't normally have been a problem, since it seemed Jonesy was someone that didn't stay in one place for very long, but the fact that his fingerprints were on the food wrapper, along with those of the two dead victims, didn't bode well. Will remembered the blue pen that he'd found when he'd dropped the young mother and her toddler at the cemetery. Would DI Mason tell him if it had been useful in any way? He'd meant to ask her earlier, but somehow, it had slipped his mind. He pressed her number again and crossed his fingers.

"What is it, Will?" she asked.

"I forgot to ask, did you ever find out if there were any prints on that pen I dropped in, the one I found at the cemetery?"

"We did actually, and they match a person we are now aware of."

"What? You mean you've got a suspect already?"

"Not exactly, but until I understand how the prints fit into all this, all I can say is he's helping us with our enquiries."

It was news to Will. Good news at last.

SIXTY-FOUR

Louise watched as Will played with cereal in his bowl and knew they wouldn't be going out today as originally planned. She could see the case was bothering him and had felt him tossing and turning in bed for most of the night. He'd arrived home and informed her no one had seen Jonesy and that he was worried about him, and all she could do was rub his shoulders and encourage him to relax. Looking at him now, it was as though he'd been through hell and back, and there was nothing that she could do apart from lend an ear and her support.

"Hey," she said, touching his arm. He laid his spoon down in the bowl and sat back in his chair, his eyes searching hers.

"Sorry, I was miles away."

"I can see that," she said. "Why don't you do what you need to do today, and I'll take the girls out for some fun, keep them out of your hair. Unless you want to come, of course, but by your long face maybe not. Don't put yourself through it if you don't want to. Maybe you're better staying here and trying to get some rest?"

"You're always so understanding," he said. "It's one of the reasons why I love you so much."

She squeezed his forearm gently then removed his cereal bowl, stacking it in the dishwasher. "Why don't you ring her?"

"Who?"

"Your DI friend. Why don't you ring her and put yourself out of your misery? She just might tell you."

"I doubt she will, but I suppose it's worth a try, otherwise I'll just sit here all day wondering."

"Then go now and ring her, before it gets any later," she instructed and busied herself wiping the table down. She hoped that the woman had some good news for her husband and not bad. Will dialled the number and waited for it to connect.

"I wondered when you would call," she said in greeting.

"Have you any news?"

"Only to say that nothing materialised at Hunsbury Hill last night. We had officers all over the place expecting activity, but there was nothing. So no, I have no news on your friend, or anything else for that matter."

"Well, that's something positive at least. There's a chance he's still alive somewhere and he's just gone incommunicado again. He might not be connected to this in any way, he might have just gone off in a drunken stupor and is laid out in some squat sleeping it off." There was hope in his voice. It didn't, however, fit with Jonesy's prints being found on the food wrappers.

"I hear you, Will," she said. "The best thing you can do is keep yourself busy. There's nothing you can do here. Carry on as normal, there's plenty of people working this case now and I can't tell you much else as you know, but thanks for your help so far."

"Thanks, but will you promise me that if you hear of anything, or if you think you have Jonesy, you'll call me immediately?"

"You have my word. Now go do something with the family, keep busy."

Rochelle had already gone, there was no point in Will asking anything else. He stood there for a moment, head bowed, not thinking of anything, not feeling anything, not wanting to do anything, but he also knew that if he spent the day in his current funk, it would be a day wasted. She was right, there was nothing he could do now but wait. He turned to see Louise making sandwiches for the picnic and wandered over, sliding a hand across her shoulder.

"I'm coming too," he said. "There's no point moping around here all day for something that might or might not happen. That is if you want me to come?"

"Of course, I'd love you to come," she said warmly. "Plus, the girls love spending time with their dad and it's no trouble to make more sandwiches. Now, why don't you go get changed and as soon as I'm done here, we'll head out?"

"Then that's what we'll do," he said.

Thirty minutes later, and with four excited children secured in their respective seats, they set off towards Wicksteed Park, a short drive away in the nearby town of Kettering. It was always nice to watch their children, full of sugar, enjoy themselves, and by the end of the day they'd be tired out and sleeping soundly on the journey home.

It was while they were driving back that Will's phone rang and, glancing at the screen, he saw it was DI Mason. Something had happened. Since Will was driving, he debated whether to answer the call with the family in the car, but he needed to find out what she had. He clicked the green button on his steering wheel and said, "DI Mason, I have my family in the car with me, do you have some news?"

There was a pause and Will suspected Rochelle was choosing her words carefully, knowing little ears could hear.

"Maybe you could meet me at the mortuary as soon as you can."

Will didn't need to ask. By her tone and the way she spoke, what she didn't say, he knew they'd found Jonesy. "I'll meet you there in an hour," he said.

Louise placed a hand on his thigh and squeezed it gently. "Would you like me to come with you?"

"I'm getting tired of going to the mortuary," he said. "But no, thank you, I'll be fine on my own. I hope this is the last time, though."

SIXTY-FIVE

SEEING JONESY LAID OUT IN THE MORTUARY WAS A LOW POINT FOR Will and he fought to contain his emotions in front of Rochelle. He doubted she'd be the sympathetic kind and thought she'd likely wonder what to do with the blubbering male at her side. The other deaths had been bad enough, but having seen Jonesy only a couple of days ago, and him already escaping the first abduction, he wondered if his own asking him to go to the police and report what he knew had put his life in danger. He also wondered, and not for the first time, what it was all for. Was someone cleaning the streets of the homeless? Did they have a vendetta against them? Or was it something else? Either way, he hoped that DI Mason and the team would find out who was responsible and put a stop to it sooner than later. He'd spent far too much time at the mortuary of recent and he didn't particularly want to identify any more bodies any time soon. Three was more than enough.

He managed to chat a little with Rochelle while he was there, though she didn't give much away. The same bruising around Jonesy's neck was evident and he pondered that. When he mentioned strangulation to her, something flickered in her eyes and

Will pressed her for an answer, but she said nothing. He assumed, by the marks on their necks, that they'd all been strangled, and with something wide, but eventually Rochelle relented and let it slip that this hadn't actually been the case. The pathologist had surmised, in the first two cases, that the victims had been sedated before being smothered. It was news to him. She wouldn't tell him any more and had likely gone out on a limb to tell him that snippet. Everything he knew had pointed to strangulation, yet thinking back, nobody had actually said it. Smothered? That took some doing. He wasn't sure if he wanted coffee or alcohol, but he needed something to lift his mood; he didn't want to bring his family's happiness down to his level after such a lovely day out. He thought about ringing Birdie, she always cheered him up, but she was also a paying client and not someone that he could pick up the phone and have a good old moan to. Or was she?

"Sod it," he said and asked Siri to dial her number. She'd want to hear about the recent update and that it was in fact Jonesy that lay in the mortuary in a cold refrigerated unit alongside Clyde and Bowie. It was only a moment before Birdie's voice filled his car, and as usual a smile found its way to his lips. It was hard not to with her.

"Hello Will," she said chirpily, almost like birdsong, and he wondered if that was why they called her Birdie. She'd never mentioned any other name.

"Hello Birdie," he said, trying to emulate her good spirits and failing miserably.

Birdie picked up on his effort straight away. "What's happened?" she asked.

"I've just come back from the mortuary and identifying Jonesy's body."

"Oh Will, I'm so sorry to hear that."

"I guess we now know who was in that cellar, we just don't

know who his abductor is. And there was another message left. 'Checkmate'."

"Checkmate," she echoed. "End of the game."

"That's all I can think of, or game's up, perhaps? Depending on your interpretation."

"What can I do to help?" she asked positively.

"I've been thinking while I've been driving back. It's obviously got to be someone that's got access to the church and access to keys. Whether they volunteer or whether they're on the payroll, I don't know, but you can't get into that cellar easily without going through the church. It would be far too difficult to get at it from the other end."

"I agree. So, we need to know who's got access, who has a key, don't we? Let me think on it for a moment," she said, and Will gave her space. A moment later, she resumed, "Right, I think I have an idea, Will. Leave it with me and I'll see if I can get this to work, then I'll tell you what it is."

"What are you thinking, Birdie?"

"Let me see if it's possible first off, then I'll fill you in."

"Before you go, Birdie," Will called out, hoping that she hadn't already gone but she had. He called her straight back. "I meant to add, I was talking to DI Mason while I was in the mortuary and she let it slip he wasn't actually strangled, none of them were strangled. But the first two did have large quantities of sedative in their system and the pathologist says they've been smothered."

"That's interesting," she said. "That puts another slant on things."

"Why do you say that, what are you thinking?"

"Sedation before suffocation really has only one purpose and that is to make it easier for the person doing the suffocating. Without a sedative they would fight just like they do on TV, get scratched even, but if someone is already sedated, they have no clue that they're being suffocated, making it far easier for the killer. And quieter. Screaming into a pillow still makes a lot of noise."

"I'm guessing you know this from prison?"

"Where else would I know that from?" she asked, a smile bouncing off her words. She had a point. "So, I'd say we're looking for a feeble man or more likely a woman," said Birdie matter-of-factly.

"Do you think the police will have come to the same conclusion?"

"I would expect so. The pathologist will have, no doubt. Pretty shabby one if they haven't done, I'd say."

"So, we're likely primarily looking for a woman, that's probably made things a bit easier. And one with access to drugs."

"Spot on, Will."

SIXTY-SIX

Birdie wasted no time calling Cynthia. It had been fun catching up with her after all the years, and she'd spent a good deal of time thinking about how much the woman had changed, and for the good, particularly with her new career that she obviously loved. It just went to show you're never too late to learn something new. Birdie had first had the idea when they'd met, vaguely discussed it with her, and so making the call to ask the question now, she already pretty much knew the answer. It would just depend on whether Cynthia would be intrigued enough to do it, and able to keep out of any possible trouble that eventuated. When she had asked about hacking into someone's computer system, she hadn't thought that she'd be asking her friend to do just that and quite so soon. Birdie had figured it might be something for the future, though the target was never going to be something as elaborate and secure as a police database or a hospital, for instance. But a church? They probably had little or no security, making it a doddle. Anyway, all she wanted to know was who was a volunteer or employee there, and whether they had access to a key. There were bound to be emails back and forth, bound to be payroll and a list of volunteers on a roster even, because she doubted those that served coffee after worship were paid employees. Churches around the country were always fundraising and relied heavily on the goodwill and support of others, there weren't funds available for wages for all. She had to find out who those people were, and she hoped there weren't too many of them.

"You want me to do what?" Cynthia asked. Her reaction didn't sound as positive to Birdie's ears as she'd hoped.

"Come ooon," she said, drawing out the last word a little. "You know you're quite capable to do it, and this is your chance to do some good, like Will and I are doing. All we need to know is who has a key to get into the church. The police are probably already doing the same thing, but we can't get access to their information, so we're doing it ourselves."

"A couple of vigilantes are you, then? Through the back door?" said Cynthia, though not scornfully. Birdie could detect the smile at the end of the sentence.

"Let's just say I'm long done being a bad girl, it's much better to be the good girl. Maybe you'd like to help?"

There was a silence on the line while Cynthia thought about it. When she finally gave a long heavy sigh, Birdie knew what the response was going to be.

"I'll give it a go," she said. "But no promises."

"Great, I knew you would," said Birdie, doing an air punch. "Their addresses would be good if you could, but hey, we'll take what we can. How long do you think it will take you?"

"Hold your horses," said Cynthia. "Let me just think for a moment."

The line was quiet while Birdie waited. She felt like whistling to fill in the space but refrained.

"Okay," said Cynthia. "I can rearrange what I've got to do today, so let me work on it now and hopefully I'll have something to you by close of play, but like I said, no promises."

"I'm excited already," said Birdie. "I'll wait to hear from you."

Birdie sat in her chair in the big house on her own, pondering what to do next. She wondered what Cynthia would come back with and googled the church in the meantime to see when the next service was. There was one later on that evening and, of course, Sunday, tomorrow. She knew which one would be the most popular, with morning coffee served afterwards. It was a chance to mix and mingle, eavesdrop and see if she could find anything out. Not from the worshippers, not from those in the congregation, but from the volunteers, the vicar, perhaps the sexton and whoever else might be willing to chat. She called Will back and told him of the plan and that hopefully she'd have names by the end of the day. Did he want to join her at church the following morning? Of course he did.

"Should we invite Stanley too, do you think?" Will asked.

"I'll ask him," said Birdie. "I don't suspect he's one for worship, though."

"I'm not a regular by any stretch – weddings and funerals are about it."

"Like so many of us. I'll call him anyway," she said. "It will do him good. Maybe the coffee and biscuits at the end will tempt him to attend."

"Well, tell him to make sure he's got shoes on, and not his slippers," said Will, laughing at Stanley's sodden feet the previous day.

"I guess we'll need picking up, then."

"Let me know what time, then leave it to me."

"I'm excited already," said Birdie. "I'll make a hero from you."

Birdie sat in the chair in the org home on her own, pondering what to do next. She wondered what Cynthia would come back with and [illegible] ponder the [illegible] in the meantime [illegible] what the next service was. There was one later on that evening, and of course Sunday tomorrow. She knew which one would be the most popular with morning coffee served afterwards. It was a chance to mix and mingle [illegible] and see if she could find anything out. Not from the worshippers, nor from those in the congregation, but from the volunteers, the vicar, perhaps the sexton and whoever else might be willing to chat. She called Will back and told him of the plan and that hopefully she'd have names by the end of the day. Did he want to join her at church the following morning? Of course he did.

"Should we meet in Stanley before, do you think?" Will asked.

"I don't think," said Birdie. "I don't expect he'll ask for worship though."

"I'm not interested in his, um, sketch — weddings and funerals are about it."

"He's at many of them. I'll call him anyway," she said. "I wish him good. Maybe the coffee and biscuits at the end will tempt him to attend."

"Will, Will? I'll make sure the sausroll [illegible], well, sort of all slip."

"And Will, lunchtime or Sunday's sadden best, the pub's about done day."

"I'll see what I can pick up, then."

"Never know what time they leave it alone."

SIXTY-SEVEN

Back at the police station, DI Mason and the rest of the EMSOU team were working furiously on the new lead. Fortunately for them, another victim meant more clues to work with, as invariably the killer got sloppier with each body they presented. The actual times in between finding each victim hadn't changed, but as they gained more confidence often something slipped. Like leaving food wrappers behind. Why take every other piece of evidence away apart from something that linked all three victims to one room?

A fisherman had eventually stumbled upon Jonesy's body after he'd gone into the bushes to relieve himself early on Saturday morning. He'd had the shock of his life and originally thought the man was sleeping off a night on the town, but when he thought about the location, he knew it didn't fit. He'd ventured over and touched him gently, not wanting to scare him, but the body had been freezing cold. He'd checked for a pulse then recoiled at the bruises on the man's neck. There was no doubt he was dead, and had likely been there all night, if not longer. Knowing from too many TV dramas not to touch anything else, he'd immediately called the police. Being Saturday morning, the few businesses in the surrounding area were not occupied, and in the absence of CCTV footage from down the lane, their priority had been to find those business owners and hope they had private security footage of their own they could tap into. There wouldn't be many vehicles that drove down the lane towards the lake.

Teams had been set up and they'd promptly gained access to the premises and were now in possession of said footage. DC Flint and a colleague were working their way through it, but since they didn't know the exact time frame, or what vehicle they were searching for, it was a laborious job. It appeared the lane was, in fact, quite popular. They knew the body had been moved and they themselves had been in the cellars underneath the church during the afternoon, so working backwards from then, they scrolled through the morning footage first. It made sense that the person wouldn't want to drive around with a body in their boot for long, they'd want to get rid of it. Would they have waited till darkness, though? Like they had on Hunsbury Hill? It was possible.

By 8 pm, DC Flint had narrowed it down to four vehicles. One of them was a black Mercedes, and when he checked the registration, he discovered it was registered to a local funeral home, Sanders and Co. It seemed an odd vehicle to be travelling down that lane, and certainly not a common vehicle to go fishing in. From the grainy prints they'd managed to get from a nearby recording, they surmised that there were two people sitting up front. They then used the ANPR cameras to retrace the journey of the vehicle and caught it on several through the town centre. Via the number plate recognition system, they then managed to track the vehicle near the funeral home and in the vicinity of the church, as well as making the journey out towards Delapré Park and the lake area. They had to have the right one. Finally, Flint cross-checked the locations with CCTV cameras to get a better look at the occupants. The images, however, weren't clear enough to do much with.

"Do you want to follow it up now?" Flint asked DI Mason. "Or wait till tomorrow?"

She looked at the clock on the wall. It was getting late, and the team needed their rest. "I'll call in on Mr Sanders on my way home. You get yourself home."

"I'll come with you," said Flint, always up for a bit of action. He had big plans; he wasn't going to stay detective constable for any longer than he had to. He grabbed his jacket and the two set out.

Flint pulled up behind Rochelle's motorbike and the two walked towards the house together. DI Mason knocked on the front door of Duncan Sanders, the funeral director. It was opened by a burly man and the two introduced themselves, flashing their warrant cards. Even though it had been dark that night, she remembered him clearly from the exhumation.

"May we come in for a moment, Mr Sanders?"

"Of course. What is this about?" If he recognised her, he didn't show it.

"You'll likely be aware of the recent murders, I expect," DI Mason said as they walked down the hallway. Mr Sanders showed them through to a warm and inviting living room where he turned the TV off. A woman stood.

"This is my wife, Monica," Duncan said. "Do you need to speak to her too? It's the police, dear," he said, turning towards her. "They're investigating the recent murders."

"Oh," she said. "How can we help? And please take a seat." She pointed to the sofa and Flint and Mason sat down.

"I'll get straight to the point," Rochelle said. "Can you tell me why one of your vehicles was down Ransome Lane late yesterday morning, heading towards the lake?" Preamble was not her strong point and she didn't feel the need to warm them up with insignificant questions.

"One of our vehicles?" asked Duncan. "Are you sure? Only we had just the one funeral on yesterday, in the afternoon as it happens, so unless somebody took one of the cars out for some other reason that I'm not aware of… I don't know why they would, though. Are you sure you have the registration correct?"

"The system never lies on that," said Rochelle. "So, you yourself, you weren't driving?"

"No, I was in the office all morning, you can check."

"We will. Who else has access to the vehicles?"

"Several people," he said. "I'd have to check the log, but I don't have that here right now."

"Could we inconvenience you to take a look at the log this evening? We'll drop you back afterwards since it's only a short run into town."

Duncan looked at his wife, who shrugged. "Might as well," she said. "Get it over with."

"I'll get my jacket," he said and left the room.

Ten minutes later, Duncan and the two detectives entered the small building that had been a funeral home and in the Sanders family for close to a century. They followed the big man through to an office, where he sat down at a desk.

"It won't take me a minute," he said by way of explanation, and Mason and Flint watched as he checked the log to find out who had taken the car.

"Well, that is strange," he said, turning to the detectives. "There's nothing written. It seems nobody took a car out yesterday. No entry. What time did you say it was?"

"We believe late morning."

"Well, there's nothing here for yesterday, other than the actual funeral we attended later on, so I'd have to ask each staff member. Like I said, there would be no reason to use the Mercedes. All the team have their own vehicles to drive to work in." The man seemed troubled. Had one of his team taken the car joyriding? It didn't make any sense.

"So," said DI Mason, "who would have access to the keys and be able to take the car unnoticed, without writing it up?"

"But that only leaves one person."

"And who might that be?" she asked.

"My sister."

SIXTY-EIGHT

A LITTLE PART OF CYNTHIA HAD BEEN THRILLED TO BE ASKED TO BE a part of what Birdie and her friends were involved in. Her new-found skills were about to come in very useful. She just had to make sure she covered her tracks well and didn't get caught. It helped that the church database would surely be pretty simple to get into, and if she could help Birdie find the person responsible for the murders, then why not? It would be a blast. She poured a large whisky and soda and took herself to the spare bedroom where she did her work. It looked a little like a television production studio with screens attached to a large workspace at various heights. She made a start.

With barely any of the amber liquid remaining in her glass, she finally had a list that her friend would need – the names and addresses of the volunteers and employees of the Church of the Holy Sepulchre. There weren't many, the exercise hadn't been hard to do, and she wondered what else might be of use to them while she was up to no good. Or was it doing good? It was tempting to do a background check on each of the names, but she didn't have the means to hack into a police database. She assumed there'd be other ways to get the information, and no doubt her tutor would be able to help, but she couldn't exactly ask him. Right now, that was way outside her skill set. She wondered what Birdie and her friends were actually looking for with the names she'd come up with – would any of them fit the bill straight off? What could the vicar, the flower arranger, the sexton and a whole bunch of other volunteers get up to that was so bad? Everybody had murder in them, she knew that. Who would have suspected her all those years ago, when she was so meek and mild, the proverbial mouse? She hadn't been the only one with murder on her mind. Cynthia scanned the list. There were five women and three men on it. It would be unusual for the vicar to be a murderer but not impossible, and the sexton would have the perfect place to bury the body since he was in charge of the grounds. Flower ladies? Coffee morning organisers? She wondered who she was looking at, which one it might be and for what reason, and figured she'd have to wait and see what transpired. Her work, for now, was done. Satisfied that she'd got everything she could, she dialled Birdie and gave her the good news.

"Have you managed it?" Birdie greeted her.

"Of course I've managed it, it only took me as long as it does to drink a large whisky and soda. I'm quite impressed with my own actions, even if I say so myself."

Birdie smiled at her friend. Look at her now, hacking into databases like it was the most natural thing in the world to do.

"They can't trace this back to you, can they?"

"I wouldn't have thought so. I've been careful, yes, but this is all in the name of justice. And hey, so what if they catch me? I'll be dead soon enough anyway."

Birdie hadn't been expecting that and wondered if she should dig a little further since it was said so matter-of-factly.

"I'm sorry to hear that," Birdie said breezily, as if they were chatting about their next holidays.

"Happens to all of us," she said. "We're all dying at various speeds, but hey ho, I'm going to enjoy what time I've got left. We're a long time dead."

Neither of them were spring chickens, though Birdie hoped she had plenty more years in her old girl's body yet.

"That's true." Changing the subject from death, Birdie said, "Can you email me the list?"

"Sure, it's on its way to you now, so it's over to you to use the information. Let me know if you need anything else, though I'm not sure what else I can provide. I was hoping to do a background check on the names, but I can't see a way to do it."

"I appreciate what you've done, Cynthia, thanks again. I'll be in touch soon, hopefully with a result."

SIXTY-NINE

WILL WASN'T REALLY PAYING ATTENTION TO THE MOVIE ON THE TV. He was exhausted, the day had caught up with him and he was ready for bed, though he knew sleep wouldn't come, not yet anyway. The girls were spark out in their rooms and Louise was glued to the ending of the romantic comedy he'd missed most of. He sipped on the last of his drink and wondered about a mug of hot chocolate to follow. As the credits finally rolled, Louise stretched, and as she turned to him with eyes a little pink and moist at the edges, Will realised he hadn't noticed her crying at the story, though he'd heard faint sniffing.

"You're a softy," he said, smiling, and received an embarrassed grin as she dabbed with a tissue.

"I couldn't help it," she said. "What a lovely ending."

"So why are you crying?" He was bemused.

"Because everything worked out for them in the end. Isn't that what life's about? Doing your bit for someone or something special? Isn't that why you're involved in volunteering at the centre? To help those in need?"

"Okay, okay," he said, putting his hands up in surrender. "I get your point. Do you fancy a hot chocolate?"

She turned the TV off with the remote and said, "I'll make it. You look done in, you've had a tough day."

"Well, I am actually," he said. "But I'm able to make a hot drink—"

"I'll do it," she cut him off, standing up.

He knew when he was beaten. "Thanks, I appreciate it."

As Louise left the living room, Will's phone pinged with an incoming text, and he saw it was from Birdie. It read, *I've got the info. Emailing it now*. Will quickly tapped a reply with a thumbs-up emoji and clicked on the email app on his smartphone. As he waited for the screen to refresh, Birdie's email came through and he read it quickly. There in front of him were the names and addresses of eight individuals, three male and five females, including the vicar, whom he knew from his work as a gravedigger, and the sexton, whom he also knew from his work at the church. "I can't see it being Joanna or Peter," he said to the empty room, "though nothing is impossible these days."

"What's not impossible?" asked Louise as she entered with two steaming mugs.

"I'm just looking at the list of staff and volunteers from the church and I can't see the vicar or the sexton being part of this."

"I wouldn't think so either," she said, placing his hot chocolate down on a nearby table.

"Well, Peter is quite generous in size, it wouldn't take much for him to overpower somebody and suffocate them, so he wouldn't need the help of drugs. Joanna is a different story, though, she's extremely petit and would need all the help she could get."

"So, who else is there?"

"I don't recognise any of the other names actually," he said, scanning the list again. "Their addresses are here so I guess I'll go and speak to them under some sort of guise, maybe be a market researcher," he said, smiling.

"Don't go getting yourself into any mischief. I understand why you're trying to do this, but if you start posing as somebody else, you might find yourself in bother, Will Peters. I know you mean well, but I'm just saying."

"I hear you loud and clear, but I've got to figure out what to do next now."

"Well, I would start with the hot chocolate and sleep on it. Then in the morning I'm sure you'll come up with the right plan."

"Did I mention I was going to church tomorrow?"

"You? Church, Will Peters?"

"I'm not an atheist, you know, I just don't go very often."

"Not at all, more like."

"I'm going to meet Birdie and Stanley tomorrow and we're going to mix and mingle afterwards, see what we can eavesdrop into or uncover. There's bound to be gossip after the recent find. Fancy joining us for a coffee after the service?"

"I'll stay here. I'm sure you don't need four screaming young ones while you interrogate little old ladies," she added, smiling. "No, you go and do what you need to do, and I'll see you when you get back."

Will texted Birdie with his plan, such as it was: *Pick you up at 830, I'll grab Stanley then we can meet before church. How does that sound?* He clicked send. A thumbs-up emoji came back. Now all he needed to do was pray that Stanley wore suitable attire on his feet and was in a good mood when he picked him up. He'd rather have a screaming child in his ear than a cantankerous old man.

SEVENTY

It was time for the second part of the plan. The killer had hoped that three dead bodies would have been enough, but since the mayor had not heeded the message and paid up, it was only fair they carried through with their threat. There had to be the desired end result or else it had all been a waste of time, not to mention of life.

The killer slipped back into the office wearing latex gloves, not that it mattered since their prints would be all over the office anyway; it was more in case they touched something they really shouldn't do – they couldn't risk it. Once inside, they made their way to the stationery cupboard and pulled out a brand-new ream of paper, unwrapped it and slipped it into the photocopier's paper tray, then pressed the start button to warm it up. While they waited, the killer removed a Jiffy bag from the same cupboard, taking care to select one from the middle of the pack. Working quickly before somebody saw the light on and wondered what they were up to, they took the papers they'd brought with them and one by one laid them on the photocopier glass to make a copy. When all ten documents had been copied, they slipped the originals back into their original envelope before putting the copies into the Jiffy bag. The killer had been tempted to write the recipient's name on the front but that would have involved their own handwriting and they weren't stupid enough to do it with their left hand to confuse things. The killer knew when the police got hold of the envelope, as they indeed would, they'd have a handwriting specialist take a look and figure it out, so it was best to leave it blank. It was actually incredibly hard to commit a crime these days, the laboratories could do almost anything and the killer prayed that forensics wouldn't find any evidence that could be linked back to themselves. They sealed the Jiffy bag up with its self-seal and carried it carefully, not wanting it to touch anything. Anyone that witnessed them would see quite literally a mail packet and nothing more – it hadn't got anything written on it, there was no story to tell.

The killer left the office as stealthily as they'd entered and headed to their car, where they put the Jiffy bag onto the plastic sheet that covered the passenger seat. They scratched their head again. The wig irritated a little and they wondered if Jonesy had had nits. Perhaps they should have washed it before using it, though there hadn't been time.

The killer drove to the town centre and parked down a side street. Pulling up the hood of their hoodie, they grabbed the envelope and, staying close to the shadows, headed across the street to a taxi rank. When they reached the first vehicle in the queue, they slipped in the back, head down, and instructed the driver to take them to the newspaper's offices on Pavilion Drive. They would have preferred a bigger paper – a national, perhaps – but that meant a longer journey, and they didn't want to risk the information getting lost, particularly as there was no name on the front of the envelope. The receptionist would likely open it, and contaminate it with her own DNA and prints, before it was passed around the small team until someone made the connection between the information within and the dead homeless men. By that stage, it would be too late for any forensic evidence to be of use.

The taxi driver tried several times to make conversation and eventually gave up. It was only a short journey and they soon pulled up outside the darkened building on the small business estate. Again keeping to the shadows of the building, they slipped the envelope into the letterbox and added a fake limp as they walked back to the waiting taxi. The second part of the plan was now in motion. The killer instructed the driver to head back before they walked the few paces down the side street to their own car. Once inside, the killer took a handful of deep breathes to steady their racing heart then reflected on what had been set in motion.

The worst of the plan was over, the documents had been delivered. All they could do now was pray that somebody made the connection fast and watch from a distance as all hell broke loose.

SEVENTY-ONE

Birdie replied to Will's text and said she'd bake scones and they could have coffee and chat at her place before they left. There was little point driving to a café when her kitchen table would work just as well, and she'd enjoy having him there.

Will waited as Stanley slowly ambled down his front path and was pleased to see he'd got trainers on again, though the laces weren't done up. Not wanting the old man to trip, he hurried from the car to greet him and tie his laces for him. "Morning, Stanley," said Will brightly. "Let me just get those laces for you before you go headlong."

"Headlong where?" he asked.

"You know what I mean," said Will, grinning.

Stanley just wanted him to say it. "You mean arse over tit?"

"If you like," said Will, standing back up and catching the man's eyes. "Are you in a good mood today?"

"I am. My daughter popped over again last night briefly. In fact, we had a takeaway together, it was quite nice for a change. Don't normally touch Indian food, but she got me chicken something-or-other. Quite tasty."

"Chicken something-or-other," repeated Will. "I've heard it's rather good, chicken something-or-other."

"Stop taking the piss," ordered Stanley. "Anyway, it was nice to see her twice in one week, I am honoured. She must be after my money, thinks I'm going to pop my clogs sometime soon. Not that I've got much, only the house."

"I doubt it," said Will as they ambled down the path together. He wondered briefly about any relative sorting through the mountains of old newspapers stored in his home. They'd need more than a domestic recycling bin for that lot when he left the earth. When he reached the car, he opened the rear door and waited for Stanley to shuffle along. It seemed odd, picking him up on a Sunday with no books in his hand to bore the long-term patients at the hospital with. His mood was different too. Maybe it was because he was involved in something, or maybe he quite liked Birdie and the prospect of coffee and cake was having a positive effect on him.

"So, we've got the list," said Stanley, leaning forward in his seat. He'd obviously not got his safety belt on.

Will noticed. "You'd better buckle up. It's the law, even while I'm driving."

"Okay," he grumbled but did so anyway, not wanting to get Will in trouble if they were stopped. He started again. "Who is on this list, anyone we know?"

"I didn't recognise any of the names actually, apart from the vicar and the sexton obviously. I don't know any of the women, although I do know a Veronica, a different one, I'm guessing."

"I used to know a Veronica too," said Stanley, smiling.

Will caught the look as he glanced back via his rear-view mirror. "That sounds ominous," he said.

"A looker she was. It was a long time ago, though, and I doubt it's the same Veronica. She'd be about my age, I guess."

"Well, maybe it is the same Veronica, maybe she volunteers at the church. It's not a particularly common name."

"I'd be very surprised if it was. I lost her at the Glastonbury festival back in 1970. Found a better suitor, I guess. Probably had bigger flares than me."

"Ah, that's a bit different then," said Will as he navigated the thin early-morning traffic. Stanley in flares made him smile. He would have been a young man fifty years ago.

It didn't take them long before they pulled up outside Birdie's place. Stanley gazed out of the window at the big house. "Bloody hell," he said. "She lives all alone in there, is she mad?"

Will grinned as he opened the car door then noticed Birdie standing in the front doorway, waiting for them both. "She likes the space, I guess," said Will by way of explanation, and the two made their way inside and down towards the kitchen at the back. The house smelled of freshly brewing coffee and home baking and Stanley curled his nose up in delight.

"Smells good," he said. "How are you, Birdie?"

"I'm good, Stanley. I see you've got proper footwear on today," she said before smiling and leaning in to give the old man a peck on a wrinkly cheek. Stanley stood frozen to the spot for a moment. It had been some time since a woman other than his daughter had kissed him, even a quick peck.

When he'd recovered, he said, "Sunday best. I thought I'd better dress properly since I'm going to church. Though I don't suppose too many do these days." Not that Stanley was dressed up, but he did have formal trousers on along with his trainers and a pullover that was clean. What more could they ask for?

"I wouldn't know," said Will. "It's been a while since I've been."

Birdie busied herself pouring coffee and placed a plate of scones straight from the oven onto the table.

"Help yourself," she said proudly as the two men found their places and sat down. Stanley reached for a scone first, split it and spread soft butter on both halves. Since they were still warm, a tiny puddle soon formed in the centre of each piece. He bit into one and devoured it quickly before picking the second up, totally unaware he was being watched.

"Did you not have breakfast?" asked Will, amused.

"No, I was saving myself. I was hoping you might have baked, Birdie," he said.

"Help yourself to another," she said before adding, "then we can get to work." While Stanley buttered and devoured, Birdie carried on regardless. "Does anyone know the names on the list?"

"Haven't seen the list yet," said Stanley, chewing.

"Allow me to read," said Will. As Will read through the list and got to Veronica, Stanley gave another grin. "I think we've established it's likely a different Veronica," said Will for the benefit of Birdie.

"Katherine Spencer," said Stanley. "There can only be one Katherine Spencer."

"And who's that?" asked Will.

"Katherine Spencer, the stupid bloody deputy mayor!"

"Of course. Now why hadn't I put two and two together?"

"That should be easy enough to confirm this morning," said Birdie. "I'll seek her out and see where she might fit into all this. But I might just add, if it is the same Katherine Spencer, I would expect she knows about the tunnels from planning meetings or whatever. They are bound to have come up in the past with discussions around developments and roading and the like."

"Nice one," agreed Will. "It sounds likely."

"I'll take Veronica then," said Stanley, wiping butter from his chin. "Just in case."

SEVENTY-TWO

THE SCONES AND COFFEE HAD BEEN A NICE IDEA, BUT IT WAS TIME for Will, Birdie and Stanley to make their way to the church – the reason why they'd come together this morning. They wanted to mix and mingle after the service, and Will just hoped that Stanley would stay awake long enough and not sit snoring through the boring parts. He needn't have worried: the service delivered was lively and reflected on many aspects of modern-day life and current events. The vicar had done an excellent job, and Will made a mental note to thank her for her thoughts and prayers at the end. He'd never been a churchgoer, there was always something in the way, something more important or pressing going on and, with a young family, it fell into the 'too hard' basket. Perhaps he'd rethink things. The vicar had delivered a sermon that struck a chord with Will and he wondered whether Louise might like to come along occasionally. Was he being realistic, though? He'd have to see; he wasn't going to commit each of his Sunday mornings just yet.

As the congregation made their way towards the front entrance and coffee, Stanley and Birdie hung back to let everyone pass through then took up the rear along with Will.

"So, as agreed," Will started, "we'll split up, get ourselves a coffee and chat to anyone we can. Is that the plan? Eyes and ears open at the same time?"

"With the emphasis on the eight, of course, who should be reasonably easy to spot," said Birdie.

"One will have a coffee pot in her hand for sure, and we know who the vicar is," said Stanley.

"And I already know the sexton," said Will. "As for the others we're not sure of, we'll take it in turns where we can. Stanley, make sure you talk to Katherine too, seeing as you know so much about her."

Stanley harrumphed. "I suppose I could give her some grief."

"Grief isn't really what we're after, Stanley," said Will warningly. "Play nice and listen hard."

"I can do that," he said.

"And what about you, Birdie?"

"I may as well chat with the other two men and see what gives, then we'll all compare notes at the end. As long as we've covered everyone, that's the important thing."

"Then let's get to it, otherwise we'll be here all day," said Will and the three branched off. It wasn't long before each of them was standing chatting to their target, cup of coffee in one hand, custard cream in the other. Will tried to not watch the others and concentrate on what he was doing as he made a beeline for one of the women, who turned out to be Margaret. She looked after the flower arranging for the church, among other things, and seemed like a sweet soul, a little overweight around the middle and friendly enough. After chatting to her about the weather, always an easy introduction, Will asked about her week. Had anything exciting happened? Apparently something had, she'd won £10 on a scratch card. After another five minutes of less than riveting conversation, Will pretty much discounted her. He saw that Stanley had moved on from Katherine and smiled as he noted the poor woman shaking her head from side to side ever so slightly as the man moved away. He decided he'd go and restore her faith in mankind.

"I believe you're the deputy mayor," Will said kindly.

"I am, yes. Katherine Spencer, pleased to meet you," she said, putting a petite hand out to shake Will's.

"I'm Will Peters. Are you a volunteer here, then?"

"Yes, I'm on the roster this week. There's not many of us now so we take it in turns. It's quite hard to get volunteers, I'm afraid. Everyone's so busy. Including me, I guess, else I would do more."

"I know what you mean," said Will and he explained his role at the centre.

"That must be rewarding work."

"It is, though with the recent deaths it's been a worry too." *In spite of himself, he found himself watching* her face for the slightest tell or twitch at the mention of the murders, but all he saw was sadness.

"Terrible business," she said, shaking her head gently again. "I hope it ends soon and they catch whoever is responsible." At that moment Will felt somebody at his side, another parishioner who obviously wanted to bend the deputy's ear about something. It was time to move on.

"I'll leave you to it," said Will, noting her turn of phrase. He rolled the words around in his head, 'hope it ends soon…', but then, didn't everyone hope the same? Perhaps he was looking at it from the wrong angle and it was simply an innocent remark. After half an hour, most of the parishioners had ventured off on their way, leaving a few stragglers to drain their cups and finish off the last of the biscuits. Stanley, Birdie and Will were among them, and after each finished chatting to whoever they were speaking to, they made their way out to the front and into the light sunshine to regroup away from eavesdroppers. A woman walked past the church with a young puppy on a lead that strained to go faster than its owner wanted it to. Will watched as the woman yanked quickly on the choke chain, which had the desired effect of bringing it back into line, all part of its training.

"So," said Will, focusing back on his two friends, "did we get to speak to everybody we needed to?"

Stanley went first, "I never saw Veronica, sadly. I was anxious to see if she was the same one, but I think I got everybody else. How about you, Will?"

"Most people, yes, but no, I didn't see Veronica either. Birdie?"

"Nope to Veronica, but I've got her address so I think we can somehow wheedle our way in and find an excuse to chat. We've just got to think of something plausible. Did you talk to Katherine then Stanley?" She was clearly teasing him.

"She's quite nice actually," he said. "Maybe I'm wrong about her."

"Do you think she is a killer, though?" asked Birdie.

"Doubt it. Nice and petite, though."

Will and Birdie groaned at the man's thought process. If nothing else, he was a good source for their amusement.

"We'll bear that in mind."

"She does fit our size profile," said Will.

SEVENTY-THREE

Birdie came up with the plan of popping around to Veronica Lauder's house and asking her a set of market research questions – a similar idea to Will's own. He helpfully pointed out she had no ID and no clipboard *to make it even begin to look convincing*, but Birdie insisted she'd be able to make it work. Finally, Will agreed to drive to the address and wait for her to return, hopefully with some answers about Veronica's involvement with the church and any knowledge she had about the tunnels. As they turned the corner onto her street, they knew it was unlikely Birdie would get anywhere. The police were already parked outside.

"Hmm, now that's a coincidence, wouldn't you say?" Birdie said, leaning forward in her seat.

"I'd say so," said Will. "Though we are all assuming it is to do with the murders."

"Of course we are," said Birdie. "If we've come to the conclusion that it's probably a slight female and someone with access to the church, I'm damn sure the police have come to the same."

Will pulled up to the kerb, staying away from the property, and turned the engine off. They sat watching.

"I wonder how long they've been in there and what they're asking." Birdie voiced.

"How did *you* get found out?" asked Will. "When they first came to your house to arrest you?"

"That was different," said Birdie, "I had to call the ambulance. Plus, I was covered in his blood and the knife was still in my hand. It all happened so quickly with me. I didn't intend to kill him, you know."

"How interesting," said Stanley. "What had you intended to do as you stuck the knife into him? Carve a slice off?"

She rolled her eyes at him. "It wasn't planned, if you must know," Birdie replied haughtily. "We'd just had a hell of a row and it was the nearest object I could reach as I saw red. Before I knew it, he was slumped on the floor. What a bloody mess too – literally. But no, by the time the police had arrived I guess I was ready to talk. It was all a bit shocking really. So, you see I'm not much help in guessing what's going on inside there unless they've got evidence and are arresting her."

"Do you think they'll frogmarch her down the path?" asked Stanley. "Like they do on the telly? Perhaps she'll be handcuffed."

"That depends on what they've got on her," said Will. "But if they do frogmarch her, you'll be able to see if she's 'your' Veronica."

"Well, I did a Google search on each of the names," said Birdie, "and there wasn't one bit of interesting information between them all."

"What does Veronica do for a living, did you find that out?" asked Will

"Actually," said Birdie, "Veronica's name did pop up on a website and I never thought about its significance until you just said. She's a funeral director, you probably know her."

"Really? The name doesn't ring a bell, but that doesn't mean I don't know her, I suppose. I don't know every funeral director, and I meet a fair few while digging graves, obviously."

"Well, here she comes," said Birdie, nodding towards the house. "There's no handcuffs that I can see. Maybe she's helping them with their enquiries down at the station."

The three stayed silent as Veronica Lauder was escorted to one of the waiting police cars. Will noticed his contact, DI Mason, along with DC Flint. He also noticed the woman's distinctive boots.

"Okay, I don't recognise *her*," said Will, "though that doesn't mean to say I haven't met her. You women are always changing your hair and whatnot," he said, turning to Birdie. "Her boots, on the other hand, that's a different story. I've seen them before for sure. What was the funeral firm called, do you recall?"

"No, but let me look now while we're waiting."

Will glanced in his rear-view mirror as she tapped away on her phone before announcing, "Sanders & Co. Here, look, there's a picture of her." She passed the phone over to Will.

"Yes, I knew I'd seen her recently," he said, satisfied. Even though it had been the dead of night, he remembered where it was. He checked the other pictures of the staff and found the one of Duncan Sanders himself. It had been Mr Sanders that had attempted to undo the catches on the casket and had ended up flying through the air, landing face down by Will's digger. "Well, that certainly is a coincidence."

"You do know them, then?"

"Kind of, I'm not sure we've ever spoken. I wonder if she and Duncan are related – maybe brother and sister? Obviously not husband and wife since they have different surnames."

"That doesn't mean much these days," Stanley piped up. "Could live over the brush?" The trio were silent as they watched the liveried vehicle pull away with Veronica inside. Will was the first to speak as the car disappeared from sight.

"I suppose a funeral director parked at the church wouldn't give anyone cause for concern with their car, now, would it?"

"I guess not," said Birdie. "And, of course, she's got access to inside."

"Definitely not my Veronica," said Stanley unhelpfully.

"I wonder what led them to her in the first place?" Will asked.

"Maybe they sussed the car, and then CCTV cameras probably," said Birdie.

"Would she be that stupid, though? Every criminal knows about CCTV cameras, it's how-not-to-commit-a-crime 101. That church couldn't be any closer to a police station either."

"Maybe they've got something else on her that we don't know about. Or she is just helping with enquiries. An employee could have taken the car and used it in the same scenario that we're considering."

"We're not going to get to talk to her now, that's for sure," said Will, starting the engine. "I may as well drop you to both back home and spend what's left of the day with my family before it's back to work tomorrow."

As Will turned the car around to head back to Birdie's place, he noticed a man walking along with a dog. It was well behaved, unlike the puppy he'd seen earlier while waiting at the church, and it gave Will an idea.

"She's only slight now, isn't she, Veronica," he said.

"Yes," the two chimed.

"How is anybody, man or woman, going to get a live man out of a cold, dark cellar and into a car without a commotion?"

"Gunpoint," said Stanley firmly. "That's how I'd do it."

"Trust you," said Birdie. "Knifepoint more likely."

Stanley raised his eyebrows and said, "You would, though, wouldn't you?"

"Fairly visual, though, isn't it, holding a knife to someone's throat or a gun to someone's back? How about something a little less obvious?" Will suggested.

"Like what?" asked Birdie.

"I noticed a puppy earlier, not long into its training and the owner had one of those choke leads around its neck. Each time the puppy strained on the leash, she yanked it back so it would learn, and hopefully quickly. Look at this chap walking his dog," Will said, pointing as they passed by. "The dog's no longer on a choke leash, he's already been taught to be obedient."

"I see where you're going with this," said Birdie. "You think maybe it was something like a choke leash around the victim's neck, hence the bruises you saw."

"That would explain some of the bruising, wouldn't it – if Jonesy wasn't strangled, if neither of them were strangled?"

"Unless you're into bondage," said Stanley. "I mean our perpetrator, not the victims. I've seen a man on a lead before," he added, shaking his head in disgust. "Bloody perverts. Anyway, it would still look odd though, the leash part, out in public."

"How about one of those shock collars?" Birdie suggested. "That way there would be no leash attached at all, it would look much more natural to any onlooker."

"Birdie, that's an excellent idea! Something so simple and easy to get a hold of."

"Bugger that," said Stanley. "Must be some weirdo."

"I think weirdo covers most murderers in general, wouldn't you say?" added Birdie.

SEVENTY-FOUR

Back at the police station, DI Rochelle Mason and DC Stephen Flint had just finished interviewing Veronica Lauder and both were feeling rather despondent.

"Coffee?" asked Flint, as they entered the incident room.

"Please, and I'd better have sugar in it as well," she said, making her way over to her desk. What a way to spend a Sunday morning, but on a murder investigation time waited for no one. She'd take some days when it was all over, recharge her depleted batteries then. Sitting back in her chair, she crossed her hands behind her head and closed her eyes for a moment, waiting for her drink to arrive. When she heard the light tap from the mug being set down, she looked up at DC Flint and said, "It seemed like everything was going to slot into place. Or so I thought."

"Just because she's got an alibi doesn't mean to say she didn't do it, as we both know," said Flint. "Everything else fits."

"It has to be somebody with access to the church and we've been through each one now. The vicar and the sexton both have ironclad alibis, so that leaves us with three other men and three women. Margaret also has an alibi, though shaky, by the way, and

I'm not convinced about the deputy mayor, Katherine, either. She is hiding something for sure. She was as cagey as a cagey thing, so we need to have another go at her. That alibi of hers is a little too convenient for my liking. A bit forced."

"Agreed. But back to Veronica," said Flint, "she went down to the lake for sure, she admits that. She picked her daughter up on Friday at 9.30 am for the weekend, took her to the pool party in town, ran her errands, then drove the daughter out for their picnic, then back home, where the babysitter took over."

"I don't understand why you would pick your daughter up in a funeral car when you've got a vehicle of your own parked at work. She went there first, remember?"

"I suppose she could have been blocked in by another vehicle. It might have been easier to take the Mercedes if it was right there."

They mulled it over, both sipping on their coffees, deep in thought. They needed a breakthrough, and fast.

"I say we give the deputy mayor another go," Rochelle said, "and we take a deeper look at Veronica."

"Katherine has also got the right phone," piped up Flint. "It fits with the information of where the photographs were taken from and the type of device used, the details you got from the image info from the text."

"But so has the vicar. An iPhone X is pretty common. That model has been out for some time and none of these people strike me as the type to keep up with the latest gadgets. An iPhone is an iPhone until you're looking for a new one because you dropped it in a puddle or did something equally deadly to it."

Flint nodded in agreement.

"When that photograph was taken, four of the eight were in the vicinity, and by that I mean the church grounds. So, let's look at the tunnels and who says they know about them." Rochelle ticked the names off on her fingers: *"Margaret and Katherine say they've heard of them, but they've never been down there. Veronica, Anne and Sandy all say they've never heard of them, so have never been, obviously. That leaves the vicar, the sexton and Ned, who have snooped about down there. We've got absolutely no* way of knowing who is lying or telling the truth, but let's go with who says they know about the tunnels for a second. If the vicar, the sexton, and Ned say they have been in them, we have to take that as gospel, pardon the pun, for the moment. Any one of them could have taken the photo at the time we have on that text message, yet only one of them has an iPhone X – the vicar."

"But with our group, it doesn't mean they used their own phone down there. They could have borrowed, say, their husband's phone, or their child's, for example. Or used a spare. I know when I purchase a new phone, I keep the old one for a backup in case I trash the screen and it has to go in for repair. We need to find out who has access to that model of phone, not necessarily who owns one."

"Agreed. Going back to who knows about the tunnel, we are looking at the vicar, the sexton and Ned, since they are the only ones admitting to ever going down there. We need to find out who has had that phone in the past and hope it was on a contract that we can see. If they purchased it outright, not so simple."

"I'll get on to that," said Flint, making a note in his day book.

Rochelle carried on, "Then somebody had to take the body down to the lake, and so far the only vehicle we've got going down there that we can connect to our little soirée is owned by the funeral home, and Veronica Lauder herself admits she was driving it, taking her daughter to the lake for a picnic. She was back at work by 2 pm and the ANPR cameras caught her in town beforehand, running errands after she'd dropped her daughter off at a pool party. That also puts her in the middle of town and near to the church at the time in question. Katherine, however, went to the office then to the doctors' mid-morning, before she carried on home with a migraine. She didn't surface from her bed until 5 pm. No one can verify her at home all day, though. And she does have the right phone, remember."

"If we forget their alibis, it fits for Veronica and Katherine, except both state they've never heard of the tunnels, though Katherine uses an iPhone X. Remember she also has a direct link to the mayor and working for the council, I'd assume the tunnels have come up in conversation somewhere in her career. Unless we've got this all wrong and it was another vehicle, and there were several that passed down that lane, we don't have anything concrete at the moment. Too much circumstantial that can also be explained away quite legitimately. We're a long way from charging anyone."

"I hear you," said Rochelle as she sipped on her coffee and pondered for a moment.

DC Flint did the same. "What's also troubling me," he said, "is how anybody would get the body out of the cellar in the first place, and alive at that. It would be hard enough for anyone, let alone a slight person like Veronica or Katherine."

"I can only assume with some sort of threat."

"Knifepoint, do you mean?"

"Or similar, yes. Perhaps even verbal: 'If you don't come with me, something will bad happen.' Maybe somebody else was being held at another location and with the threat of them being harmed – your child, for instance – you'd do anything to prevent it, wouldn't you?"

"It wouldn't be the first time someone's child had been used as leverage in a kidnapping."

"We still haven't figured out why the perpetrator is doing this. I'm not buying because they are homeless men, that is no reason to kill them, and I'm not buying cleaning the streets up either. I know we've gone over this before, but it has to be something more."

"It's not common for killers to kill simply because they can, there's always a reason or desire behind it. This has taken some planning, and there have been three in quick succession. Normally, a serial killer doesn't attack with timings quite so close together, so I'm thinking it's not a fix type thing. No one is doing this for kicks."

"But they are doing it to send a message, and that's via the torsos of the victims, remember. The mayor himself has been of no use to us at all."

"We need to have another go at him."

"I suggest we get the team together again and refresh. If there's going to be another body, it will be soon going by *what's happened so far*. Yes, we've disrupted their operation somewhat, their location, but that might not stop them, only slow them down. However, there's a chance it will push them into making a mistake. They'll feel more pressured, no doubt."

"You're forgetting the actual messages, though," said Flint.

"How so?"

"The last one said 'checkmate'. Game over. I take that to mean the killings are finished."

"Maybe." Rochelle played with her bottom lip as she pondered. "What happens after checkmate in a game of chess?"

The two locked eyes at the realisation.

"Holy hell."

"Let's hope not."

One game over. Was another about to begin?

SEVENTY-FIVE

Stuart McGregor was always on the last minute and had been the same all through his life. As a full-time reporter at the *Chronicle*, it was a wonder he ever hit a story deadline, but somehow he managed to never let the paper down. It was a standing joke with everybody in the small team, so when he walked through the door at 8.59 on Monday morning, it was no different than any other day of the week. The bright and breezy young man was well liked by everyone, his long, fine hair, which he wore tied up in a tight bun, the envy of most of the women in the office. He relished the attention it brought him. As a single man he was constantly on the lookout for his next date, though none of his colleagues were his type particularly. He was the only one under forty and they teased him rotten, but it was all in a day's work and he thoroughly enjoyed his job. He didn't plan on staying for much longer, though. He'd big plans to move down to London and write for one of the national newspapers, live the big dream. But for now, the *Chronicle* was where it was at.

As he walked through the open-plan reception area, he flung both arms wide and shouted at the top of his voice, "Good morning, team!" He waited for the chorus of 'good morning, Stuart' back before heading across to his desk. It was a daily, light-hearted moment and one he took great pleasure in, though he knew when he moved to London, he'd have to drop his grand entrance. For now, the team enjoyed his company and spontaneity, and he'd carry on lifting spirits where he could. He stopped at the desk of a fellow staff writer and perched on the corner casually.

"How was your weekend, Bruce?" he asked teasingly, knowing full well that he'd been out on his first hot date in a long time after a recent split. "What was she like?"

"I'm not telling you anything," said Bruce coyly, though by the look on his face it had gone well.

"Are you seeing her again?"

Before Bruce could answer, a shrill scream from behind them reverberated around the office. Everyone stopped what they were doing and turned towards where the noise had come from: Amanda on reception. She was up and away from her desk, hands fastened tightly across her mouth as if she'd seen a giant rat and the action protected her. The terror in her eyes was evident even from a distance, and as she screamed again, Stuart rushed over and was by her side in a flash.

"What is it, Amanda?" he asked eagerly.

She was staring intently at something on the desk in front of her. She finally lowered her fingers but visibly trembled. A couple of the other ladies had gathered around, and Bruce found himself standing next to Stuart.

"What the—" said Bruce. There on the desk was a picture of a naked torso with a message written across it in blue ink. He could only assume, as Amanda obviously had, that the person was dead.

"Don't touch it," said Stuart, taking charge. As the rest of the office gathered round, Amanda started to relax a little, though tears streamed down her face and somebody placed an arm around her shoulders.

"Does anybody have any tweezers to pick the pages up with? Because I'd say that's a dead body." He pointed to the picture.

"I would too," said Bruce.

A hand passed Stuart a set of tweezers and he gently picked the first page up, the photocopy of the naked torso. He laid it to one side, but underneath was another with a different message clearly visible.

"Dear god," said Stuart.

He looked through each of the documents carefully, each one indisputable in terms of what it depicted.

"Is Gillian in?" he asked.

"Editor's not due until ten today," a female voice informed him.

"You'd better give her a call on her mobile, she needs to see this, and pronto."

The woman moved away to make the call.

"Who has touched these?" Stuart asked.

"Only me," said Amanda, finding her quivery voice. "I was just opening the post."

"Go get a sheet of flipchart paper from the boardroom," he instructed a woman on his right and she scurried off.

"What do you want that for?" asked Bruce.

"So I can lay these out without touching them and have a good look at them properly before we call the police."

"What are the rest of the pages?" asked another voice from the rear of the small crowd.

Stuart used the tweezers to lift a document covered in text. They waited while he read a little.

"Apart from the bodies, they look to be copies of contracts between our council and a company called Oneland Developments," he said, scanning the parts he could see clearly. There was also a printout of invoices paid to Oneland Developments. As he lifted away another document, he could see who the directors were and began to snigger in a derisory manner. He read some more, realisation of just what the documents meant dawning on him.

"What is it is?" Bruce asked.

"Well, well, what do you know," said Stuart smugly. "What I appear to have in my hands, ladies and gentlemen," he said dramatically, "are documents that show our good man the mayor has been siphoning off public money to his own development scheme, the facility for the elderly that's being built. He's been double-dipping. I'd say these invoices are more than likely fictitious and they add up to a cool two million."

A chorus of disgust filled the air.

"How do you work that out?" asked Bruce.

"Because I know who's building that development, and now I know who the directors are behind the company. When I've looked before, I've always hit a brick wall, a shell company with more layers than an onion, so it's been impossible to confirm anything. But this here," he said, pointing to a document, "links it all together. Contracts for the boys, I'd say, and the mayor is one of the boys. Jammy whatsit. With the invoices on top, he's more than creaming it in. We'd better call legal into this too. We'll need confirmation this is kosher and we can use it."

"Where has it come from, do you think?" Bruce asked.

"That is the multi-million-pound question. Who would know? It's been sent anonymously, of course; someone dropped it in. I also suspect it's someone that's involved in the recent deaths, else how would they have pictures of three bodies that we're assuming are dead?"

"Is there a note?"

"No, but the person that dropped these off must be in possession of the originals, because these are copies, and must be linked to the deaths, which is why we need to talk to the police."

"Don't you want to write the story and publish it first?"

"It wouldn't be wise under the circumstances, not with the

murders. I don't think Gillian or legal would go for that. Yes, I can write it up. It's going to take some extra digging, mind, as I haven't got everything I need here, although there's plenty to be going on with. We've got to be careful on this, we've already had three deaths. We can't be selfish and put more lives at risk."

The phone on Stuart's desk rang in the background and went unanswered as the group stood looking at the printouts before them. Stuart's mind raced ahead full speed at the opportunity, yet his moral compass was steering him in another direction. Could he take advantage of what lay before him and at least print the story of the background to the development now he'd got evidence of the corruption?

What he was struggling with were the dead bodies. They had to be connected to the documents, or else why send them all at once? He needed more.

SEVENTY-SIX

It had certainly bothered her being questioned. The whole experience had been unnerving and not something she ever wanted to go through again. But she understood that in order to catch the murderer everyone was a suspect, though the police had narrowed it down to a select few, she being one of them. She wondered how, what the criteria had been for her to be on the suspect list; what had prompted them to question her? They were too close for this stage in the game.

She had risen early and headed to work, wanting some time on her own to think things through. Life was hard sometimes, and she didn't like the fact that she was beginning to struggle, but there seemed no answer to their problems, not for the foreseeable future anyway. It was only going to get worse. A coffee shop tempted her in with the promise of freshly baked muffins and she headed inside and ordered a large coffee to go with one. The aroma was welcome to her nostrils and she found a seat at the window and made herself comfortable. Outside, people bustled by on their own way to work, but she didn't feel much like rushing, not this morning. She had always enjoyed being an early riser, it gave her time before her family got up to do her own thing and not worry about anyone else's needs but her own, if only for a few delicious minutes. This morning, she'd slipped out of the house before anyone had woken and left them to it, sure that her husband could cope for once. He'd think it strange, her not being there, though he could always call her, make sure she was all right. Her coffee arrived and she ignored it for a while, watching in the distance the comings and goings of other human beings, each with their own worries of varying degrees, coping in their own way.

Today, somebody at the newspaper would find the evidence she'd so carefully planted and make a decision about what to do with it. All she had to do was make sure that they knew the photographs and evidence of corruption were linked, in order to do maximum damage to the man she despised so much, the man that had stolen from someone so precious to her.

The shock collar had been a fascinating tool to use, and she'd witnessed first-hand the startling evidence of what the human mind succumbed to when persuaded by pain. Now, though, she needed to find one last volunteer to help, her masterplan almost complete. There was no way she could risk making the call herself, or writing a note, but she'd plans for the next best thing. After the delivery of her important message, what would happen next was down to the gods. She thought about her daughter, about to face such disappointment and upheaval, the driver for what she was doing. Her mission was almost complete – just one final act before the curtain came down to reveal the real criminal. And it wasn't her.

She knew just where to look for the right person to deliver this particular message. That part wouldn't be any harder than picking up the others had been – all keen for the money, such as it was.

Another hour later and it was time to go, so she gathered her things and left the café and half a mug of cold coffee behind, heading back to her car. She knew where to drive to, where they hung out, and it wasn't long, travelling through the backstreets, before she had someone in her sights. The young man looked like every other homeless person, unkempt, thin and in need of a good meal. Often they wore spaced-out expressions – some from chemicals, some from desperation. With her target chosen, she pulled into a side street that was more of an alleyway and jumped out. As casually as she could, she made her way back towards the young man, keeping her head down as she went. As he began to walk past, she called out.

"Excuse me."

The young man turned. "Hello?"

"Hi, I wonder if you'd like to earn a little cash?"

The man paused then said, "Doing what?" Cagey.

"I just have a small job, a message to be delivered, that's all. Nothing more." She watched his eyes as he considered what to do. It wasn't someone she knew this time, so they didn't know her either.

"What does it entail?" Still suspicious.

"I just need you to make a phone call at ten past nine on the dot. I'll tell you what to say. I need to make sure somebody gets a message is all. Can you do that? I'll pay you ten pounds."

"Ten pounds? And all you want me to do is make a phone call?"

"Yes, I have a phone with me."

"What do you want me to say?"

"I've got it written down here for you. Here," she said, pulling a piece of paper out of her bag. She handed it over and waited until he'd read what it was. She noted his raised eyebrows – did he think she was the killer? "The number to call is on the page at the top. Just make sure you get to speak to the right person – Stuart is his name."

"What if they don't answer, or are not in?"

"Then you'll need to try again, because I'm not handing over the cash until I know the message has been delivered, right?"

"I suppose," he said almost sullenly, shrugging.

"I'll stay with you, to make sure it's done. This is important."

She edged him towards a doorway. As the young man dialled the number, she marvelled again at how easy it was to use someone that wouldn't dream of going to the police unless their life depended on it, and that would soon fade, once again, into the background. Finding them again would be virtually impossible.

Perfect.

<h1 style="text-align:center">SEVENTY-SEVEN</h1>

Stuart was studying the documents when Bruce entered the conference room. "I've just had a weird phone call," he said. "Actually, you have."

"Oh?" said Stuart, only half-listening.

"Yes, and it's to do with these documents."

That caught his attention. "What do you mean?"

"I just took a call and I'd say the person was almost certainly reading from a script, because it didn't sound very natural at all."

"What did they say?"

"They insisted on speaking to you actually, but as you're busy, I pretended to be you."

"Thanks… I think."

"They said they wanted to make sure that the package had been received and that someone was taking the contents seriously, that the two things are in fact linked."

"Well, we kind of figured they are linked. What else did they say? Do you think you were talking to the killer?"

"Now, here's the interesting part, the caller said that they had been blackmailing the mayor and threatening to go to the press with what they knew about his corruption and involvement in the elderly facility and the fake invoices. They had killed three people because the mayor had selfishly refused to give into their ransom demands, and he'd let them die."

"You're kidding me," said Stuart, incredulous.

"I'm afraid I'm not, my friend. It would seem that the mayor has ignored the ransom requests and had not paid up the half million pounds demanded of him and they were now seeking help from the press, read *us*, to get the word out that not only is the mayor corrupt, but heartless and soulless to boot, with three deaths on his conscience. Obviously, the killer couldn't go to the police, but wanted the world to know what was going on, and why."

"What is so important for somebody to kill over local government corruption?" asked Stuart.

"I can only guess there's a good deal more behind it that we don't know about at this stage," said Bruce. "I wish I could have asked a couple of questions, but once they'd delivered their message, they hung up. We have no way of finding out who it was."

"A male voice?"

"Male, yes, but like I said, it was stilted, not real, so I suspect it could be somebody else reading, maybe even someone the killer had coerced."

"You think there might be another murder?"

"I don't know what to think, but I know this: the police need to be involved now."

"I agree, this is getting too dangerous," said Stuart. "It's a wicked story, though, deaths apart. Just the corruption aspect on its own and now we've got proof that it's jobs for the boys and the mayor is involved. He must be making a packet on the development, he's one of the main contractors, or his side company and wife as a director is. There is no reason why we can't carry on with that part of the story. Plenty of evidence here," he said, waving at the documents laid out in front of him. "And public interest too.

Imagine the revenue this will bring the paper! The follow-up stories could go on for weeks, go national even."

"What if what they said is correct and the mayor knew about the kidnappings and refused to do anything?" Bruce let the thought dangle in the air. "I wonder if the police are aware of any of this going on in the background?"

"Well, I think we should speak to Gillian first, let her decide." Stuart looked at his watch. "She'll be in shortly, so we can see what she wants to do then, and in the meantime, we write up as much of this as we possibly can. What a hell of a mess that's about to unfold. He doesn't stand a chance of being re-elected now. Then again, that could be the reason for the timing. There'll be more than the mayor and his wife that falls out from this lot." Realisation of what it meant filled his head. "I can see the headlines now," he said dramatically. "Mayor ignored ransom demands – three dead."

"Maybe we can work on the headline a bit," said Bruce with a smile.

"Yes, you're right there. But I tell you what, this is going to sell some papers, this is going to put the town on the map. This is going to get us the coverage we need."

"You mean *you* the coverage *you* need, Stuart," said Bruce.

"Well, that of course. It won't do my career any harm, as long as I do a good job, get the angle right, but I can't do that in twenty minutes."

"I guess you'll be pulling a late one today then," he said to his friend.

"How can we get a trace on that call now, how can we find out where that call was made from?"

"The phone company, perhaps, but I daresay the police will be able to find out about our incoming calls a lot quicker. That it went straight to your landline, and didn't go through the switchboard, will hopefully makes things easier."

"Fingers crossed," said Stuart. "Now, if you don't mind, I've got work to do. Oh, and Bruce?"

"Yes?"

"While it's fresh in your mind, write down every word that you can remember the caller telling you, so we've got it. If nothing else, to give to the police."

"Will do."

SEVENTY-EIGHT

While Stuart was trying to figure out his next move and tackle the story of a lifetime, Will was having a second cup of coffee in his kitchen before setting out for the day. He didn't feel like he'd had much of a weekend. It had been such an emotional time with everything going on, particularly seeing Jonesy laid out on a trolley in the mortuary. Having then spent most of Sunday with Stanley and Birdie at the church, he felt like he'd missed a chunk of time to recharge his batteries, both mentally and physically. He was tired of death.

There was always something going on in his life and, like everyone, he had varying degrees of problems that rose and invariably sunk away again. Will and his family were very lucky that nothing major had impacted on their lives together, though if Will paid it some thought, his own past had certainly dished that aspect out in spades – but it was now ancient history. Jonesy, Clyde and Bowie had been enough death to last Will till the end of his days, and he hoped it would be some time before any of his girls had to bear witness to it themselves, or before it crossed his path again. He scanned through the paper in front of him, glancing at the images, not really paying any attention to the mayor's re-election campaign, before loading his breakfast things into the dishwasher. It was time to leave, though he hadn't any firm commitments until he was due to take Sanjeev to his weekly eleven o'clock appointment at the hospital. He wondered how the young man fared after his own weekend, how different it would have been than what Will himself had done. Will also remembered he'd made a mental note to try harder with the guy, that he could well be lonely and in need of a friend. He wasn't strange, he had a condition, something that he had to deal with, and that's why he took him to his counselling sessions. It wouldn't be easy for him to build relationships, not on a friendship level and probably not on a more intense level, husband or wife, say, whichever he chose. He filled a flask with more coffee for later and grabbed a protein bar from the cupboard then headed out to his car, on his way to the town centre to wait for someone needing a ride.

His phone buzzed with an incoming text and he asked Siri to read it for him while he drove. It was from the Towcester Road Cemetery sexton – a grave needed digging. He instructed Siri to reply that he was available to do it later on that afternoon, and he hoped he had everything he needed in his boot, so he didn't have to drive back home beforehand. The mention of a grave made him wonder again about burying Jonesy, Clyde and Bowie. With no relatives and no one able to contribute to the cost of a funeral for the three of them, it would be down to the council – a public health funeral. While a public health funeral sounded like something for the diseased, it sounded marginally better than a pauper's funeral. He should make enquiries to see when the police planned to release their bodies and find a spot for them to be buried. He would offer to do the honours himself. It made sense that the three of them went into the same grave together. He doubted any of them would mind; they might even smile about if they were watching the proceedings from above. He'd have a word with DI Mason later, it would be a good excuse to call her.

"Sod it, I'll do it now," he said to the empty car. "No point in waiting."

He instructed Siri to call her and waited for Rochelle to come on the line. When she answered, he noted she sounded drained, just as he had felt yesterday afternoon, and assumed that the case was getting to her too. Being of ill health, she needed a break.

"You sound tired," he said, stating the obvious. "It's Will Peters here."

"Thanks for that compliment," she said flatly. "What can I do for you, Will?"

"I was just wondering when the three might be released? I guess we should make enquiries on getting them buried soon, since I dig graves and all."

"I suppose you do," she said. "I'll double-check if it's possible to release them."

"It is not up to me," started Will, "but since nobody's come forward to claim them, family-wise, I mean, it sounds like it will be up to the council to do the honours. They were still people – homeless or not, they were human beings – and they deserve to be sent off properly instead of being stored in a cold fridge, not that they can stay there."

"I don't doubt that," she said, altering her tone and adding more compassion.

"I'll wait for your call, then." Changing the subject, he said, "How are you feeling? How is the treatment going?"

"That's two questions, Will, neither of which are your business."

"Don't be like that," he said. "I'm genuinely interested how you are doing."

Rochelle must have caught herself because she paused for a moment before answering. There was no point being grumpy about it, though she certainly wasn't over the moon about her illness. "Fine, thank you, and to answer the other question, apart from the tiredness, also fine, just one more week of radiotherapy to go. It was caught good and early so my future is as bright as yours. I'll be back to normal soon enough."

"Glad to hear it," he said, adding a smile to his voice to try and lighten her mood. "I'll wait to hear from you, then I can liaise with the council about their arrangements."

"I'll be back when I know more," she said before hanging up, leaving Will feeling a little sorry for the woman. He wished he could make her feel better somehow, lighten her load. He suspected she was carrying the burden all on her own.

STUART PORED over the documents in his editor's office. The paper's legal representative perched on the corner of her desk, his sharp navy suit adding formality to the occasion. Gillian Roper, with all her years of experience at a newspaper, would hopefully throw light on what to do next. Had it been up to Stuart alone, he would have written and printed the story and then gone to the police, but it wasn't his call with something so important. He also didn't want any more lives to be lost – three deaths in a week was already three too many, and if there were a fourth, it would have been on his conscience. Still, it was the scoop of the century and he knew it could make his career if he handled it well.

"While these documents explain obvious corruption on the mayor's part," said Gillian, "they are certainly no reason why somebody might kill. I find it hard to believe that just because he's on the take, that he's behind the company building the elderly development, that that's reason enough for someone to kill three people."

"I don't get it either," said Stuart, "but that's all we have to go on. It's a shame we can't ask the person that dropped the package off some more questions."

"That would be too easy, I suppose," she said. "But at least we had the anonymous tip-off and confirmation that the two events are linked. So, here's what we know," she said, sitting back in her chair and crossing her legs. She counted out on each finger as she went: "One, the mayor is up to his eyeballs in the doo-doo. Two, somebody has found out; I'm assuming it's someone close to the paperwork rather than a family member, so maybe a council employee. Three, the kidnapper gave ransom demands that were never met and three people lost their lives. Four, this person is serious, so will they kill again? And five, there has to be another reason, other than the mayor getting even fatter on the side project he's running. We've certainly got a story," Gillian finished. "I think we should get it written up, see how it looks, then I'll give the mayor a call so he can seek advice and give us his side, though I rather doubt he'll talk to us. Right now, I'm calling the police."

The man in the navy suit nodded his confirmation.

"I think that's the best course," Stuart said, relieved.

"Right, then you've got until 10 pm to get this finished."

Since Stuart had had the rug pulled out from under his feet before, he jumped from his chair and almost ran back to his own to add some flesh to the bones of what he'd already started.

SEVENTY-NINE

Editor Gillian Roper picked up her phone and searched for the detective's details before making the call.

"I think it's best you come into the office as soon as you can, you'll want to hear this," she said.

DI Rochelle Mason didn't know whether to be angry or ecstatic at the editor's news. As she sat opposite her more-acquaintance-than-friend, the pieces started to fall into place. The mayor, she knew, was involved up to his weak neck, since he'd finally told them about the texts he'd received. If only he'd said something earlier… He had been released on police bail and hadn't said much more, despite her heated questioning methods – too feeble and likely too ashamed of not saying something sooner about the ransom demands. Three people had died needlessly because of him and she wasn't going to let that go.

When Gillian Roper had delivered what she knew, it was over to DI Mason to make the most of the extra evidence.

"What I need to do now," she said to Gillian, "is find out who

329

called that number and where from. I'm taking these documents with me, though I suspect you'll already have copies and I doubt very much there'll be any usable forensic evidence on the ones that were sent to you."

"Stuart was very careful, he handled everything with tweezers. Nobody's touched them except Amanda on reception, but like you say, chances of there being anything useful on them are virtually nil."

"I guess I should thank you for sharing these with us anyway, it does place some pieces of the puzzle together."

"We should work together more, we need each other. I hope that CCTV footage I've given you helps too. You might make something of the figure delivering it, but it's not very clear. It's over to you now, the story will be printed just as soon as we've spoken to the mayor and asked for his side of events."

"I get you've got a job to do, but I really do wish you'd phoned us as soon as you'd got this. We might have been able to do something sooner. Now, the caller will be long gone."

Gillian shrugged. "We'll agree to disagree on that, we've held nothing back from you. We work in different industries, private and public; our wages rely on us selling newspapers, your wages rely on taxpayers. It's as simple as that."

It was back to money.

"Right then," said Rochelle, standing. "I've got to go, but let me know when you run this, won't you?"

"I can do that. Like I say, we should work more together, have a mutually beneficial working relationship."

Rochelle nodded her agreement.

As she left the *Chronicle* building, heading towards her bike, she glanced around at the cameras outside that covered the area where the package was dropped off. She didn't often drive her motorbike so soon after her treatment, but when Gillian called, it had been easier to slip into her leathers and drive across instead of waiting for a taxi, it was only a short journey. It was important that she worked with the editor, often a mine of information and one of her sources when it suited the woman. The police needed the press on their side and vice versa – editors were always looking for a scoop. Still, it had been worth a visit. She mulled the documents and their implications over as she flew back through traffic towards the satellite office and the rest of the EMSOU team.

EIGHTY

As Will steered his car into Greenwood Road, he marvelled at the fact that, apart from a quick drop off on Friday, it had been a whole week since he'd last pulled up outside the young man's brick terraced house to take him to the hospital for his session. It'd been the day after the exhumation, tiredness the reason he'd had fallen asleep waiting for Sanjeev and the reason why the lad had wandered off on his own. Will had then experienced the wrath of Sanjeev's father. And Dr Kumar had been clear about what would happen if it ever occurred again. There was no reason why it would, but it played on Will's mind as he waited outside the young man's house.

Will knew what would be taking place on the other side of the front door, that it would be at least another five or six minutes before he saw the whites of Sanjeev's eyes and then there would be several more minutes waiting as Sanjeev checked and double-checked and checked again that the front door was locked properly. Will hoped that Sanjeev was having one of his better days. After a full five minutes, Sanjeev finally made his way away from the front door towards the car. Will quickly jumped out to open the back door for him – anything to speed up the mission to get Sanjeev to his hospital appointment. As usual the young man wiped the seat three times with a cloth which he carried in his manbag before deciding it was safe to sit down. Thinking back, Will couldn't remember seeing him do that when they were all in the car together on Friday, though he didn't ask about it. The last thing he wanted was to upset him about why he might or might not have done something in the recent past. It was Will's task to deliver Sanjeev to his therapy session as close to on time as he possibly could, and they set off towards the general hospital. Remembering his own mental note to engage the young man in more conversation, he made a start.

"So, Sanjeev," he said. "What did you do over the weekend?"

"Same as usual, nothing," came the reply.

"Did you go out at all?" Will asked.

"Only to Aldi."

Will debated whether to tell him about what had been going on in his world, and since the conversation was falling flat with the questions he'd already asked, he figured it might be a way of engaging him.

"Well, I had quite an interesting weekend," he started. He waited to see if Sanjeev would enquire about it, but he didn't, so Will pressed on anyway. "Did you hear about the third death in the town, by chance?" He looked in his rear-view mirror, searching Sanjeev's dark eyes, but nothing seemed to register, and Will wondered if he kept abreast of local news. Maybe he wasn't interested or had missed the story. A couple of beats passed before Sanjeev answered.

"Tell me."

Will smiled and told the story of what he knew of each of the three deaths, in case Sanjeev hadn't been aware, and particularly of the visit to St Sep's on Friday afternoon, after they'd dropped Sanjeev back home. He drew the line at telling him about the tunnels and their adventures down there and what they'd found, and kept it to specifics that he might have read in the newspaper. He chanced another question, "Did you know there were supposed to be tunnels underneath the church?"

"Yes, I know of the tunnels," said Sanjeev bluntly. "I've been down there once."

That surprised Will, because it wouldn't be clean, not in the way that Sanjeev liked things.

"When was that? Can you remember?"

But Sanjeev had gone, his mind on something else, and Will never did get an answer to his question. He tried again with a different subject, reverting back to the weather. It was every British person's fallback conversation starter, but in this case Will got nowhere. By the time he pulled up in front of the hospital doors that Sanjeev needed, his mouth was dry from talking, mainly to himself. Sanjeev had stayed silent for the most part, but Will hoped the young man appreciated his trying.

"I'll wait for you," he said. "And I won't fall asleep on you this time, I promise. I'll be right over there." He pointed to an empty space, hoping he could get to it while Sanjeev made his way into the unit and that no one pulled into it in the meantime. He was in luck. As Sanjeev's glossy black hair vanished inside the building, Will reversed into the space so he was pointing in the right direction, ready for the off, when Sanjeev returned. Not risking a nap, he pulled out his phone and flicked through the apps, trying to find something to amuse him before finally giving up and deciding on people watching for the remainder of the time. In his head, he tossed around what they had done over the weekend, what they'd discovered, though there wasn't a great deal of anything that was concrete evidence, it was all assumption. He wondered how DI Mason and the rest of her unit were faring. They certainly had greater resources at their fingertips than he, Birdie and Stanley ever would. He checked the clock. Another five minutes and Sanjeev would be making his way out.

As he sat there watching the door, he saw a familiar face leaving the building, though it wasn't Sanjeev's. Could it be…? He sat up taller in his seat, straining to double-check who he was looking at through the windscreen. There in front of him was Katherine Spencer holding a youngster's hand. The two paused for a moment and Will watched as Katherine turned as if she was waiting for someone else to come through the door. A couple of seconds later, she was joined by a woman that Will had only just recently become acquainted with, Veronica Lauder. She also held the hand of a child. As Will looked at the four of them, from one face to the next, he realised something else the two women had in common, apart from their matching Chequered coats. It pulled at his chest and he sighed loudly at the injustice of it all. Yes, the two women knew one another from the church, but there was something else, maybe something even more special that bound them together. Beside each of them stood a young child, each wearing a smile as big as a boomerang, and both using crutches. As Will looked closer, there was no mistaking who their mothers were – they were holding hands with them. As the group slowly moved away, Will watched the children, their legs moving awkwardly compared to their mothers', their disability clear for all to see.

He spotted Sanjeev heading his way and debated what to do. Common sense prevailed, he could hardly run after the women and children – what would he say exactly? Plus, he had a duty to look after Sanjeev, and get him home safely. He was about to start the engine and pull forward when he spotted a taxi pull up further down, and saw the unmistakable blue hair of DI Mason as she got out the rear seat, there for her own treatment.

"I'm ready," said Sanjeev, pulling him back to the present. "Please take me home."

EIGHTY-ONE

WILL KNEW BY NOW THAT IT WOULD ONLY BE FIFTEEN MINUTES OR so before Rochelle would have had her radiotherapy and would be back outside, ready to get back to work. His quandary now was what to do with Sanjeev, because he didn't want to miss the opportunity of 'accidentally' bumping into DI Mason when she returned after her session. Yes, he could ring her, but face to face was his preference, and either way there was the problem of what to do with his charge, who was waiting patiently for his lift back home. As he thought about what he'd seen only moments ago, he wondered about the greater implications and if there were indeed any. Just because two women had something in common concerning their children, did that make either of them a murderer? Through his own investigations with Birdie and Stanley, he'd deduced that the killer was someone slight who was connected to the church, and maybe the police had come to the same conclusion, but now seeing these two suspects had children with disabilities, he wondered if the motive was buried deep in either of the women. He thought about Bowie, Jonesy and Clyde, and how they'd suffered the bruises around their necks, the messages on their chests, and he struggled to find an answer as to how it all fitted together. He needed more. He needed knowledge that he wasn't privy to rather than his own logic and that of two old people going into overdrive and coming up with something that could quite possibly be so off course it wasn't true. As DI Mason walked into the building for her treatment, Will heard Sanjeev trying to get through to his brain while he was ignoring him. The young man needed certainty as to what would happen next.

"Sorry, Sanjeev," he said. "I was miles away. What was it you said?"

"Please take me home," he said simply.

"Do you have anything else you need to do in town? Somewhere I could drop you, perhaps?" Will already knew the answer – but he'd been to the library on Friday, hadn't he? Maybe he'd like to go again.

"No," said Sanjeev flatly. "Please take me home."

Will knew he couldn't get Sanjeev back to Greenwood Road and be back at the hospital in time for DI Mason to come out. He needed something else, he needed to occupy Sanjeev in a way that he would be happy with, and preferably one that didn't take Will too far away. Then it jumped out at him – the café! He'd been there with Birdie.

"Sanjeev, would you like a cup of coffee?"

That flummoxed him and Will could see the thought process whirring round inside his head, the young man wore it on his face.

"Perhaps I can get you a sandwich? It's lunchtime, after all." Will was hopeful. He'd remembered the café that he and Birdie had sipped coffee in not that long ago, and it was only around the corner. "How about if I get you a takeaway, would that be better for you?" asked Will, figuring that it would help with the cleanliness issue, that Sanjeev might be happier sipping from a cardboard cup than sitting down at an alien chair and table. Maybe he had a wet wipe in his bag?

"How about it?" Will tried again. "I'll walk with you and you can choose, and then we can either come back to the car and eat, or we can stand over there by that bench," Will said, pointing. "What would you prefer?"

Again, Will could see confusion as the young man sorted the words out in his head. He tried a different tack. "Let's walk," he said and headed slowly towards the café, hoping that Sanjeev would follow and enter without any fuss. Maybe his issues only arose when he touched something and if he didn't need to touch anything there wouldn't be a problem? The two entered the café and Will led the way with Sanjeev at his side, conscious that what he was doing could backfire on him big time, but hoping that it would pay off and help get Sanjeev out more and being sociable. They joined the short queue.

As they waited, side by side, to be served, Will heard a voice call out to Sanjeev. The young man turned his head at the same as time as Will to see a man now standing next to them. He was dressed in scrubs.

"Father," said Sanjeev.

"Hello Sanjeev, what are you doing here?"

Though the question was asked of his son, the man's eyes were directed at Will, who tried to read his expression. Was he in trouble again?

"Hello Dr Kumar," said Will. "I'm pleased to meet you finally." He put his hand out to shake. The man looked down at it and eventually took it.

"May I ask what you're doing here?" he asked. His tone oozed displeasure.

"I thought Sanjeev might appreciate a coffee and a sandwich before I took him home. Is there a problem?"

"No," he said. "Have you bought coffee for Sanjeev before?"

"Sadly, no. I thought it about time I did, though," said Will. "We are just heading back to the car; we don't have a lot of time." He pulled out his best smile – Will wasn't going to be intimidated by the man.

"Carry on," he said, as Will picked up their order and prepared to leave. "Nice to finally meet you."

"Likewise," said Will. The pair said their goodbyes and hurried back outside to the car. He was pleased neither Sanjeev nor his father had been an issue in the moment, and that he'd been able to finally meet the surgeon, but he also hoped he wouldn't later find himself in trouble for digressing from the usual plan. Back outside, Will waited patiently with Sanjeev as he sipped his drink and they waited for Rochelle to leave the hospital. He knew that while he had Sanjeev on board it would be difficult to drive her back himself, but still the plan was to accidentally-on-purpose bump into her and he was going to do his damnedest to make that happen. He was about at the bottom of his coffee when the door finally opened, and DI Mason locked eyes with him. He pretended to look surprised, told Sanjeev to stay put, and walked the three or four paces across to her.

"Am I supposed to believe this is a coincidence?" she asked testily.

"It is indeed fortuitous," he said, "because I have something you might be interested in."

"What's that, Will?" she said, looking for her phone, no doubt to organise her taxi back.

"I suspect you've come to the same conclusion as I, that it may be between two women, Veronica and Katherine, and I guess you've already done your background, but I just wanted to inform you of something you may or may not already know. It might help."

"And what's that?"

"They both have disabled children who have difficulty walking unaided. I'm no doctor, but maybe something like muscular dystrophy? I don't know, you'd have to check."

"What's that got to do with anything?"

"It could be a reason, another commonality. I'm saying, if you didn't already know, it might be another lead for you."

"I thought I'd told you to stop playing Sherlock."

"I can't help it," he said, pasting his best smile on his face. "Anyway, it's over to you, I just thought you might like to know." He held up his hand in a light wave as he returned to a waiting Sanjeev and the two went back to the car. He didn't bother to offer her a lift back this time.

ONCE BACK AT THE STATION, she headed for the office of DCI Karen Miller, and filled her in what she'd learned. Something told her to throw in the titbit that Will had shared with her, what Katherine and Veronica had in common other than the church. She'd learned early on in her career not to leave the slightest thing out; nobody knew the level of importance that any one piece of information could have on a case.

She'd sent the original Jiffy bag, which was now safely enclosed in an evidence bag along with the documents, on to forensics for further analysis. She doubted if there'd be much to look at, but they might get lucky.

"I've got DC Flint putting pressure on the phone company," Rochelle said. "We need to know where they called in from. I just hope it wasn't a damn disposable again."

"Have you seen the footage from the newspaper's cameras as yet?" Miller asked.

"Not yet, ma'am, though the editor says there's nothing to see."

"Doctored?"

"Doubt it. Why would they? Apparently, a shape can be seen, but no detail. Perhaps when we add the other local businesses' footage to it, we'll see more. Fingers crossed for a slip up on the killer's part. We need so much more to be able to charge anyone at this stage and we're not even close."

"Boss!"

The two women turned to where DC Flint was frantically waving his arms in the air.

"You'll want to hear this," he shouted as he made his way over.

"Go on."

"The phone call was made from a disposable again, but tech have managed to narrow the location right down to Bridge Street."

"Excellent!" DCI Miller said. "I want that camera footage."

"Ordered it, off to get it now," said Flint. His smile couldn't have been any wider, his excitement at the breakthrough on full display. It was well overdue.

"I'll come with you," said Rochelle, suddenly feeling a lot less tired than she had been only minutes ago. Would they finally see the face of their killer?

EIGHTY-TWO

As the pair pored over the screen, the caller could be clearly seen at the allotted hour. Flint slammed his fist down hard on the desk.

"Got you!"

Over his shoulder, Rochelle looked at the surrounding details of what else was going on as the male made the call.

"Not so fast," she advised as she pointed to the screen. "It's obvious he's reading from that piece of paper in his hands, and that fits with what we've been told, that the call sounded stilted, but who is the woman? She moves away quickly after the call, as if she doesn't want to be there."

"We need to follow both of them, see who they are."

"Get the dots joined up with local camera footage and see if you trace either person back to a vehicle. Either or both had to get to that spot somehow. Let's hope it was with their own car. Then cross-check that with ANPR. Start that back from the beginning again," she said. "You take the male and I'll take the female, and we'll jot down everything we can see."

After half a dozen more playbacks, there wasn't much more of note.

"Female. Long, dark, straight hair and I'd say around five-five. Chequered coat. Could it be the deputy mayor? Fits her profile more than Veronica's, though it's almost impossible to confirm yet, way too grainy."

"Male. Unkempt, slim, collar-length hair, maybe five-nine? Hoodie and parka-style jacket. Popular with street people. Another homeless person?"

"It's something to consider, isn't it? Three deaths, all of them rough sleepers. Are we looking at our next victim, do you think? I was hoping the 'checkmate' message was the end of it."

"A game of a different kind, like we talked about?"

"Perhaps."

"The killer sent those images and documents to the newspaper. Surely nobody else would have access to the torso pictures."

"Agreed."

"Our mayor hasn't coughed up the cash, so they've given the story to the *Chronicle* to expose him – at great personal risk to themselves, I might add."

"Something is extremely important to them. Why else would you risk it? They didn't need to send the images. The documents on their own would have exposed the corruption side of things."

"I agree. They wanted to make sure the world knows what he is responsible for. He could have stopped the deaths and what better way than to publish such graphic images?"

"The newspaper won't print those, will they?"

"Well, which family members are going to complain? There's no identifying features on either, they could be anyone, and since nobody has come out of the woodwork, despite us trying to trace any loved ones with so little to go on..."

"Somebody is pretty upset about something and prepared for the fallout should they themselves be exposed, that's for sure."

The two sat in silence while they thought through what was

being said. Will's comment about seeing Katherine and Veronica at the hospital with two young girls... Could there be a connection?

"You have children, don't you?"

"I sure do, why?"

"What would you do for them? How far would you go if their world was in trouble, say?"

"In trouble? In the worst possible way, do you mean?"

Rochelle nodded.

Flint answered almost immediately. "Cliché, but I'd go to the ends of the earth. There's nothing I wouldn't do for them if I had too, and I'd suffer..."

"The consequences afterwards," she finished with him.

Realisation dawned on them both. "It's a parent, and I think I'd go out on a limb to say *she's* a parent, which fits with the victims being drugged before being smothered. Both Katherine Spencer and Veronica Lauder have children with walking difficulties. We need to find what connects those two children with the corruption aspect, because it could be they're linked. Add that to the extra CCTV footage and hopefully we'll get a clearer picture of just who was involved in that call."

IT WAS AROUND 8 pm that evening when they drew a little closer to knowing *who the killer was*. After hours of trawling through footage from various cameras in the town, it had been a chequered coat that had got them that bit closer. DC Flint had spotted it again. Though the wearer no longer had long dark hair, and while it could well have been someone else with the same coat, the ANPR data had shown which of their two female suspects had driven their vehicle into town that day and within the time frame they were looking at.

"Bring her in," DI Mason instructed.

"It will be my pleasure," said Flint.

EIGHTY-THREE

MASON AND FLINT WERE GLAD TO BE FOLLOWING THE CASE
through as the local detectives. Even though the EMSOU team were running things, it was a privilege to work alongside them and be involved. It wasn't often the town had murder investigations to work on and the experience for them both would not harm their careers. Since their discovery from ANPR that Veronica Lauder had been in town that morning, they had picked her up from work and she was waiting for her solicitor so that they could begin a formal interview. DI Mason had a few harder questions for the woman to answer this time around. While she waited, she called her acquaintance at the paper in the hope that she'd change her mind and wait to print the story.

"Not a chance," Gillian reiterated once again.

"Thought not, but I had to ask. Now I need something from you, if you want to help."

"What's that?"

"All hypothetical, of course."

"I wouldn't expect anything else."

"Right. Well, hypothetically, what do you know about children with walking disabilities?"

"Nothing at all," Gillian said. "But it's a lead you're following up on."

Gillian's light laugh filled Rochelle's ears loud and clear. Obvious, yes, but worth a try. Sometimes a reporter knew a lot more about the town's goings-on and Rochelle wanted to tap into that knowledge vein.

"Okay, I know, I know, pretty obvious," Rochelle admitted. "Tell me."

"You'd have to ask Stuart, he's our local hive of information, but I'm afraid he's up to his eyes in it. I believe there's a big story about to break anytime now."

Rochelle wanted to jump down the phone and slap some sense into the woman, but cooled her temper.

"I'll take my chances. Kindly put me through."

Rochelle heard the phone click and wondered if she'd been cut off. Just as she was about to toss her own phone to one side, a male voice finally came on the line.

"Stuart?" she asked hopefully.

"Yes, DI Mason, what can I do for you?"

"I'm told you're the fountain of knowledge and I need to hear what you know around children's disabilities – maybe walking disabilities, locally."

Silence replaced their words, and after several beats, Rochelle checked they were still connected.

"Hello?"

"I'm still here, just thinking. Give me a minute."

She could hear a tapping sound as his fingertips flew across a keyboard, and she hoped that, instead of focusing on his scoop, he was finding what she was after.

Finally, he said, "Here we go."

She waited, refraining from letting out the screaming fit she was holding inside.

"Sunny Nook is closing down."

"The care home?" Suddenly it seemed so obvious. "Tell me what you know."

"Since paid placements were scrapped and personal budgets were issued directly to the families with kids in need, the home is no longer viable. They can't plan ahead any more because they've no idea how many weeks families will book their services for. They've been used to having core regular residents, but the 'less desirable families', shall we term them, would rather have that money paid directly to them so they can go away on holiday, for instance, instead. Not what it's intended for, but that's the less motivated of society for you. The disabled child goes without their support, and the family go to Spain off the back of it. The home can't balance its books and the casualties are the legitimate residents that need the support the home offers."

Rochelle digested what she was being told. Was it reason – personal enough, perhaps – to make the mayor pay? For three innocent young men to die?

"I'm guessing you think that's the link?" Stuart asked.

"I'm not saying anything yet. When is it due to close, the home?"

"End of next month."

Rochelle hung up without saying goodbye; he'd get over her rudeness, no doubt. DC Flint was at her shoulder and she turned to look up at him.

"Did you catch that?"

"Makes sense," he said. "I'd be angry too if my little one counted on that type of support and it was suddenly taken away."

"Not in cutbacks, though."

"No, but it's still a strategic local government decision. It will have been decided upon and signed off on by the mayor or someone high up in council, I'm guessing."

"Back to him again, another common denominator in all this sadness."

"If Veronica Lauder and Katherine Spencer have disabled children, do you think both women are involved in this elaborate plan?"

"It's a fair point, and one we should look into because it would explain a few things. Katherine Spencer could easily get access to the relevant documents, whereas Veronica Lauder has easy access to drugs, and both have access to a black Mercedes."

"First thing's first: are both their children currently residing at Sunny Nook? Check that. Then let's look at the crossovers, such as their vehicles, alibis, and see if they have the same coats even, and turn over every other piece of evidence, no matter how small. If they each have access to a black Mercedes, maybe the plates have been swapped at some time then back again. They could have done that to try to confuse us."

"On it, boss," he said, half-sprinting back to his desk to make a start, leaving Rochelle deep in thought. She needed to update DCI Miller with their latest theory, though she'd wait for Flint to confirm the connection first. It only took a moment before he had the answer.

"Boss," he shouted across the room. "Affirmative to both kids at the home."

All they needed to do now was bring in Katherine Spencer and let the two women know the other was also being questioned. There was no other tactic quite like it, each woman motivated to spill before they were stitched up by the other. Who was going to get in first?

EIGHTY-FOUR

ACROSS TOWN, WILL WAS GETTING CHANGED INTO HIS gravedigging clothes, which thankfully were still in the boot of his car. The image of the two women with their children outside the hospital doors had not left his mind. Was there anything in it? What he didn't know, of course, was what was going on in the background, the evidence of the corruption that had been conveniently deposited at the newspaper's offices, and what was now slowly unravelling back at the police station after he'd reported his observation of the two women and, more importantly, their two children.

Approaching the small digger, he started the engine then paused in his seat for a moment as the gentle throb worked tiny ripples through his body like a decrepit massage machine. It was better than nothing, he mused, as he dropped his head back and leaned into the vibration. In a perverse sort of way, the motion eased his tired bones a little. He'd called Birdie on his drive over to the cemetery and updated her on events. She hadn't offered much back by way of possible explanation and had vowed to fill Stanley in. They'd agreed to talk after he'd completed his work, but for now, he'd a grave to concentrate on digging.

. . .

ON THE OTHER side of the cemetery, making her way up the path with a small bunch of flowers in her hand, was Katherine Spencer. She made her way towards a grave she knew so well, the place where she often came to chat to her daughter. Oh, how she wished they could converse in person. What would she have to say about what had been going on? In another couple of weeks, she'd have been fifteen, had she still been alive, had the driver not taken her tender years and tossed them away as roughly as they'd tossed her body off the bonnet of their car. The coroner had ruled it an accident, and no charges had ever been brought, but Katherine knew differently. Amelia Spencer had lain in a coma for three days before finally passing away, and there wasn't a day that went by that Katherine didn't think about her. She removed the old brown stems and headed across to the rubbish bin to dispose of them before rinsing and refilling the stone vase with fresh water from the fountain. Once she was back at the graveside, she kneeled and tidied the edges of debris and replaced the vase by the headstone, which she wiped with a cloth from her bag. Satisfied everything was in order, she transferred a kiss, via two fingers, to the name carved into the marble. Amelia had only been eleven years old. She stayed and chatted for a few more minutes before making her way back down the path towards the entrance and back to work.

THAT WAS when Will spotted her, or rather her coat. A closer look told him his mind wasn't playing tricks on him. Once he knew for sure she'd left the grounds, he turned the digger off and trotted across to the spot where he'd just seen her. Quickly, he scanned the headstones looking for the reason for her visit. It only took him a moment to find what he was looking for: Amelia Spencer. He did the rough date calculations, deceased at age eleven. Realisation hit him – he'd already been to the spot once before, and recently. It had also been the place where he'd found the blue pen, the one he'd dropped into the police station. He made the call without hesitation.

"Yes, Will," she said, short and exasperated.

"The blue pen I dropped in."

"What of it?"

"I'm at Towcester Road Cemetery and I've just seen Katherine Spencer visit a grave. She has a daughter buried here, and it was around the same spot where I found the pen."

All he heard before Rochelle rang off was: "Spencer has just left the cemetery on Towcester Road, find her!"

Will went back to his digger, wondering what he'd just set in motion. By the time he'd reached it and turned it back on, blue lights and sirens filled his senses, and he could guess the rest.

What he didn't know, not for sure, was why.

EIGHTY-FIVE

IT HADN'T TAKEN LONG FOR KATHERINE TO BE SWIFTLY PICKED UP and driven to the police station for questioning. As she was escorted down a bland, concrete-walled corridor, she'd been shocked and surprised to see Veronica being escorted into a room not far ahead of her. The strategic move on the detective's part had the desired effect and Katherine immediately called out to the other woman; the set-up couldn't have worked any better. Both women now knew the other was in the building and helping the police with their enquiries. Who would crumble first?

DI Mason started with Veronica Lauder. The woman, she had to admit, surprised her with such a stoic attitude and gave them precious little. Even when CCTV footage and ANPR data explained her movements, she sat stony faced and refused to answer their questions, but DI Mason was used to such behaviour. Time would see her relent eventually; it always did with those that were not hardened criminals. Being left to stew was also an opportunity to think of a way out – for themselves.

After a full twenty minutes of getting nowhere, Rochelle swapped rooms to start the interview with Katherine Spencer.

"We know you took copies of those documents," DI Mason said, "so why don't you tell us your side of the story? At what level was your involvement in the master plan, and the deaths of three young men?"

Nothing.

"They weren't meant to die, were they, the three men?"

Nothing.

"Unless you start talking like your friend next door, you're going to take the rap for this. How does that make you feel?"

Nothing.

"This isn't the TV, you know. If you don't speak, we'll have no choice but to hold you, and what will happen to Saheli then?"

At the mention of her daughter's name, something flickered across her face. DI Mason knew she'd hit a nerve.

"Look, think of your family now. Think of yourself and how you are going to support your daughter. The more you can help us sort this mess out, the better it will be for you in the long run. Don't take the rap for something you didn't do yourself. Murder is a serious offence and carries a heavy prison sentence."

"What will happen to her now?" Katherine asked quietly.

It was a start and Rochelle knew she had to keep her talking. "That's what you need to concentrate on, looking out for her, for her future. Wouldn't you like to be a part of it?"

Katherine nodded.

"Then tell us your version of events."

And so Katherine was the first of the two to incriminate the other. An hour and copious notes later, DI Mason went through the same exercise with Veronica, who had since lost some of her stamina to stay quiet and eventually gave them her side of what had happened, incriminating Katherine to take the fall. By 5 pm, both women had told the exact same story almost word for word and the detectives were no further forward in making a charge stick. DI Mason sought advice from the SIO on their next move.

"Stalemate," she offered DCI Miller. Realising her choice of word, she added, "Huh, more bloody chess terminology." Tiredness swept over her as the two women stood by the vending machine. She pressed for a Snickers bar and waited for it to drop. "They'll both be charged with murder at this rate, which is stupid, though you can't argue their loyalty to the cause and each other."

"Maybe a night in a cell will encourage one to start telling us what really went on. Unless, of course, they did in fact split the tasks and both committed the murders. In that case, nothing will change. Factoring in either stolen documents or illegally obtained drugs really isn't going to add much to their sentences. They're going down for fifteen plus either way, though if we're talking two or more victims, my money is on a whole of life order," said Miller.

"I need to spell that out more. If they are each figuring that they'll be sentenced to fifteen and be out in eight, say, a whole of life order might just be the ignition to start the fire under one of them. If either is responsible for none or one death, premeditated or not, that's a huge difference in sentence. I know which I'd rather receive."

"Try it," suggested DCI Miller. "Have another go at them both in a couple of hours, but don't go on too late. We don't want to fall foul of their eight hours' uninterrupted sleep time and give the defence unnecessary loopholes."

"We might need an extension on this one, though let's hope not."

"I think we might see some action from Spencer first. Lauder has shown no signs of giving, not yet. Mark my words, Spencer will be the first one to sing. She's already lost one daughter; she'll not want to lose another. With a fifteen-year sentence, the child will be in her thirties by the time she comes out."

"Let's hope she sees sense, then. It can't get more personal than this, it's a sad state of events all round."

They were about to move away from the machine when DC Flint found them.

"Boss!" he shouted, catching their attention as he approached. "Katherine Spencer's daughter was killed while on a zebra crossing. And guess who was driving and got off?"

"Don't tell me our blasted mayor again, surely not."

"No, it wasn't, this time. It was his wife, Barbara Hayhurst. The coroner put it down to accidental and so nobody was ever charged. A freak accident by all accounts."

"This really can't get any more personal."

"It's even more motive, though," added DCI Miller.

EIGHTY-SIX

It was Katherine Spencer that saw sense first. At close to 10 pm, she made a formal confession of her part in the plan and implicated Veronica Lauder as the one who had committed the murders. She told of meeting the woman at the support group and various specialist appointments both their girls had on a regular basis, as well as seeing her at Sunny Nook. They'd become close friends, their daughters and the church a common bond between them, until one day Katherine mentioned some of the dealings she was privy to at the council, the fictitious invoices and how she knew they weren't right. When the personal budgets were introduced instead of the regular paid placements at Sunny Nook, and the home started to experience difficulties, as did others, the two women talked about getting revenge.

Their plan was simple, make the mayor pay. Katherine thought the ransom demands would be met, and they'd be able to give the money to Sunny Nook – maybe a novice assumption in hindsight. When Clyde was killed, she wanted out, it wasn't what she'd signed up for. But things spiralled quickly out of control and Katherine couldn't see a way to stop it, she was in too deep. She'd been dragged along, caught in a fierce wave she wasn't strong enough to swim away from. Veronica, she said, was fine with the deaths, used to them even, because of her line of work, but Katherine wasn't that cold. In the end, all she could do was expose the corruption and let Veronica carry on with her own warped ideas, and hope to distance herself from them. Her daughter was more important than any more plans of revenge, and certainly any more deaths. Veronica had been a lone wolf in that respect, motivated by her own twisted mind more than doing anything more positive for her daughter.

During searches of both their homes, an iPhone X was found in Veronica's daughter's wardrobe, tucked inside a coat pocket. It was currently with digital forensics for analysis. Even if the images had been deleted, they would likely still be stored in the phone's 'recently deleted' folder, which most people didn't realise even existed. At the very least, it had Veronica Lauder's prints on it. There was also a set of distinctive boots, like wellies, and samples of the dirt caught between the ridges of the soles had been compared with both the cellar floor and earth from Hunsbury Hill Country Park, where the bodies had been found. There were matches for both. The final nail in Veronica's own coffin was Jonesy's hair caught up in the wig he'd worn on his final day. Since Jonesy had known nothing of what had happened to him that first time at the cemetery and Veronica Lauder refused to elaborate about the botched attempt, they'd probably never know what really happened that night.

DI Mason returned to her desk, exhausted.

"That's it for tonight," DCI Miller said, approaching her.

"I'll not argue with that, every part of my being is screaming for sleep."

"It's a good result, though a tad unusual, and both women are safely tucked up downstairs. We're nearly done now, just the formalities."

"What a sad mess on so many levels."

"Yes. The human race will never stop surprising me. Nice work, though, you and DC Flint."

"Thanks, ma'am, I appreciate it."

As DI Rochelle Mason made her way to the locker room to change into her leathers, she wondered about calling Will and telling him the news. Tiredness told her it would have to wait until tomorrow.

EIGHTY-SEVEN

IT WAS a bittersweet day for Will as he dug a hole deep enough to hold three people. He'd volunteered to do the honours; it seemed right that he take on the funeral responsibilities for the three young men. When Duncan Sanders had found out about his sister's involvement in the crime, he'd offered, if Will was okay with the suggestion, to be the funeral director free of charge. It had seemed a little perverse when it was first suggested, maybe a little close for comfort to the woman that had caused their deaths in the first place, but when Will chatted to Louise about his quandary, she made him realise one sibling couldn't be responsible for the other's actions. Duncan hadn't been involved at all, and since he was offering to help, it was a far better solution than a public health funeral from the council itself. The issue Will then had was where the plot should be. It really couldn't be at the Holy Sepulchre, that would definitely be too close to their deaths for comfort, and so Will finally made arrangements for a plot at Towcester Road Cemetery. It was somewhere where Will himself spent time as he dug graves for the newly departed and he could see the lads got a visitor occasionally. The vicar, Joanna, agreed to give her time and conduct the service, and a wreath for each of them was created by Louise and the children out of foliage from Stanley's garden and flowers from Birdie's. They took pleasure in the fact the young men would at least have a decent burial and, at the very least, three of them would attend the undoubtedly small service, which was scheduled for 2 pm later that day.

By 11 am, Will had made the final touches to the bottom of the grave, laying leaves and wildflowers as he liked to do so no coffin rested directly on the soil itself. Satisfied his work was done, he parked his digger back behind the shed, changed out of his work clothes, and made his way back across town towards Moulton, and home. Louise had taken the day off work to support him and attend alongside him and had organised a funeral tea at Refresh with the help of Hazel. Everything was in place; he could do no more now until it was time. Louise greeted him at the door when he arrived back and held him for a long moment. Neither of them spoke. When he finally pulled back, he said, "This feels highly unusual. I'm not sure if I like this feeling or not."

"I can understand that, Will, but from this point onwards, we'll be there to say goodbye as we would at anyone else's funeral we'd find ourselves attending. All you have to do now is have a hot shower and get changed. Your part is over, though I do have to say, I've a feeling Clyde, Bowie and Jonesy would share their appreciation of your efforts if they were with us now. Most would have let the council do their bit, but not you Will Peters. You're a wonderful man, husband and father, and I couldn't wish for a sweeter soulmate to spend my life with. I'm so very proud of you." Louise planted a kiss on his lips to stop him speaking and he kissed her back. "Now, shower!" she said, changing the mood with two simple words, and Will made his way upstairs as directed. As water ran down the drainpipes, Louise hoped that the day ahead would be as joyous as any funeral could be, a celebration of life itself rather than death.

She drove them to the service at the funeral home where the three coffins now lay. It was only a small room, since they weren't expecting more than a handful of mourners to attend and pay their respects, but as Louise turned onto St Giles Street, Will sat open-mouthed at what lay ahead of them. The road was almost blocked with people, some congregating by the funeral home and some heading down towards the square. As Louise navigated the heaving street, Will spotted a blue flashing light on the other side of the crowd and groaned.

"What's going on?" Will said. "Surely all these people are not for the boys, are they?"

A burst of siren urged people off the street and onto the foot-paths to move the crowd out of the way. As the liveried vehicle made its way through, he recognised the woman sitting in the passenger seat. DI Rochelle Mason smiled directly at him as the car pulled alongside his own. He wound his window down.

"You again," she said warmly. "I figured you'd be behind this commotion." Then, ignoring Will for a moment and still grinning, she directed her comments to the driver and said, "You must be Louise. Pleased to meet the woman behind the man." She waved 'hello' in her direction.

"And you," Louise called back.

"If you can turn your car around, and follow us, we've a change of venue. We'll take you down to the guildhall. Mr Sanders thought it best under the circumstances and has arranged for the service to take place there. We'll find you a place to park – wouldn't want a ticket today, eh?" She wound her window back up and Will and Louise followed as instructed, gobsmacked at the turnout. By the time they parked up, the street looked like a fire alarm had gone off nearby and half the town centre had evacuated to the same spot. Will couldn't believe his eyes.

"We need to find Birdie and Stanley," he said to Louise urgently. "Stanley is wobbly on his feet at the best of times." As if on cue, a faint beep-beep followed by a booming 'coming through' made him turn, then smile. With Birdie bringing up the rear, Stanley navigated his way through on a motorised mobility scooter. He was clearly enjoying himself. Will glanced at the man's feet, out of habit, and grinned at the white trainers glaring out from under formal black trousers. At least he wasn't in his slippers again.

"Wicked turnout, Will. It's like the old days on the Wapping picket line, I just need a placard in my hands."

"Nice ride," said Will, looking the machine over. "Present to yourself?"

"From my daughter. Said I need to get out more. Apparently, it suits me."

Will could only smile.

"Hello Will, Louise," Birdie said brightly when she could get a word in. "I can't believe my eyes."

"Neither can I," he said. "I'm stunned. I suppose we should find a seat inside before they all go."

"Follow me," instructed Stanley and they made their way forward behind the scooter. The scene resembled Moses and his staff at the Red Sea and the parting of the waters, though Will doubted Moses had had a horn like Stanley was now using.

The service was a bit late starting – an hour late, actually – and Will hoped the knock-on effect with the committal service and later tea at the centre wouldn't be too disruptive, but it was out of his control now. Sitting up front with Louise, Stanley and Birdie around him, he heard DI Mason's voice once more. "Room for a little one?" Everyone shuffled a seat along and Rochelle sat down next to Will.

Smiling, Will said, "It was at an exhumation I first met you, if you remember. It's fitting this time it's a burial, don't you think?"

"It looks like there's a lot of people on the young men's side from the turnout. And you were expecting a handful."

"I was clearly wrong."

"You weren't wrong with finding their killer though. Your help turned out to be invaluable, and for that the team thanks you."

Will wasn't sure how to respond and was saved from doing so by the funeral service starting. He, like the rest of the congregation, faced forward and focused on the reason they'd come together in the first place.

EIGHTY-EIGHT

AS THE INFINITELY SMALLER GROUP MADE THEIR way from the graveside and back into town for the funeral tea at Refresh, Will remembered he had an outstanding question for DI Mason. With all the goings-on, he'd almost forgotten to follow it up, but since his headspace was now much clearer, he'd pulled the question out from one of the quiet places in his brain. He made his way over, having told Louise he needed a moment.

"I've been meaning to ask," he started, "that night at the exhumation, and the brass plaque above ground…"

"I wondered when you'd get around to that," she said and grinned. "You strike me as someone who never leaves anything undone."

"That's me. So, did you ever figure out how it got there?"

"It was the son actually. He'd been convinced his mother had been buried alive and had opened the grave himself. It must have taken him ages to remove all that soil by spade, but he admitted when the coffin was finally exposed, he couldn't get the catches off to double-check inside." Will remembered the clasps being tight; Duncan Sanders the funeral director had had to do the honours in the end. The rest was history, though it made a funny story. He couldn't help the grin as he remembered the events of that night.

"He dislodged the plaque in doing so?"

"Apparently. Though if he'd known, he'd have taken it with him or buried it again. The fact it was found above ground, he can't explain. Must have got caught up somewhere along the line."

"And just why is your hair blue? It's a fairly common colour now, I suppose, but on a detective? I wouldn't have thought it allowed."

"Are you always so nosey?"

"Inquisitive, I'd call it."

"A spot of undercover work, and I can tell you blue stain appears to hang around longer than the box might have you believe." It explained it perfectly.

Louise wandered over and placed her hand in Will's.

"It turned out to be a lovely day, and I don't just mean the weather," she said, looking across to the sun getting lower in the sky. Stanley and Birdie made their way over too, the ground a little uneven for Stanley's steering abilities and his curses could be heard long before he reached them.

"Where's the tea? I'm parched," he announced.

"Come on, Stanley, let's get you a cuppa and an egg sandwich," Will said as they moved towards the car park.

"Bloody hate egg," he mumbled, just loudly enough for Birdie to hear and swat his shoulder with her gloves she was carrying. She bent down to his level and whispered in his ear, bright red lips serious.

"Remember, Stanley Kipper, just what I can do with a carving knife. Now stop your grumbling or else I'll remind you."

"I like a feisty woman," he said before winking.

Will couldn't help but overhear the exchange and rolled his eyes towards the heavens, feeling the weak sun on his face. They were perhaps a little unconventional, but the three had made a pretty decent team getting to the bottom of the case.

"Last one to the car is a rotten egg!" he yelled as he set off at a slow trot. He was almost there when the mobility scooter flew past him, its occupant waving his fist in triumph.

"Keep up, Will!" he shouted.

"Reminds me of your story of old Sims," he said to Birdie as she caught him up. "All he needs now in that basket is a false leg."

"Well, maybe I could oblige, with one of his real ones…" It was Birdie's turn to wink.

ACKNOWLEDGMENTS

This book is most definitely a work of fiction, though some of the physical places featured are indeed real. If those places are not portrayed entirely accurately, that's my doing to make it fit the story – it is a work of fiction after all. Many believe the tunnels under Northampton do exist, but others say they are simply a warren of underground cellars. I'll leave you to decide should you ever look into their existence yourself. The Refresh Centre is entirely fictional, though there is a real-life version that does a wonderful job supporting homeless and disadvantaged people in the town.

I've had some excellent input with my research, but I'm conscious of protecting my source, so I'll leave the name out, just in case. Let's just say, you know who you are and your insight into certain events has added so much more to the story than Google ever could.

Not forgetting my editors, Jenny and Jon, whom I thank for their sterling advice and accuracy. It's a pleasure to work with you both as usual.

I always enjoy hearing from readers, so do drop me a line about anything to do with my books at linda@lindacoles.com.

Finally, thanks to you, the reader, because if you didn't buy my books, there would be little point in me writing any more.

KEEP IN TOUCH

If you'd like to keep in touch via my newsletter, and grab Hot To Kill for FREE, use this link to leave your details:

https://geni.us/lindacolesnewsletter

Enjoy,
    Linda

Keep in touch:
www.lindacoles.com
linda@lindacoles.com
<u>Follow me on BookBub</u>

ALSO BY LINDA COLES

Jack Rutherford and Amanda Lacey Series:

Hot to Kill

The Hunted

Dark Service

One Last Hit

Hey You, Pretty Face

Scream Blue Murder

Butcher Baker Banker

The Chrissy Livingstone Series:

Tin Men

Walk Like You

The Silent Ones

The Will Peters series:

Where There's A Will

ALSO BY LINDA COLES

If you enjoyed reading one of my stories, here are the others:

The DC Jack Rutherford and DS Amanda Lacey Series:

Hot to Kill

When a local landscaper vanishes, Madeline Simpson knows she was the last person to see him alive – because she killed him.

With a serial sex offender on the loose, Detectives DC Jack Rutherford and DS Amanda Lacey already have their hands full. It's only when another death occurs that a link between the two cases comes to light, and Madeline finds herself the focus of their investigation.

While attempting to keep her deadly secret, Madeline stumbles upon clues that point to the true identity of the sex offender. She's closing in when tragedy strikes, and the death toll increases.

But DS Amanda Lacey has no idea how close she is to the killer as her work and personal lives collide.

How long will she have to wait to find out the full truth?

If you like interesting characters, imaginative story lines, and British crime drama, then you'll love this captivating story.

The Hunted

The hunt is on...

They kill wild animals for sport. She's about to return the favour.

A spate of distressing big-game hunter posts are clogging up her newsfeed. As hunters brag about the exotic animals they've murdered and the followers they've gained along the way, a passionate veterinarian can no longer sit back and do nothing.

To stop the killings, she creates her own endangered list of hunters. By stalking their online profiles and infiltrating their inner circles, she vows to take them out one-by-one.

How far will she go to add the guilty to her own trophy collection?

Dark Service

The dark web can satisfy any perversion, but two detectives might just pull the plug…

Taylor never felt the blade pressed to her scalp. She wakes frightened and alone in an unfamiliar hotel room with a near shaved head and a warning… tell no one.

As detectives Amanda Lacey and Jack Rutherford investigate, they venture deep into the fetish-fueled underbelly of the dark web. The traumatized woman is only the latest victim in a decade-long string of disturbing—and intensely personal—thefts.

To take down a perverted black market, they'll go undercover. But just when justice seems within reach, an unexpected event sends their sting operation spiraling out of control. Their only chance at catching the culprits lies with a local reporter… and a sex scandal that could ruin them all.

One Last Hit

The greatest danger may come from inside his own home.

Detective Duncan Riley has always worked hard to maintain order on the streets of Manchester. But when a series of incidents at home cause him to worry about his wife's behaviour, he finds himself pulled in too many directions at once.

After a colleague Amanda Lacey asks for his help with a local drug epidemic, he never expected the case would infiltrate his own family… And a situation that spirals out of control...

Hey You, Pretty Face

An abandoned infant. Three girls stolen in the night. Can one overworked detective find the connection to save them all?

London, 1999. Short-staffed during a holiday week, Detective Jack Rutherford can't afford to spend time on the couch with his beloved wife. With a skeleton staff, he's forced to handle a deserted infant and a trio of missing girls almost single-handedly. Despite the overload, Jack has a sneaking suspicion that the baby and the abductions are somehow connected…

As he fights to reunite the girls with their families, the clues point to a dark secret that sends chills down his spine. With evidence revealing a detestable crime ring, can Jack catch the criminals before the girls go missing forever?

Scream Blue Murder

Two cold cases are about to turn red hot…

Detective Jack Rutherford's instincts have only sharpened with age. So when a violent road fatality reminds him of a near-identical crime from 15 years earlier, he digs up the past to investigate both. But with one case already closed, he fears the wrong man still festers behind bars while the real killer roams free…

For Detective Amanda Lacey, family always comes first. But when she unearths a skeleton in her father-in-law's garden, she has to balance her heart with her desire for justice. And with darkness lurking just beneath the surface, DS Lacey must push her feelings to one side to discover the chilling truth.

As the sins of the past haunt both detectives, will solving the crimes have consequences that echo for the rest of their lives?

Butcher Baker Banker

A cold Croydon winter's night and pensioner Nelly Raven lies dead and naked on the floor of her living room. The scene bears all the hallmarks of a burglary gone wrong.

It's just the beginning.

Ron Butcher rose to the top of London's gangland by "fixing things". But are his extensive crooked connections of use when death knocks at his own family's door?

Baker Kit Morris will do anything to keep his family business alive. Desperate for cash, he hatches a risky plan that lands him in trouble. As he struggles to stay out of prison, he forges an unlikely friendship with an aging local thug.

And then there's the Banker, Lee Meady, a man with personal problems of his own.

Just how does it all fit together?

As DC Jack Rutherford and DS Amanda Lacey uncover the facts surrounding the case, the harrowing truth of the killer's identity leaves Jack wondering where the human race went so badly wrong.

The Chrissy Livingstone series:

Tin Men

She thought she knew her father. But what she doesn't know could fill a mortuary…

Chrissy Livingstone grieves over her dad's sudden death. While she cleans out his old things, she discovers something she can't explain: seven photos of schoolboys with the year 1987 stamped on the back. Unable to turn off her desire for the truth, she hunts down the boys in the photos only to find out that three of the seven have committed suicide…

Tracing the clues from Surrey to Santa Monica, Chrissy unearths disturbing ties between her father's work as a financier and the victims. As each new connection raises more sinister questions about her family, she fears she should've left the secrets buried with the dead.

Will Chrissy put the past to rest, or will the sins of the father destroy her?

Walk Like You

When a major railway accident turns into a bizarre case of a missing body, will this PI's hunt for the truth take her way off track?

London. Private investigator Chrissy Livingstone's dirty work has taken her down a different path to her family. But when her upper-class sister begs her to locate a friend missing after a horrific train crash, she feels duty-bound to assist. Though when the two dig deeper, all the evidence seems to lead to one mysterious conclusion: the woman doesn't want to be found.

Still with no idea why the woman was on the train, and an unidentified body uncannily resembling the missing person lying unclaimed in the mortuary, the sisters follow a trail of cryptic clues through France. The mystery deepens when they learn someone else is searching, and their motive could be murder…

Can Chrissy find the woman before she meets a terrible fate?

The Silent Ones

An abandoned child. A missing couple. A village full of secrets.

When a couple holidaying in the small Irish village of Doolan disappear one night, leaving their child behind, Chrissy Livingstone has no choice but to involve herself in the mystery surrounding their disappearance.

As the toddler is taken into care, it soon becomes apparent that in the close-knit village the couple are not the only ones with secrets to keep.

With the help of her sister, Julie, Chrissy races to uncover what is really happening. Could discovering the truth put more lives at risk?

A suspenseful story that will keep you guessing until the end.

ABOUT THE AUTHOR

Hi, I'm Linda Coles. Thanks for choosing this book, I really hope you enjoyed it and collect the following ones in the series. Great characters make a great read and I hope I've managed to create that for you.

Originally from the UK, I now live and work in beautiful New Zealand along with my hubby, 1 cat and 6 goats. My office sits by the edge of my vegetable garden, and apart from reading and writing, I get to run by the beach for pleasure.

If you find a moment, please do write an honest online review of my work, they really do make such a difference to those choosing what book to buy next.

Thanks,
Linda